MARY MALL[illegible]

Liberation At Last

Love After Death I

First published by sweetspotbooks.co.uk 2024

Second edition

ISBN: 978-1-0687857-0-2

Cover art by Sarah Nagalewska (Hawkeye Designs)

This book was professionally typeset on Reedsy.
Find out more at reedsy.com

To my dearest mother whom I loved, love and will always love from the bottom of my heart

PEACE

Contents

Acknowledgments

To my two sons Matthew and Daniel who have come through me into this realm. You have both, in your own unique way, taught me so much about myself, about love and about life. Thanks to you I am the woman I am today. I love you.

Chapter 1

It was a crash-landing.

Who would have thought, that having left his car in the capital's car park a couple of hours earlier, he would have to come back shortly after to find it written off - a total loss. He had not been speeding, neither had he suddenly stopped dead in his tracks on a busy road. For heaven's sake, his car was parked - stationary - in the city's car park where nothing ever happened. You always found your car where you left it and how you left it, on your return at the end of your work day, bar some pigeon poo every now and then.

Until today, that is.

More worryingly is the fact that he shall not be getting any compensation for the damage, as this would be deemed an *act of God*. An act of God for what? An act of God to punish him? To punish him for what? Like everyone else on this earth he had his faults, of which he was aware, but deep down he was one of the good guys who tried to do good and avoided doing bad when and as often as is humanly possible.

That morning he had set off whistling to himself, thinking how sweet life had been since this beautiful girl had entered his life. She appeared as if out of nowhere. He hadn't seen this one coming. He didn't know much about her, but she touched something deep inside within minutes of meeting her. It was love at first sight, on his part. She was one of those whom although he had only known a mere couple of months, felt as if he had known her all his life. She was a friend, a lover, a companion and a soul-mate all rolled into one.

Thanks to her presence in his life, he was now oblivious to the off-hand comments his colleagues made at work to undermine his authority. So lost in love was he that not even the screeching din outside his house at weekends, as the house next door was being demolished and rebuilt, bothered him. His nostrils picked up only the aroma of her rose-scented skin and shut off the smell of sweat everywhere and on everyone. As his eyes beheld her splendour, he began to see beauty in everything, everywhere. He was well and truly in love. And nothing else mattered.

After depositing his car in the car park like any other morning, he had walked to work with a song in his heart and a sense of gratitude that surpassed the mundane. This morning's events were totally unexpected- like a bolt out of the blue. A bolt, indeed! Where had she fallen from, this demented woman? It's true that people who decided to commit suicide had to do it somewhere, but to crash-land, bum-bang right through the roof of his car was a bit more than he could fathom that morning. He would have to see it, to believe it.

The phone call from the police made everybody want to poke fun at him at work. He had dropped his coffee and rushed to the scene as soon as he had been summoned. He hadn't been the first to get there. The police had beat him to it, the ambulance -how futile for someone who was so obviously dead - and lots of other people had gathered by his car, by the time he got himself there.

CHAPTER 1

Curious passers-by were ushered to move on by the police. Exclamations of horror, lamentations and wailing resembling that of an animal which had just been maimed, filled his senses. Suddenly, it seemed much hotter and the stench of sweat and death infiltrated his nostrils, suffocating his lungs. The stuffiness in the air, the heat, the noise all suddenly began to get the better of him, inducing a feeling of being slowly smothered. He found it hard to breathe.

It wasn't a pleasant sight to behold, let's face it.

His car was, indeed, demolished. The body work crushed. You wouldn't have guessed that one human body crashing from that height, at that speed could cause such damage – but hey, there was the evidence staring him in the face – fact, not fiction.

The colour red. Not his favourite colour. It had never been. He had always preferred blue. When asked, he always undoubtedly went for blue, without hesitation. But today, red seemed to be the colour of the day and splattered all over what had just been his beloved new metallic blue car, was red everywhere. It was hard to comprehend that all that blood could splatter from just one dead body. He was sure that in Hollywood movies, in which everything is over-the-top, the amount of blood shown in casualties is quite realistic.

Why on earth was he thinking of colours and films? More pertinently, who was this woman, who on this day had decided to end her life and ruin his own day in every single way? Couldn't she have fallen on one of the other cars on either side of his, perhaps? Why his?

It did feel as if life had singled him out on this occasion. He hoped that this spate of bad luck didn't come in threes. He couldn't afford another car and with Christmas just round the corner and most of his Christmas shopping not as yet done, life didn't seem so sweet after all. He hadn't been prepared for this sudden turn of events. The whistling and singing in his heart seemed to be slowly fading away, as was the colour from his face.

He fainted.

Eventually, as he came round, he hoped that it had all been a bad dream. He imagined that suddenly his sweetheart would come and soothe him, reassuring him all is well and will be well. Her kind words and melodious voice, her warm smile and twinkling eyes would be enough to bring colour rushing back to his face. Alas, when he opened his eyes the same scene he had been so keen to blank out, accosted him once again, with a vengeance.

It was only then that he began to seriously wonder who this woman could have been. Surely, she was someone's daughter, wife, mother, lover, sister, friend, helper, colleague or acquaintance. She must have fulfilled some sort of role in life which had made her important, if not indispensable to some. For a moment there, he stopped his thoughts in their track as the shocking truth of a particular one caught hold of him. He suddenly realised that it could have been his own mother, his own sister, his own friend, or his own lovely, kindhearted, dark olive-skinned girl. He momentarily forgot about his car being wrecked, about not having enough money to replace it or about not having it to run errands during this busy festive season. For a brief moment, he was touched. He was touched by a deep sorrow and a compelling sense of compassion.

He looked carefully at all the people gathered here now. The young fair lad, with hazel- green eyes leaning carefully over her shattered body caught his eye. This young fair lad let out an anguished cry of "Mum, why?" and burst into floods of tears. It started off like a soft sob, but became louder and shriller until gradually, his tormented cry filled the stuffy stench-filled air. It was heart-breaking to watch a young lad who was barely eighteen losing his mother like that and finding her like this. His heart went out for him, despite the fact that he did not know this man from Adam and that this tragic accident had cost him his car and a lot of money, as well as upsetting his peace and quiet and all his plans for Christmas.

There was something about this lad that continued to captivate him. He wished he could read what was going on in his heart and mind just by looking at his hypnotic hazel-green eyes. He couldn't, of course, but he could somehow imagine. He had been trying to be compassionate and put himself in other peoples' shoes for quite some time now and had managed, on occasions, to do this fairly well. He wasn't so sure about this one though, as who could actually put themselves in this lad's shoes today?

Possibly, like him, this lad had set off for his day's work with a song in his heart and a spring in his step. Possibly, like him this lad had, up until this moment in time, been happy with his life and the little blessings it had been bestowing upon him. Possibly like him this lad had been looking forward to a good, productive working day with some fun to follow in the evening with family and friends.

Possibly, unlike him, this lad would never recover. He would be able to get a new car, somehow. He would manage to get the Christmas presents sorted, somehow. Moreover, he would regain his peace and sense of tranquility as soon as he went back home to his dark olive-skinned sweetheart. But, the life of this nameless lad with the deep hazel-green eyes had been shattered, forever. And just as that bloody motionless body would never regain life, neither would that boy regain his innocence, or the joy of living that had now been decimated, any time soon.

The first question we all ask is, *why*? Why this woman? Why this lad? Why today? Why his car? Why a few days before Christmas? He himself wondered if she could have waited a few more days, when his car wouldn't have even been in the car park as he would have had time off work. Or perhaps, could she have done it later on in the day when he would have clocked off? Or earlier, when he wouldn't have arrived? All these thoughts, amongst many others, raced through his simple mind filling it with a thud - thud - thudding - causing a full-blown migraine.

Yet again, he thought how selfish to have such thoughts when he would soon walk out of here intact and bar money for a new car to be found, his life would be back on track. Yet, the life of this lad leaning over his mother's dead body might take many years to recover, if ever. This lad left the house in the morning hoping it would be a morning like any other, and yet it was that morning which would change him for the rest of his life.

One single act committed in a single moment of utter and sheer despair changes the course of many lives - forever. He hoped and prayed that he himself would not have to face such a tragedy, ever in his lifetime. He saw in this lad's eyes, heard in his anguished cry, smelt in his shortened breath, the love he had had for this woman – the mother who had ushered him into this world one day, not too many years prior to this moment in time.

A moment in which time stood still.

This lad's love for this woman shone right through the anguished torment. He decided that no son should ever have to see the woman who bore him into the world, in such a state. He continued to wonder if there had been any other family members present and possibly others who had not seen or heard, as yet. His heart went out to them, although he didn't know them. Perhaps they too were at work having a business-as-usual kind of day, until hit by this bombshell. He felt for all those whom a moment in a day comes to shatter and change them and their lives as they know it - forever. From this point forward, there is no turning back.

Will his curiosity ever be satiated? And why did he have this urge to know? It wasn't as if it were any of his business really, was it? His race was always accused of being busy bodies, minding everyone else's business, but never attending to their own. Maybe, he wasn't as liberated as he thought he was. But, compassion was there in plenty– not a bad start for a person trying to open his heart to love, whistling whilst dancing to life's bitter-sweet symphony.

Chapter 2

Her spirit, one the other hand hadn't left the scene of the *crime* just yet. They always say, and many believe this might be true – that especially when one dies an accidental death – their spirit hovers for some moments before it moves on to another realm. She had wanted to run, she had wanted to hide, but her spirit wouldn´t go anywhere. Frozen, it hovered over the aftermath of her pre-planned, premeditated death.

She watched, astounded by the fact that she had finally found the courage to do what she had wanted to do for the last fifteen or twenty odd years. They say that you need more courage to live than to die, but they didn't know what they were talking about. The courage to die was true courage. The courage to die, to face an unknown reality, an unknown state of being leaving loved ones behind, was a courage which only came through - yes, through what exactly?

Was it courage?

Or was it despair?

Presently, there were too many questions clamouring for her attention and she couldn't answer any of them, not right now, anyway. Her body had just been shattered, as was the wholeness of an innocently parked car, and that of all those who had been left behind. She didn't know if it were through courage or despair. All she knew was that she was there - on the other side.

She remembered calling out the name of her eldest daughter, as both her feet had left solid ground and were kicking madly in mid-air. Why had she done that? Was it to make sure her eldest daughter's name was the last thing she uttered before her body hit the ground? Or rather, crashed through the car? She hadn't factored that into the equation - this wasn't a plan she had thought through thoroughly. And it weren't as if her eldest daughter could save her now.

She knew her eldest daughter had been trying to save her for most of her living life. She knew too, that if it weren't for her and for her most beloved hazel-green eyed son, she would have done this much sooner. She knew that forty-three was no age to die. And yet, it was no age to exist as unhappily as she had. For a split second on her way down she felt liberated – totally and utterly free. Until her body crashed through the stationary car with a great big thud.

She realised, as her spirit hovered momentarily over the scene, the catastrophe she had caused. But, it was too late for regrets. It was no use crying over spilt milk. What was done, was done. She couldn't rewind, neither could she turn the clock back.

Was this a mis-take? Had there been another way out of all the anguished pain - a way which did not involve taking her own life? Had she tried hard enough to keep going? Explored every alternative? Looked at her predicament from every different angle possible? Left no stone unturned? She couldn't take all these questions being fired at her and felt the urge to tear her hair out. It's just that as she tried to reach for her hair, she realised that there wasn't any there!

She made her way to where her youngest son was as he leant over her mutilated, lifeless body. She tried to dry his tears. She whispered softly in his ears, telling him how much she had loved him all those years . She told him that he had brought her such joy, love, laughter and fun. She reminded him of how she loved it when they went out shopping or walking and how funny she thought it was when people mistook him for her boyfriend. She scrubbed up well and always looked so young and beautiful, especially when she could find the strength to make an effort to dress up.

Why couldn't he hear her? On this side, or rather the side she now found herself in, the sound waves travelled differently than they did back here. That's the reason why he couldn't hear what she was saying. She soon realised that, indeed, being on the other side made communication to those here, a bit tricky.

But will he ever know in his heart of hearts that none of this was his fault? Will he ever know that all the love he had lavished on her would never be lost? Would he ever be told how much her heart leapt for joy when his keys turned in the front door lock as he let himself in ravished, rummaging for food? Would he ever know the pleasure she felt in making him the most deliciously filling meals even when she was listless, tired and depressed? Would he ever be told that he was the light shining bright in her darkness, the song in her heart, the treasure she valued over everything and everyone else? How will he ever find out that he was the love of her love and the life of her life? Who will tell him?

She had never wanted to burden him with her troubles and her sad life-story. She had wanted to spare him at all costs. She had never let on how depressed she had been, how her life had been disappointment after disappointment, and a series of shattered dreams and broken promises. She had wanted to love him as she had never been loved. She had wanted to nurture and keep him safe as she had never been herself. She had wanted to protect him from her sadness and pain, from herself and her heart-breaking reality. So he had never really known the travesty of what she suffered and endured in love and in life, up until then.

Giving birth to him had been a doddle compared to when she had done it seven years earlier. In the latter she had thought she was going to die and that her body would give in. She hadn't been ready to die then, not at barely eighteen. Now, at twenty-five surrounded by family and friends she was ready – to give birth. Giving birth to him had been a ray of hope in this mundane and harsh reality she inhabited. And now in hindsight, he was the best thing that had ever happened to her since leaving the land Down Under. As he grew older he continued to bring her joy, warming her heart with gratitude, at having been gifted this life of which she had felt utterly and truly unworthy.

The birth of her eldest daughter had been a different story. She had been barely eighteen at the time and totally unprepared for motherhood. For who is at that age? She had hoped she would be able to go to college and study to become a school teacher. Becoming a school teacher in that day and age had been quite fashionable and she cut the grades. She had always passed her exams with flying colours and all her teachers had urged her on. But, her dad and destiny had other plans. She would live to regret not having stood up to her dad, taking the path of least resistance into the future. She hadn't planned on getting married so young and having a daughter at barely eighteen. But, it was a fiat accompli. She had made her bed and now she must lay in it.

She hadn't spared her eldest at all! Why such a compulsion to protect the youngest and expose the eldest? Where was the fairness in that? Hadn't she loved her eldest daughter in the same way she had adored her youngest son? She would need to suspend judgement on this one until another time. It was all getting a bit too chaotic and far too confusing. Thoughts of her eldest daughter instantly transported her to where she was - at a stranger's house violently throwing up down their toilet b0wl, at the breaking of this devastating news. She was lying on the floor in a heap overwhelmed and overcome by grief, guilt, desolation and utter despair. She hadn't thought her mother would have gone through with it - not today, anyway.

She wanted to reach out and give her eldest daughter a big hug to reassure her it hadn't been her fault, but her arms failed her. Not having a human body was frustrating, as much as it allowed her to teleport to different places on a whim. Eventually she decided that the best thing to do at this point in time -although she wasn't in time - would be to stop and wait to see what happens next. There was nobody here to greet her just yet, but maybe that was because she had been an uninvited guest and they hadn't been prepared for this eventuality, not here, nor there.

She would have to hold fire for a while and be still, until her judgement was due, fingers crossed it would be soon. It was no use trying to sort out, judge and analyse all her intentions and actions now – it was pointless at this point. She would have to hope that the God she believed in would judge her less harshly than she had always judged herself. She also hoped against hope He wouldn't take too long in coming.

Hopefully the God she believed in was a merciful Being and would forgive her what she wouldn't or couldn't forgive herself. Perhaps, this God was much more compassionate than she could ever be towards herself or anybody else. Perhaps, rather than throwing her in a place of infinite infernal damnation, her God would eventually welcome her into His kingdom. She had yearned to enter His kingdom all her life, but after her two year love affair with Greg she doubted she ever would.

The God she believed in had sent her signs and signs and more signs, telling her loud and clear that her transgressions had been absolved, they had all been forgiven and forgotten. Her two-year long, love affair with her husband's best friend waived away as if by a magic wand, so contrite had she been. But, why couldn't she forgive herself? Why did she have to torment and beat herself up everyday with futile feelings of guilt and shame? Why hadn't she seen how useless feelings of guilt were? Why hadn't she been able to love herself as her Creator loved her? Why hadn't she trusted His forgiveness? All these questions, and more, crossed her mind as her spirit continued to hover in a state of being neither here nor there, yet seemingly everywhere.

She might have to wait to be judged, although she hoped it wouldn't be too long a wait. She always believed, for so she had been taught, that judgement took place instantaneously, but it turns out that this was fanciful and wishful thinking. She might be judged quite soon on the one hand, but then have to wait until she was completely justified and purified before she could enter His kingdom, on the other. She wasn't sure what the protocol was and who would guide her to where she needed to be. This was all very new to her and she didn't want to jump the gun, as she had already done. So she hovered in an unfamiliar place, in an unfamiliar state of being - still shell-shocked. Who would support her now, given her eldest daughter wasn't there to prop her up in her hour of need as she had always done? She'll just have to wait and see.

Things weren't moving fast here and she wasn't going anywhere in a hurry. She had always had the patience of a saint. She would wait for her husband to leave the house in the morning before she got up. She would wait for her children to go to school so that she could go back to bed. She would wait for enough money to be saved to buy new mahagony furniture, a brand-new oven, a new dress, new curtains, new lace doilies, new table-cloths, new shoes - new whatever was needed. She would wait for friends to come round to keep her company, sparing her her own. She would wait for someone to wake her up inside, she would wait for passion to return and love to revisit - but they never did. Finally, hope gave way to despair and she would wait for death. Death was the only certainty in life. But, the more she wished and waited for death the more it eluded her, like water slipping right through her fingers.

To wait...and to wait... and to wait....had seemed her mission in life. And why the thing which she had waited for and wanted the most would never come, she never understood. There was no doubt she was patient, but life was taking the mickey at this point and she was going to show it who is boss.

She would wait no longer.

She would put a stop to all this waiting once and for all.

She would not wake up another morning hoping it would be her last.

She would make it her last.

And so she had.

If only she knew how true the saying in her mother tongue: '*kemm konna ahjar meta konna aghar*', roughly translating as, *we were much better off, when we were worse off*, is.

Waiting is the last thing she imagined she would have to do on the other side. Here she didn't have a clue how long she would be waiting for and it was killing her! Oh, no it wasn't! She was already dead. As dead as a dodo. Life was in control after all, even after death. There seemed to be no escape of this waiting, neither here nor there, she bitterly thought to herself.

From the corner of her eye she caught a glimpse of a flash across the ether. She hoped it was someone coming to greet her or even better judge her, at last. But no, it wasn't. It was a big burly man, sweating droplet after droplet of fear, moving closer to her corpse. She didn't wish to see him, neither did she want him to see her like that. Was there a way he could be spared?

She moved a bit closer. The stench of his sweat intermingled with fear filled the air. How did she dare look into his eyes when she knew what she would see there? This humble fisherman had loved her. She knew and saw it in his eyes, with her own eyes - or not, as they had popped out of her body upon the crash, or so it had seemed.

She had been the best thing that had ever happened to him. She had touched his heart and opened it to love. His eyes sparkled with love and devotion, and although his lips never uttered a word of it to her, it was written all over his face. It's true she had had an affair with his best friend for two years, but he was willing to let that go and start afresh if only she would too. Would she ever be able to love him once more, as she had done before? This tricky question they both asked themselves, time and again.

What does it take to fall in love with someone with a renewed vigour? Questions such as these tormented him day and night. Maybe, deep down inside, he knew the answer, but chose to brush it under the carpet. It was much easier believing she would love him again, and that indeed, she did. It was far less heart-breaking to believe that his love and effort to keep her were fruitful, than to admit that they had been in vain. Deep down the pain of this unrequited love shot right through his heart like a poisoned arrow tearing it apart. He watched silently as she lay in a pool of blood, her body burst, his heart split into a million pieces.

She on the other hand, had thought it much less painful (for him, not for her) to pretend. By pretending she loved him again, he would be spared the pain that this raw naked reality now exposed. He might not be able to handle it. The truth hurts. Her charade had shielded him from it, as on an illusionary level he was hers and she was his. Truth begged to differ. And in her heart and mind its voice incessantly sang its truth song - reminding her that this charade was wrong.

She never gambled that as soon as her feet left solid ground and her body lay lifeless, shapeless, and formless she would get to see it all as clear as daylight. She saw the awfulness of all the pretending and that the poor sod didn't have a clue. Or perhaps he knew, but his love for her was stronger than she or anyone else had given him credit for.

Did she respect him? Yes, most definitely. The answer to that came quickly. There was no humming and harring in this case. He was an honest, honourable, loyal, hard-working husband and a good provider. Yes, she had a lot of respect for him, always had and always will have.

But love?

That was another matter. That was a matter of the heart, not the head. She knew that she had not been true to her heart and hence her body laying lifeless now. To be true to one's heart sounds so simple, and yet it is one of the most difficult things to achieve in our lifespan on earth. She wondered if there were people out there who lived life truthfully – authentic people, they were called - if she remembered correctly. People who had been true to their hearts, allowing it to guide them rather than over-riding its dictates by the thinking, and over-thinking of a deeply conditioned busy mind. Such people had the audacity to recognise and acknowledge what they felt and acted upon it, or not - with no drama, but with a sincerity of heart. There was a simplicity in their honesty and a freedom in their truth.

Was it the truth that had set her free, or the travesty of pretending which had brought her to this state of being? *The truth shall set you free,* someone had once said. Did they mean now on earth, or thereafter? Or both? Or neither? Those who shy away from truth -and choose to live a lie - it began to dawn on her, created a much greater pain than the one they had tried to run away from in the first place. The real pain in their hearts will find a way to come out even if it meant through extreme measures - like suicide - it will find a way to be expressed. She concluded that authenticity hadn't been one of her fortes, believing that living a lie was a much easier and a much simpler option, than expressing and living her truth.

So what happens next? she wondered. The pain of beholding this truth in her soul of souls (her heart was shattered by now and had bled to death) and seeing it in the depths of her spirit, was unbearable. Moreover, the pain that this had caused and was causing everybody who loved her began to dawn on her, taking hold of her spirit little by little until she didn't know what to do, where to go and whom to turn to. She found herself in a fit of frenzy and panicked.

Suddenly an angelic entity came to her rescue. It may have been her very own guardian angel, whom she had prayed to daily during her life on earth. Its warmth felt familiar. It held her hand, or rather sustained the space she inhabited, with love. She felt strong, stable, and safe wrapped in Its loving embrace. Its presence bore no judgement. How she would be judged and by whom she still did not know, but for now suffice it to say that she felt OK.

Resting in this warm loving embrace, lots of insights came flooding through her at the speed of light. White flashing orbs of light gushed through the vortex of where centre of the top of her head used to be. She didn't know where these realisations were coming from. But, this steady stream of consciousness, flowing like refreshing rivers of crystal-clear water, came gushing in, bringing with it renewed ways of seeing and being.

It came to her that this next chapter of her life - for her conscious awareness lived on- will not unfold as she had always believed it would. Judgement wouldn't be procured by an old Man in a white long beard, flaunting a long white robe, sitting on a white fluffy cloud. She wasn't quite sure, as yet, how it actually worked. She would have to wait and see. For this moment (not) in time, she just allowed herself to be.

Chapter 3

In the meantime, it seemed as if she could only watch, wait and trust the process. But, it didn't feel as if she had been here long enough to trust the process. She didn't know what the process was. On the other hand, it didn't seem as if she had a choice. Some would say, *go with the flow*, but there wasn't much flowing at the moment, either. It all seemed stuck and stagnant with nothing to do and nowhere to go.

Things had settled slightly, but it was getting quite long drawn and boring, although the transition itself seemed to have happened in a flash. It began to dawn on her that time was now measured differently on this side or *the other side,* depending on which side you were experiencing it from. She had no way of telling how long she had been in this watching and waiting place or state of being, in earth time.

It had already seemed like infinity, but that couldn't be right. It couldn't have been all that long, surely? How would she be able to tell? Who would help her now? She, herself, would have to figure a way out of this conundrum, as soon as possible. She had got used to getting her own way on the other side – the label of being *mentally ill* had served its purpose well, then – but, will it now?

As her human body was being transported from the scene of

the crime to a hospital mortuary nearby, she sneakily peeped at the watch on the paramedic's wrist. It showed it to be one in the afternoon. So all this waiting was only two hours' worth of earth time? Shocking!

Is this what infinity is - time going on forever, or never?

Being here didn't give her the quick fix she was after. This state was incongruent with her idea of the after-life, as a state of sheer and utter bliss, where her soul would be liberated in an instant and rested in peace, forever. The idea of a fairy-tale, happy-ever-after ending, was all a scam after all. She would sue the institution which mis-sold her this state of being as heaven, were she still on earth. She hadn't bargained for this waiting, watching and seeing nothing and everything, all at the same time.

Now that she was being given the chance to see things as they really are, she wasn't so keen on doing so. How blessed to have eyes, but not see. How damned not to have eyes and see. To be able to see is imbibed with a sense of responsibility. Oh, not responsibility! She'll have to wait a long time if she were going to be made to look at that. This was a rabbit-hole she wasn't as yet ready to dive deep into.

Her eldest daughter at times had accused her of getting away with murder under the guise of having been *mentally ill.* The label had absolved her of so much. Had she used that label to shirk responsibility for her behaviour, to get away with being totally selfish, self-absorbed, self-cherishing – shunning the needs of others always in favour of her own, concerned only with her own comfort, rest, well-being, sense of hurt, rejection, injustice and injury? Responsibility is a heavy theme she would have to come back to, suspending all the questioning, for *another time.* Time seemed to be the only luxury her soul possessed at the moment, so much of it that it seemed to flow infinitely. She had wanted to escape from it and yet here she was again, bound by it.

The ambulance comes to a sudden halt with a jolt. She had never noticed so many potholes in the road as much as she had today. Maybe, her husband had failed her in so many ways, but not when it came to driving. He had been an exceptional driver and either avoided the potholes altogether, or drove so slowly that he eased the bump every single time there was one.

She watched dumbstruck as her body, bashed and bathed in blood, was transported to the old cold morbid mortuary. It smelt of death, although it's hard to define and describe what death smells like, she debated within herself. Well, it wasn't exactly designed to be a seven-star hotel, was it? A part of her had hoped it would have flowers painted on its walls, and angels on the ceiling to get her into the mood for where she was headed. She hadn't expected it to be a plain white ice-cold place. How she longed to see familiar faces who would soothe and comfort her.

And the familiar faces did come. They didn't look happy, comforting or soothing. In fact, she wasn't quite sure whether it was anger or fear she depicted in their saddened demeanour and heavy hearts. She wasn't sure if her eldest daughter would be summoned to identify her carcass. She remembered calling her name as she was being pulled down by that strong gravitational force -gravity - as she committed the greatest travesty of all time.

That cry – was it regret? Had it been that just as both feet found themselves kicking in mid-air she had had a change of heart? No, it had felt like total and utter freedom for a split second. But, freedom always comes at a price, *always*! she believed. And what would the price be this time? she pondered. Were the rules here the same as on earth?

So many questions and so few answers. Yet not to worry. She had an infinity, it seems, to sort them out. So was her perception of life-after-death being sweet-tasting like milk and honey flowing from heaven, taking her to a state of being overflowing with life, love and light, a fallacy? At this moment in time the answer seemed to be a resounding *yes*.

Will she ever win? she asked herself, feeling defeated in death as in life.

"Hang on, what's he doing here?" she hissed.

She was grateful for the distraction, she had to admit. Things here we not as clear-cut as she had been led to believe and finding her way around was tricky, very tricky. It was quite confusing and becoming a bit overwhelming.

Anyway, what was he doing there? she pondered, whilst he pouted staring at her bloody body, impassively. He was a part of the reason why she had done this today of all days, and maybe he knew it. And yet if the wedding still went ahead in six months' time, then a big part of having committed suicide today, so close to Christmas and to her daughter's engagement to this man on Christmas eve, would have been in vain. What a waste of a perfectly timed death that would be! she thought morosely.

Who did he think he was, looking at her as if he knew her, as if he got her, as if he cared? All he cared about was getting her eldest daughter to marry him, knowing she would make a fantastic wife and an amazing mother. After this unexpected turn of events her daughter wouldn't want to forge ahead with the wedding, and would definitely defer or cancel the engagement which was due to take place in a few day's time. She was sure of this. This act of hers wasn't as selfish as it seemed, after all. There was her daughter's future at stake and her suicide would take care of that. Her suicide killed two birds with one stone - her own misery and her daughter's upcoming engagement and marriage to this soulless man.

She seriously doubted this young lad, who had never shown any emotion, had been capable of love. Her eldest daughter would need a man with love and passion pulsating throughout his heart, mind, body and soul. A man who would fall head-over-heels in love with her, and love her unconditionally. A man who would protect her from the harsh world outside and offer her a safe place to hide when she needed one. She knew her eldest daughter much more than her eldest daughter ever knew herself. She knew her needs more than her eldest daughter knew her own needs. She knew her eldest daughter and her eldest daughter knew her much more than either of them knew themselves. And she knew, more than her daughter, that this young lad wouldn't cut it.

A doctor.

He wanted to be a doctor.

Her daughter would marry a doctor who would take care of other peoples' needs, cure their illnesses (or so you'd hope!) and be there for them. But would he be there for her? If the past were an indication of the future, then he would not, from what she had already seen. But how could she relay this to her eldest daughter from here? Her eldest daughter hadn't believed her whenever she had tried to touch on the subject when back on earth, believing she had an ulterior motive. If she were guilty, it was only of wanting to see her daughter happy - loved, respected and valued, which she seriously doubted this lad had it in him to do. Alas, now her daughter would have to open her eyes and see for herself. If this didn't stop the forthcoming engagement and upcoming wedding from going ahead, then nothing would.

The man she had called *husband* for many years had come from the scene of the crime to the mortuary in time. In that dark, cold, sordid room she could see as clear as daylight that he still loved her, in spite and despite all that they had gone through. She saw it so clearly now that her heart ached with the pain he was feeling. How was it that she had never perceived it to this extent before? Was it at all possible that his fits of rage, anger and fury were all down to a fear- a fear of losing her -or a fear of actually never having had her? Maybe, just maybe, in his heart of hearts he knew she had never loved him.

She lied. He believed her lies. She almost began to believe her own lies herself. Then suddenly one day the lie took on a life of its own. It took on its own shape, form and personality, colouring hers and his perspectives, beliefs, attitudes, actions and decisions with its deceit-tinted glasses. It temporarily shielded both of them from the truth.

Is this what had actually made her mentally ill? All this pretending, separating her from what is real and true? Was she mentally or spiritually ill? Was there a difference? And if there were, what was the difference? There had been a great disparity and conflict between what she had perceived as reality and wanted to embrace as reality, and the reality and truth itself, it began to dawn on Amy, as she began to perceive the growing gulf between the two.

She hadn't wanted to live like she had, but she didn't know how to change it - or more precisely, she didn't want to change it. She carried on with her everyday business going through the motions of daily life on autopilot and out a sense of duty and obligation. Her body was present performing the daily physical tasks of cleaning, cooking, ironing, baking, cleaning, cooking, ironing, baking, shopping, with more of the same. Yet, her heart and her mind were back in her home country, Down Under. Her heart and her mind had been stuck there for the last twenty odd years, frozen in a time-capsule where she had been held by her lover Greg's warm embraces, shutting out the rest of world, daring (to have an affair) and not caring (about the aftermath). Affairs are so exonerated by the media, she maintained, but in reality it left people shattered and feeling very empty inside. The glamour of it was shown, but not the sense of feeling used and abused when the lover went back to their other beloved, bound by law but not by love.

She had never recovered from that and whatever reality she was faced with thereafter, she couldn't cope with. So she absented herself from the present moment. Wherever she was physically, she wasn't present mentally – mentally she was constantly in Greg's strong arms covered profusely in his passionate kisses, swathed in his warm tender caresses and intoxicating silent whispers of sweet nothings. She could still feel his lips softly, yet urgently kissing the nape of her neck, sliding down her chest to her small, yet firm breasts, making her go wild with love and passionate abandon. He had liked running his dexterous fingers through her short, dark hair amongst other sensitive spots on her body which made her writhe in sexual excitement and pleasure, filling her with sheer ecstasy.

It all always seemed as if it had just happened a moment earlier, or was just happening now, instead of many years before. She swore she could still catch a whiff of his perfume lingering on her languidly lying naked body. The smelling, the tasting and the eating of this delectably delicious forbidden fruit so many years ago, always seemed so concurrent, making the past ever more real than the present. She wanted to push the memory away - she fought it tooth and nail - and begged it to go away, but it faithfully followed her night and day. The ghost of this forbidden feast haunted her waking hours and permeated her artificially induced sleep.

To her these memories were as real, as real as can be - much more real than the food she ate, the hot chocolate she drank, or the biscuits she dunked into her tea. More real than the broom she would hold whilst sweeping, the water on her body whilst bathing or the bed she would lie in whilst sleeping. Evermore present than her daughter, son or husband and more real than the sky, the sea, the sand and the air she breathed - was his essence and presence, everywhere.

Like an obsession, his presence would not let her rest. Or perhaps, being obsessed she would not let it go. Some would argue she couldn't, whilst others would disagree and maintain she wouldn't! Either way, she was bound in chains, enslaved by a past which she couldn't or wouldn't extricate herself from. She tossed and turned in a dark deep sea of yearning for what was, could be or could have been. There had been no rest for her mind, no respite for her soul. The electric shock convulsion treatments (which had already been banned in most European countries at the time), which had been administered many times with the hope of making her forget, had the opposite effect. Sadly, it seemed to make the distant past much more present and real, the memories much more vivid and the need to go back much more pressing, making her present much more depressing.

That is where she had wanted to be. She had never wanted to leave. He had promised he would leave his wife and be with her and hers, forever. But like many men, he was a coward, she asserted. It was him not keeping his word that had actually destroyed her. Or had it? Had he shattered her dreams, her life, her hope for and promise of love, security, passion and protection or was it her inability to let it go that had done that?

And protection? Protection from whom or what exactly? Even if he could protect her from her angered and humiliated husband in his fear and fury, he would never be able to protect her from herself and from the hell on earth she eventually created for herself and for all those around her - to punish herself for her transgressions.

It hadn't mattered that they had been both married at the time, that they both had children and that Greg and her husband had been besties. He didn't give a toss and eventually neither did she. They both had everything to lose and what would they gain? And more importantly, what would she gain? Their lives could be shattered in one moment, just one moment is all it took for them to be found out. Yet, they didn't care. As far as they were concerned it was all worth it. They were young, reckless and in love. And they had the audacity to believe that true love conquered all.

That's what she couldn't take, in her embodied life. After all that had happened, how come true love had not conquered all? How could he leave her, abandon her and act as if none of their encounters, and moreover their love, mattered when it came to the crunch? He chose his wife over her – the wife he had so bitterly complained about time and time again, the wife he would slag, the wife he would proclaim not to love any more. Had it actually been love, true love? Or now come to think of it, was it merely lust, passion, and a bit of fun on the side from where he had been standing?

She had given him her heart, mind, body and soul and hadn't kept anything back. Maybe she had given too much? Maybe there is a part of her, she should have kept for herself! It was too late now and besides, all this thinking, wondering, pondering, musing and inquiring had made her very tired. She longed to shut her eyes and go to sleep as she had done for all those years on earth. Shutting her eyes and sleeping had been the oyster shell which had held and protected her, in moments of darkness and doubt such as these. She chose when to wake up if to wake up at all, when to sleep, how long to sleep for, when to open her eyes and how long for - she had complete control.

Well actually it wasn't her who decided, was it really? Thanks to advances in medicine chemicals and toxins pumped into her body, to numb her mind, were doing it for her! So she wasn't in control, after all! Blessed, blessed and more blessed are those who have eyes and shut them to sleep and slumber. She thought that now she would be allowed to sleep forever. Not for one minute had it occurred to her that this was the point of no return where her eyes would stay wide open to see, her ears unplugged to hear and listen - whether she liked it or not - sleeping was not an option, only being awake was.

Her reverie was thankfully interrupted by someone who seemed to get paid for covering up lifeless bodies after everyone had left. What a way to make a living. He came around checking up on them one by one on tip-toes! She couldn't fathom why someone would tip-toe in a room full of corpses; it wasn't as if they were going to be woken up now, was it? Or rather, it wasn't as if they were ever going to be allowed to go back to sleep – ever again, is it?

Chapter 4

This state of being was proving to be too much for Amy – how is she going to survive being awake the whole time? I'll let you know this wasn't like watching tellie, either. Watching tellie always manages to distract you from whatever it is you're running away from. As you watch others struggle, you are absented, albeit momentarily, from your own struggles. The characters on tellie are often faced with much harsher realities than your own, so your plight seems significantly easier compared to theirs. Alternatively, they live in blissful realities to which you are briefly transported, abstracting you from your own gruelling harsh reality.

The modern opium of the people. Distraction. It worked. But, here it was different. Here you were watching what you really did not want to see, and you weren't given a choice about what to watch. You just had to stay there with your eyes and ears wide open, watching whether you liked what you saw and heard, or not.

There were no TV Guides to offer choice upon choice of what to view. You could not flick though pages telling you when your favourite programme was going to be repeated, should you have missed it the first time and there was no switching channels if you got bored or didn't like what you saw.

Not that people seemed to get bored nowadays. People seemed to be getting dumb and dumber and less and less discerning as to what makes good TV viewing, Amy asserted. The more *real,* obscene, rude and loud people were on screen, the more successful the programme became. A shame, really.

Anyhow, all in the name of free will and freedom of expression, I suppose. Yet, how free were they, really? How free was she, actually? Hadn't she thought prior to being here that she would be free forever? Free from all the thinking, the over-thinking, the analysing, the judging, the blaming, the naming of intentions, actions, constantly being pulled in different directions by conflicting thoughts and emotions? Didn't she believe that now she would be liberated from guilt, from shame, from the mundane, from things that didn't matter, or shouldn't have mattered, but did? Hadn't she hoped she would be set free from her attachment to a past which bound her like a heavy iron anchor deeply embedded into the bottom of a deep dark sea? She hoped she would be liberated from the longing of being back in her long lost lover's arms and free from the yearning of being kissed incessantly by his soft, tender lips. She believed she would be freed from memories of a dead past that seemed so alive, present and real, robbing her of life in the present, stealing her peace, controlling her every thought, dictating her state of being, tainting her world-view with a deep sense of loss and a heart-breaking grief which would not leave her.

She had hoped her suicide would liberate her spirit from all of this. But, alas!

She had hoped she would be liberated from the soul-destroying routine of everyday life, where one day merged into another, with nothing new, exciting or mentally stimulating to ever come along to break the cycle. She longed for a change in direction, and what better way of changing direction was there than this?

Or so it had seemed!

She imagined herself being free from her own self-judgement which was not sympathetic to her story– *a saint with a history* she would call herself on one level – *in your dreams* her harsh, self-deprecating voice would mock! She envisaged a state of being free from her desire to sleep and slumber day and night shutting herself from herself and from those self-judging violent voices which never shut up. She thought she would be free from her desire for peace, tranquility and calm which seemed to elude her, the more she desired them.

Now it seemed she couldn't win either way, neither here nor there.

Hadn't that Man she believed had been murdered for speaking Truth once proclaimed, "Peace on Earth to all men of good will?" It's true she wasn't a man, but wasn't that just a figure of speech meaning that the peace that was there to be had, was for everybody? Why had she been missed out and left behind? Why was it that the harder she tried, the more she failed? Didn't *goodwill* mean that she did not wish anybody any harm? Of many things she had been guilty during her life on earth, but never had she wished anybody any harm, not even her harshest critics or worse enemies.

It was a heart-breaking sight which stopped her in her musings and jolted her back to the present moment. It wrenched her heart to see all those people congregated together under one roof. There was deadly silence, despite the number of people present. You could hear a pin drop. They all looked despondent, to say the least. It seemed as if they were gathered to commemorate her life and give her soul a good send-off, as it were.

She wasn't sure about this. What does a good send-off actually mean? Who were they doing it for? Was it actually for her that they were gathered there, or for themselves – a way to connect to their own grief through someone else's? In actual fact, did it really matter to her what they were there for? They had turned up for some reason or another and that should be enough - end of story. She should be filled with gratitude that so many had taken precious time out of their busy schedules to come and bid her farewell. It wasn't her job to judge them; it would be her job over the next many moments of forced, continued wakefulness to procure her own judgement in some way, not knowing how yet. She wondered whether her self-judging voice would still be as strong, as opinionated, as obstinate, and as unforgiving as it had always been or whether it would mellow, having taken a hit. Perhaps, formed and informed by what it continues to see and hear about her, it might grow in love and compassion towards her and her plight.

But, back to the here and now.

It felt as if anybody and everybody was here – the whole island, it seemed. Family and more family, friends and more friends, acquaintances and more acquaintances, people she had liked, people she had disliked, people she had been totally and utterly disinterested in, people who had brought her pleasure, people who had brought her pain, people who had valued her, people who had devalued and humiliated her - the list was endless. She saw people, people and more people. She didn't even know that so many people knew who she was and was shocked at how they all seemed to know what she had done.

From where she was standing – well, not actually standing – she couldn't explain at the time what position her disembodied being had assumed – this was all a bit too much. It were as if she had suddenly caught a glimpse of the enormity of what she had done and saw how loudly her actions had spoken. She perceived the impact of her deed, not just on close loved ones but, on many others. Her suicide had shaken the tiny village to its foundations and the island to its core.

She would have to pay for this in some way, but how, she would have to wait, to find out. A lot of good would come of it too, she tried to justify to herself. And she was right. Her sacred benevolent Creator always turned bad things to good for those who loved Him. And loved Him she had done with all her heart.

Was this waiting a part of her purification process? her conscious-consciousness wondered. Being in this place of watching and waiting was in itself a painful state of being. The constant state of wakefulness added to the discomfort. If purification included pain and discomfort, then she was in the right place or in the right state of being, for that matter. Pain almost always invariably is there to tell us something - to show us what needs changing - the more we ignore its message the sharper it gets, and the louder it shouts, until its message is heeded.

Her body may have died, but her consciousness lived on. It was much more aware than ever before. She had a gut feeling, well now that she didn't have a body any more, she wasn't sure she could call it a gut feeling, that this state of being wasn't going to last forever. It was a stage, amongst the many stages before the final destination. But she also knew she wasn't going to go to a better state of being any time soon, not unless all this s**t (not that she should swear in church) had been cleared and her soul cleaned, cleansed and renewed - made as white as snow - ready for the next realm after this.

She had hoped that by *crossing over to the other side* as so many people referred to it, her life as she knew it would come to an end. She hadn't bargained that it would have to get worse, much worse, before it actually got any better. Having waited for so long to die, she would now have to wait goodness knows how long to live.

Oh my goodness! There he was again. That dark, handsome well-built man with a tough exterior as his manual jobs demanded, yet within whom a soft, tender and compassionate heart resided. She may have had something to do with the hardening of his heart, the sense of his soul being lost and his spirit crushed, she admitted to herself.

He had been very handsome in his youth – a *teddy boy* back in the day, with a long curl casually drooping over his tanned forehead. His deep, dark eyes had always been his best feature, and many would back Amy on this one. It were as if all the love his heart couldn't contain came shining right through those eyes, which were almost as black and as sparkly as a summer's night sky shimmering with starlight. He was a good man. She knew that. But, she had been so wrapped up in her own little drama of losses and grief that she had never really given him and how he felt, much thought. She actually blamed him for her misfortune most of the time. Why such a pang of pity now? What good was that going to do? She tried to move as close to him as she could, to see what she could catch a glimpse of, in those mysterious eyes of his. It hadn't changed from what she had seen earlier, but reinforced it further still. He had loved her, and always will.

He couldn't begin to process the sense of loss he felt in the pit of his stomach. It felt as if it had been ripped wide open, oozing ounces and ounces of pain-stained blood. Death had dug its unrelenting scathe into his ribs so that he could hardly breathe. It was best not to think, feel, or move. So he just sat there, motionless and numb.

As he sat in the front pew waiting for the funeral service to begin, he remembered the first time he had laid eyes on her. She had been the most beautiful girl he had ever seen and he had seen many in his day. He had girls falling at his feet every day before that day- and many years thereafter. There were blond girls, dark girls, young girls, older girls, well-off girls from well-to-do families, less wealthy ones, but he had never been interested. His mum had given up on him ever marrying. To every girl's mother who had approached her, hoping her daughter would be the chosen lucky one, she would say to give up hope as he wasn't interested in dating or in getting married. He was too busy fishing or getting himself into trouble playing pranks on unsuspecting passers-by or on innocent local fishing-boat owners. He was a free-spirit and lived a carefree life.

When younger his mum was the one who wore the trousers in the house, as they would say back in the day. She was the one with the business acumen and the money, whilst his dad -a very quiet, unassuming shy man would go about his business, silently. Whilst she hustled running the little village grocery shop, he welded ships at the local dockyards. There were many things that united them, but one thing that did divide them and cause many endless arguments and sleepless nights. This was their son Mike. The pranks he was constantly playing on villagers and the trouble he was incessantly causing every Tom, Dick and Harry caused a rift in the couple, especially since the mother sided with Mike against his father's *better judgement* of the boy needing discipline and a good hiding every now and then.

On the other hand, they both concurred that he should be sent to a public school. They were not academic themselves, but since very well-off they had wanted him to have the best start in life. On this they both wholeheartedly agreed. Uniforms were tailored, school satchels ordered, school shoes bought from the Capital, ready for the big day.

But how would he be made to go? He was as strong as an ox and as stubborn as a mule. He believed that school was for wimps and for people with nothing better to do - stuffy people - who enjoyed reading about life, rather than living it. Life in the great outdoors, underneath the eternal clear blue sky, constantly sniffing in the fresh salty sea air is what rocked his boat– the school of life, in the long run, taught him all he needed to know.

He flatly refused to go and played truant more often than not. You could safely say that school wasn't going to be the way forward for him and that the money his mum and dad spent, had been totally wasted. When he did go, he was so rude to the teachers that he got severely caned, so much so, that he wouldn't be able to walk for a week, and so would go fishing instead.

Fishing had always been his passion. In fact, it was the sea that had been the love of his life. His mum would have bet her whole fortune on him never getting married, so much in love with the sea he had been. He bought, made up and sold numerous little boats and was well known in that neck of the woods for his dealing and wheeling in sea vessels. He was known to have *borrowed* , but never returned, a boat or two on occasion for a night or so and avidly remembered for burning one, just for fun.

Miles out at sea he would forget the world with all its cares and its pressures to conform, to perform and to succeed. He didn't care for any of these. All he had ever wanted was a quiet life in which he could fish and be happy. Whether he would ever fall in love or not he did not know, neither did he care. The only thing he did know is that he had to be by the sea. When out at sea, he was at peace - you could almost say, it felt like being in a trance. Looking out at the dark sea in the dead of night, with the sound of waves lapping gently against his fishing boat as if they were making love to the vessel, filled him with an indescribable joy. Every time it felt as if his whole being became the sea itself and a sea of calm washed over him. He made being out at sea all night, to an untrained layperson's eye, seem as if it were a doddle. He never grumbled at how hungry he was when he returned to land at four, five or six o'clock in the morning. He never complained how his shoulders, back and neck ached after lifting tons of heavy fish into his tiny boat. He would be too elated, and filled with such a sense of achievement after every catch, to complain. He would be proud at having worked honestly for a living, making his own way in the the world, depending on nobody but himself and on what divine providence decided to grace him with that particular night. It wasn't pride as in an arrogance, but a pride as in the satisfaction of a job well done. And when back empty-handed, as sometimes happened, he maintained that one had to take the rough with the smooth in life and just carried on.

He often wondered, when miles away from any sign of human habitation, how his life would unfold. One thing he was quite clear about was that he had wanted to be independent and free. Conform, conform, conform - had been his dad's motto in life. Well, he would do anything, but! Wasn't conforming the same as dying while you were still living? What was the point of life if you didn't explore the endless possibilities, push your boundaries and dare to do something different, and be different? "I am not a sheep," he would say out loud to the fish at sea, in the dead of night, as the stars watched over him and the sea provided for him.

It came as a shock, however, to his dad more so than to his mum when he announced that he had bought a one way ticket to the land Down Under. Many people had left the island in search of better job prospects down there and they knew of many friends and relatives who had upped and left their homeland in search of a better life. For him it wasn't so much the allure of a better life as much as wanting to be independent, making it completely on his own.

His dad's nagging to conform had urged his free spirit to fly further and soar higher.

He had looked at his father at times, and vowed he would kill himself should he ever end up like him. He was hard-working and a very respectable member of the local community, a regular church-goer and a dedicated family man and Mike respected him for that. But, he could not and would not conform to anybody's expectations of him and would not be told how to live his life by anyone, be it an individual or an institution.

He was a bit more like his mum if truth be told, who

wasn't your regular stay-at-home mum like many of her contemporaries. No. She had business acumen, which ran in her side of the family, and used it successfully. She made a lot of money which was a blessing, as there were many mouths to feed. She was also a seamstress and sewed half of the brand new dresses worn by numerous females on the first Sunday of August during the long-awaited and much anticipated, village festa (Maltese for fiesta).

Her heart wasn't in the village festa this year, however. Her eldest son was leaving.

She didn't know when she would ever be seeing him again. She had loved him like none of her other children, which is not really fair as a woman should love all of her offspring equally, surely? But, no matter how much she rationalised it in her head, her heart pounced with joy every time he called her 'Ma'. He would leave the week before the village festa which means that this would be the first village festa she would have to celebrate without him - it wouldn't be the same! She would miss him like crazy, although he had always been getting himself into mischief and had neighbours threatening to kill him as he had burnt their cat alive, their boat, or their dog, a bit of an arsonist really, when you come to think of it. He would take refuge and sleep in the mortuary nearby many a night, to escape his father's fury, knowing that his dad would beat him black and blue as soon as he heard of his, yet new, misdemeanour.

Before he went to sleep he would take a bite to eat and rest his weary head by the foot of the cold metal bed. There had been times when he would go to bed knowing his dad was out on the prowl trying to give him a belting or two. On nights such as these he would ask his unsuspecting brother to sleep in his place. Swapping sides, he would silently chuckle inside. This was a clever and clearly premeditated move to make sure his brother got the lashings in his place. By the time his dad realised he was beating the wrong son, his brother would have already been beaten to a pulp. This would buy him time to pounce out of bed and dash out of the house like a man possessed. And sometimes possessed seemed to be quite an accurate description of him, many people in the village would say. But he was her son, nonetheless, and she couldn't bear to imagine life without him.

She had bought him the best suitcase on the market and showed a very brave face in public. She smiled as she proudly announced to her regular customers that her eldest son, was turning a new leaf; some sense had been knocked into him and he was going to emigrate to work.

However, that smile was only there to mask the pain of her impending loss. What was there to be proud of really? He would go and only God knew when she would ever see him again. Her husband on the other hand, would not talk about it, not with her, not with his own brothers and sisters, nor with friends (not that as a busy family man he had any), not with colleagues – nor with anybody else! He just went into himself as if this were the death of his eldest son and he needed to grieve. Perhaps, a part of him felt responsible for this loss. He had been a harsh disciplinarian as most dads back in his day were and his free-spirited son would not be broken in. He needed to fly the nest, to be free to take to the sky or sail across the sea.

The big day came and went in a flash. He'd enjoy the voyage which was going to take about four weeks on that imposing ship which had pulled up at the harbour a couple of days prior to the big event. There were tears of sadness, of loss, words wishing him luck, words giving him advice, words hoping the best for him, from all and sundry.

Needless to say, he was a youth just turned eighteen full of a zest for life, for adventure and new beginnings. He felt courage in his loins and hope in his heart. His gut ached, not from fear, but from wanting to go and conquer the world and from a heartfelt desire to be who he was meant to be – fulfilling his destiny. His gut ached from a yearning to do away with all the pressure to conform and please others that came from living on a very tiny island. He would set himself free as he set sail to enjoy the luxury of anonymity. He stood up, straight and tall, on the front deck counting his blessings, whilst looking forward to the new life which awaited him. He did not know a word of English, nor did not have a job lined up in advance, but he was not afraid. There would be nobody to meet and greet him on the other side, yet he had a vision and a dream which he believed in and this urged him on.

If only he had known then what he knew now, that all his dreams would one cold sunny winter's day be crushed to smithereens. If he had known, he most certainly would have never set foot on that godforsaken continent of an island. If only he knew then, that the quiet, simple life his soul had always yearned for would elude him in the land Down Under, he would've never set foot on it. But alas, he didn't have a crystal ball which would tell all.

So he honoured his heart which wanted to set sail and be free and for doing that, he had no regrets. He had no regrets at having met her either, of having fallen in love with her, of having given her his heart, mind, body and soul. He loved her then, and he loved her now with a love that transcends space and time and nothing and nobody would get in the way of that.

And now bearing her lifeless body as it lay motionless in its coffin it all seemed to him as if he were watching a sad film in sepia of someone else's funeral -not his beloved Amy's. A stranger's. This couldn't be happening to him. She would not do this to him and to them. She would always be there.

As the coffin was brought to the centre of the aisle and was put down on the cold marble floor, he couldn't help but wonder how it had all come to this.

Chapter 5

He had always preferred freedom to love, but somehow he longed for the love of this woman even if his freedom were jeopardised. He knew she would be the making of him and because of her he would be a new and better man – reformed even. Don't get me wrong, he was naughty but not nasty, not a nasty bone in his body. And as to his heart, he began to feel it opening up to love and to be loved, through the beauty and warmth exuded by this woman who melted him like the sun back home in the Med, melts ice-cream.

There she had been, minding her own business at the bus stop, when he started chatting her up. She was a very beautiful, shy, coy young girl. He was twenty-one - and this was his first love. Love at first sight.

Every time he saw her his heart pounded with excitement and a yearning deep inside to get to know her, to be with her and to one day marry her. This is what filled his day and night dreams. He would imagine his life in pictures - in colour, not sepia -of how happy she would make him and how happy he would make her. In his eyes their life together would be picture perfect. Other people's marriages failed, perhaps. But, they would live happily-ever-after.

He wasn't academic and could hardly read or write, but

he was picking up English at the speed of light. He was a fast learner and very determined. Necessity was the mother of invention, she had always maintained and in his case this couldn't have been truer.

So it wasn't a matter of luck, but more of a cunning plan that he had befriended one of her brothers who in the end had set him up with her. He didn't think he could be this happy - that life could be this perfect. He knew now what his heart had been destined for and understood why he hadn't ever fallen in love before - because none of the other girls were her - as one of his favourite oldies sung.

His heart burnt with a passion that all the love songs in his era sang of. He enjoyed the bliss of this perfection and match made in heaven. Mike couldn't believe his luck when she agreed to marry him only after a very short engagement. He was the happiest man on earth and would say so to anyone who cared to listen. But he was a very private person when it came to matters of the heart, so not many knew.

It was a simple wedding. She wasn't into lots of fuss, this woman. She was the embodiment of perfection in his eyes and could do no wrong. His love for her was unfathomable and he never doubted her love for him.

He would be hers for keeps and she his, forever.

That word *forever* is a toughie, as many of us know. It was only after four years of marriage that she declared she had been having a love affair. It had been going on for two years right under his nose, right under his roof and slapped him right in the face.

He wasn't even sure he believed her. A Brazilian author once wrote something along the lines that people would rather believe a lie than the truth, Amy recalled. He decided he wouldn't actually endorse that truth unless he saw with his very own eyes, heard with his very own ears and experienced with his very own being the affair she claimed had been going on behind his back for so long. He had been convinced that it was all a story made up to make him jealous, so that he would start giving her a bit more attention and tender loving care, since that had waned soon after the *'I do's'* were exchanged.

He had decided he would keep watch, like they did in the films he had watched at the drive-in with her. He would spy on them, only because unless he caught them red-handed, he would not believe. He had to witness it with his own eyes. And so they did meet on that fateful day. And so did he see with his very own eyes and hear with his very own ears.

As hard as he tried he could not etch what he saw and heard that day, out of his mind. He wished a magic potion would make it vanish into thin air. But alas, instead of getting fainter, the snapshot of the obscene scene grew bolder, and like a hallucination, its shape and form danced dementedly in front of his very own eyes, changing colour, shape, depth and width, morphing into a vision which would haunt him by day and torment him by night, for the rest of his life. As the secret skeleton had come out of the closet to see the light of day - his own light was darkened, and he felt his life-force slowly slipping away.

His dreams swiftly shattered. What was left of his heart, mutilated. His days of innocent freedom and abandon over. He changed overnight.

He became very highly strung and anything, no matter how minor, would be enough to tip him over the edge. His angry outbursts saw him foaming at the mouth like an other-worldly, or under-worldly being, terrorising all and everything in sight. On the outside it was business-as-usual, but inside he experienced death with every breath. Inside, there did reside chaos, confusion and a carcass for a heart beating the drum-roll of death.

He was out of his mind with the questions which faced him that day and forevermore, thereafter. That she didn't love him any more seemed obvious. Had she ever loved him? Had she loved him on their wedding day? Why did she marry him in the first place? Why his friend? Or rather why his best friend? Did she seek Greg out? Did he seek her out? Did it matter? Did he still love her? Would he ever be able to get past this? Would his heart ever heal? Would he ever be able to forgive her? Would this excruciating pain ever subside or even better, go away altogether?

He was an anguished soul, being pulled in this and that direction by the desire to forgive her and keep going as if nothing had happened on the one hand, and the urge for revenge and punishment, on the other. He was constantly being torn between these two opposing factions. Most of the time it felt as if he were going mad - schizophrenic even! The fury he felt was in direct proportion to how much he had loved her, doted on her and trusted her. He was no mathematician, however he knew that it hadn't been reciprocated in the same way.

The only solution he could think of would be to go back to his own home country, which he had missed, but had hoped not to return to in a hurry. Or at least not to return to, in circumstances such as these. He had to leave. He had to get away from this place. Yet, he wasn't going anywhere without his little one, their little Marie, you see! In the meantime, he had fathered the most exquisite four year old one could ever imagine. Her inquiring big brown eyes, long auburn curly hair and air of confidence, coupled with her innocence, won the heart of everyone.

Amy hadn't remembered their home-country, having been taken to the land Down Under only at nine months old. She didn't speak the language, nor did she know anybody there, bar Mike. Leaving the land Down Under had never been a part of her dream. She wanted to stay, keeping her little Marie with her family - she didn't want to go away.

But Mike wanted to go.

Mike needed to go.

And he definitely was taking his little Marie with him, no matter what. He had made that crystal clear. It was a battle of wills. A tug-of-war ensued, fought over by a desire to make the pain go away. But the pain had set up shop in their lives, and it did not stop, no matter what. Neither of them, wherever they turned to, could find any respite or peace day or night. He knew leaving with Marie would destroy Amy and perhaps this is what Mike had wanted at the time. He wasn't in the right state of mind to analyse or discern the right course of action in terms of intention, morals or ethics. He felt that being the injured party, it was his prerogative to make that decision. He would have to evaluate later the integrity of his intentions and actions, when not at the mercy of so much anguish and pain. He just wanted to jump ship, and so he did.

Amy, on the other hand, wasn't just going to give up Marie just like that. Having Marie hadn't been easy. It was a difficult pregnancy and Amy thought she would die during childbirth. Having been born at only seven months Marie had been incubated at the local hospital, for the first seven weeks of her life, until she was fully recovered and well enough to be taken home. Amy's body and mind took longer to heal as she had been pulled and prodded in every direction at barely eighteen years of age. She was a girl needing to be taken care of herself, now a mother of baby girl needing her constant love, care and attention.

It was hard, without a shadow of a doubt. But Amy had had her mother's support and her three brothers' dedication to her, and to her little one. All their love, attention, energy and time had been invaluable as each played their own part in making this new arrival, having made it through by the skin of her teeth, most welcome. Grandma Jo almost loved Marie more than she loved Amy. She couldn't bear to be without her. She would have her every day whilst Amy was at work at the office. She took Marie out shopping, to the swings, to the park and everywhere the twain went, everybody thought that Marie was Grandma Jo's own daughter. Alas, all three brothers doted on her too. The eldest brother would buy her copious amounts of toys, the middle lots of lovely clothes, whilst the youngest would feed her playfully when she didn't want to eat, which was often. This love which Marie was surrounded by for the first four and a half years of her life, gave her a solid foundation for what was to come. There were hard times ahead and she needed all the love and attention she could get.

The house sold quickly and cheaply. Tickets booked. Cruise ship boarded. The tri-une headed back to his home country. The four week voyage was hard. He still loved her, that he couldn't deny. The love he felt for her at the altar, he still felt now. The heart which contained that love had been decimated, but the love itself had intensified -perhaps, that's what hurt does, Amy wondered, in the middle of this mess.

He had set the intention to forgive her and move on, just as the ship left the dock and headed to the open sea. So, why hadn't he? What was it that stopped him? It was that image. That frightful picture in his head had captured both lying stark naked on his (their) matrimonial bed, and immortalised it. He witnessed, in shock, their bodies intertwined, sweating in the throes of pressing passionate kissing and urgent caressing leaving no body part untouched. Her soft moaning and musical groaning in pure unadulterated pleasure assailed him as he slowly approached the bedroom door. They hadn't heard him silently sneak in, so immersed in the present moment and in each other they had been. He had caught them red-handed, and couldn't deny what he hadn't wanted to believe was true. I leave the judgement of Amy, dear reader with you, for now. Perhaps, you wouldn't be as harsh on her, as she had been on herself, for the rest of her days.

He didn't swear. He didn't lash out. He didn't do or say anything. He just left the abominable scene as quietly as he had come in. It was not his crime - although what he had just witnessed had been criminal. If it had been any other man he may have recovered quicker. But Greg had been his best-mate! And her, he had trusted and loved with all his heart.

He thought that being back under the eternal blue skies of his homeland would ease the pain. He hoped that being thousands of miles away from the scene of the crime would make the memory grow fainter, its hold on him weaker. How wrong could he have been! Not one day passed in which that scene would not play on his mind as if in a loop, with the sounds and smells of that day accosting his senses in every way.

How do you run away from a demon who seems to be

taking hold of you, possessing you, owning and constantly tormenting your very heart, mind, body and soul? Work. Work. And more work.

He kept himself so busy that he didn't have any time to think or to look at his own thoughts, let alone listen to them. When not working, he would drink. Ah, the benevolence of being drunk. What a balm to his mind and spirit. No image, mental or otherwise would get past the alcohol, one of the most addictive and lethal legal drugs around. And so he proceeded to work and drink, and drink and work, round the clock, so that there was no space for any image or thought of that day to dock in the port of his conscious aware mind.

It turned out that the senses could be numbed, the mind blanked, but the raging inferno inside could not be quelled. It would burn and churn inside his body like molten lava under the earth's crust and like a volcano every so often, very often when Marie was still only very little, would erupt. It was an active volcano, its eruptions growing stronger, steadier and deadlier as time went by. There were casualties.

The chattels would be smashed to smithereens with plates, sometimes empty, sometimes full, flying to the ceiling whilst decorative ornaments hurtled through space at times just missing Amy or Marie by an inch of their life. Sofas were seized and smashed. Mike's cursing of all that is sacred and divine shattered glass, and whilst losing leave of his senses, some other dark force took over, procuring this devastation and destruction. It sometimes seemed as it Satan himself were in the room with a legion of seven other demons securing Mike's soul as their own. How could such intense love, coexist with such extreme anger? Was it anger, in actual fact, or hurt? Or were they one and the same?

Presently he stared at the brown wooden box across the aisle in the middle of the church. He couldn't figure it out! It was all becoming so confusing and he began to feel quite uncomfortable sitting in the front pew. His thoughts were conveniently interrupted by the organ playing the opening hymn.

What had his Marie chosen for this? he wondered. It was lucky she had made it through, alive to this day, but he didn't want to go there, just now. He was very proud of her. He admired her courage and fortitude, in stark contrast to his inherent cowardice. Her strength put his weakness to shame.

It wasn't until she was older and stood up to him, telling him that she wasn't taking his mad outbursts of physical and verbal violence any longer, that he really started to notice and respect her. On that day, he had met mettle with mettle. Marie was only fourteen at the time and had shown admirable courage and fearlessness. He had to respect her for that. It's as if stooping to his level, shouting, swearing and stamping her feet, she had finally reached him in the deep, dark recesses of his own demented self-centered existence, where he nursed his wounds with the diligence of mother nursing her newborn child. She had found a way in. From then onwards their relationship blossomed. He recognised that she was no ordinary daughter, for she had stood up to him more than any man.

He had nearly physically killed her once. Suddenly, as she stood up to read the First Reading he was overcome by an immense sense of shame. This daughter had brought him nothing but joy. She had loved him much more than he deserved. And yet, he had nearly murdered her over two mouthfuls of lemonade which she had drunk whilst he had been out fishing.

He blamed his youngest son. But no, it wasn't him, Amy had vehemently reassured Mike. Mike and Amy argued, neither of them knowing how the little amount of lemonade Mike had left, had halved in size.

Marie's blood flushed out of her body as she was rudely awakened by this shouting in these ungodly hours. She assumed the fetal position, covering her head with her hands to protect herself as much as she could from what, she could only guess, was coming. Her frame froze in terror as she heard Mike thumping towards her bedroom door, breathing heavily, frothing at the mouth, uttering swear words which would make Satan himself shudder. At five o'clock in the morning, sweating like a pig from a nights fishing trip, the demons tormenting his soul once again took hold of Mike's senses, whilst he himself lost leave of them. He forced open the door. His hand raised ready to strike to the rhythm and the beat of the wrath contorting in his head. He beat Marie black and blue. It all came back to him as he sat watching her read from the front pew.

This memory had etched its mark onto Marie's soul and as much as she had forgiven Mike - she could never justify the act. This brutal attack on her life, by her own father at barely fourteen, marred and scarred Marie's being for many years after that. For every time she put a foot wrong, as we all do in life, she would be terrified that consequences of grotesque proportions such as on that day, would accost her.

Why had he done it? Who or what was it he had wanted to disfigure that day? Did she still remember? Had she forgiven him? Had he forgiven himself? are some of the questions which flooded his mind as he watched her, in awe, standing tall at the lectern.

He wasn't sure how well he actually knew her at this stage. She had held it all together and given him strength. A sense of shame overcame him. Silent tears formed and filled the whole of his left eye and the whole of his right eye, balancing on the cusp, on the verge of falling onto his dark, weather-beaten face. Finally, they strolled down steadily. He couldn't stop them.

She had been the backbone of the family. She had shown admirable fortitude. Not only had she got a degree from the local university (of which he was very proud), the whole village, yes the whole village literally adored her. All the mums had wanted their sons to marry her. She was a very altruistic person and had been doing voluntary work in the local childrens' centre since the age of fourteen. Wherever he went he would meet someone who would be singing her praises and this made him a very proud father.

None of this was any of his doing. It wasn't because of him as much as it was in spite of him that she commanded such a presence in the community, earning people's love and respect. He knew it. And that knowledge hurt. He could attribute merit to himself regarding her education, and how he paid for her private tuition and urged her on, but regarding her popularity and her standing in the community, that had all been her own doing with the help of Grandma Jo and some well-trusted friends, one of whom had been like a surrogate father to her.

Victor, a very holy man - a saint - many would agree, had run the catechism centre Marie frequented religiously between the ages of fourteen to twenty, in their local village. He acknowledged Marie's strengths and filled her with confidence.

He believed in her, respected her and loved her during a time when she didn't think many people did, especially not her mum and dad.

Victor looked up at her now reading in church at her own mother's funeral and was filled with pride that this girl, whom he had loved like a daughter, had done so well for herself. He knew he had played a crucial part, but that to him was an honour, rather than a chore. He had helped Marie build the foundation on which the rest of her life would rest - it was a solid foundation, made of stone, not sand - and would put her in good stead for what was to come. He did this not just for Marie, but for hundreds of youths in their village and across the whole island, you see.

During her most formative, sensitive teenage years he nourished and nurtured this precious soul making sure she knew what she was capable of, helping her reach her full potential and realise her life-purpose. He prayed she would get through her mother's suicide in one piece and would be able to continue to grow and flourish in the face of this adversity.

Mike also looked up at Marie reading with a mixture of admiration and pride, then back at himself with an increasingly growing sense of shame. What in Jove's name had he done to deserve such a pure soul for a daughter, who lavished so much love on him? It had never crossed his mind that today he would be sitting in the front pew watching her read at her own mum's funeral, with her mum not sitting in the pew, as she normally would do - but is dead instead, boxed in a coffin in the middle of the church.

Now as he faces the big brown box in the middle of aisle with tears still streaming down his face - the biggest weakness, the greatest vulnerability - he faces himself. He's not exactly sure what he's crying for. For what could have been, maybe? Self-pity, perhaps? A sense of futility? What he could have done differently? All sense of hope had left him. It all seemed so final now. And that's because it was.

Chapter 6

She wore white that day.

She wore white today.

She was dead that day, she is alive today.

Being in church, she saw as if it were yesterday, the day her and Mike had promised to love each other, for better or for worse, in sickness and in health, in poverty and prosperity, until death do they part. Mike had kept his promise. He loved her now as much as he had done when he promised he would. But had she?

The pain she had caused him cut through her to the quick - or rather reverberated throughout her ethereal body - she could feel it in the depths of her being. But not just the pain she had caused him, for hadn't she hurt herself in the meantime? Her unwillingness or inability to let it all go - whether through pride, ego or an exaggerated sense of culpability - had hurt both him and her. And not being able to accept her Creator's or her own forgiveness, how on earth was she ever going to be able to accept Mike's, which was tainted with so much hurt, anger and an unconscious desire to make her pay?

He on the other hand, was constantly assailed by the mental image which had accosted him that day. It followed him faithfully through work, rest and play. He wanted to forgive her and start again - he really did. But when forgiveness seemed so close at hand, the image would flicker bright in the night-light and blight any hope of a clean slate.

This is what this was now - a clean slate.

This is the time and place she would have to forgive herself and come to the realisation that guilt is a wasted, useless emotion. It zapped all of life's sweet juices from its victims and injected a subtle poison, slowly and insidiously through its jagged teeth. Was it that the guilt never left her? Or that she had never let it go? She didn't know.

Many people had wanted to help her carry the burden, or lighten the load. Other people wanted to help her get rid of it, ditch it, put it down, leave it behind, but she couldn't or wouldn't. She had clung to it as if the very essence of her existence had depended on it, as if without it she would die. She had defined who she was not through her divinity, not through her love, but through her guilt and *sin,* for want of a better word. Strangely she thought, as much as she had perceived her sin as her pitfall, it wasn't. What had it been then, that had brought her to her knees?

"If it weren't the sin itself, what is it then ?" she demanded to know. Luckily, nobody could hear her outburst. She looked and examined closely and patiently this time. It faintly began to dawn on her that it wasn't so much what she had done, as much as the attachment to it, which was keeping her captive. How does one let it go, drop it, surrender it? How does one suddenly stop blaming themselves, stop being angry at themselves, stop hating themselves for what they had done? Is it a decision that they make, consciously or unconsciously? And if so, how and what tools help bring this letting go about?

Only Amy held the key to her own liberation and nobody,

no matter how much they loved her and had wanted to set her free, had the power to do anything on her behalf, on the earth plane. Not even Jesus himself - who had come to show her and us how to set ourselves free —could do it for you, or for Amy - that was a great fallacy, Amy began to see. Only she could do it - her Master went before her to show her how to turn the key, to claim her freedom and sovereignty. But she had to turn the key and take full responsibility for her own salvation.

This was a lot to take in, in such a short space of time. She was feeling quite overwhelmed and overcome by a slightly increasing feeling of being trapped - a sense that there was no escape from this current state of being, in which she would have to take full responsibility for the life she had just ended, evaluating and reviewing so many different aspects of it. Being in church seemed to be the perfect place for it, but not today. The energy in there was too intense.

For a start there was Marie reading Psalm 23. She had been a firm believer in the after-life being a better place, hence she did what she did. She had previously believed she would be transported or teleported to a place of pastures green, with crystal-clear waters flowing. But here she was hovering about still in a state of anguish, with many more questions than answers. Where were the pastures green, the greenest ever seen? And the streams of milk and honey? The milk and honey would be of no use to her body now, although cossetted in that stuffy wooden box in the middle of the church it might make her smell a bit nicer. Her carcass could do with a bit of perfume. And as to her soul, it yearned for a break from this incessant thinking, over-thinking, analysing and over-analysing. It yearned for rest, and conveniently the words "may she rest in peace," resounded throughout the church, from the ardent congregation. But only the words - her state of being was a far cry from their prayer and her wish.

Anyway, why hadn't He come to judge her yet?

Would He wait until the church service was over and she was put six feet under?

Every morning as she slowly and deliberately opened her eyes, she would curse the daylight and had done so for far too many years to count. She would be able to see nothing else but her pain, which she nursed patiently and lovingly like you would your most beloved wounded pet. This cycle she created, seemed to create her and there didn't seem to be an end in sight. There was no light at the end of her tunnel. She would push herself, with much effort through a door, as it were, feeling some brief relief, hoping for better things to come. Six feet further along, she would be faced with another door and yet, another - always with a hope which was never fulfilled. It was an infinite corridor of doors for rooms with plain white ceilings and floors.

She had tried consistently and made various efforts to get out of this self-centered, ego-cherishing, pain-inducing loop, but as going through one door just led to another and then to another - with no end in sight - hope began to wane, giving way to despair and the spark of life she tried to rekindle constantly within her, faded before it were even given a chance to ignite!

At other times when in between white ceilings, floors and closed doors she would catch a glimpse of the pain she caused others, mainly her Marie. She would momentarily see the anguish and fear in her eyes and wondered if they disappeared, if she would. They would all be much happier without her, she reassured herself. Marie would be so relieved. And why wouldn't she be? It was a rhetorical question, which Amy asked for all the wrong reasons, she now realised.

Ever since a child Marie had felt responsible for Amy's well-being, providing her with all the love and reassurance a child of six can give and which Amy, whole-heartedly received. And what did Amy give her back in return? She looked at Marie now with a mixture of pity and compassion. It was too late to feel concern for how Marie had been feeling all through her life as she presently walked down the aisle after having finished reading. It was even harder for Amy to make out what her eldest daughter, the daughter she bore at barely eighteen – and not out of love, she had always reiterated to make sure that Marie got that loud and clear, not out of love - was feeling.

My goodness, she sounded very confident and clear. Marie stood straight and tall at the pulpit managing those lovely words of farewell to her, very well. She thanked the congregation for their presence too. They didn't have to be there, but they came in drones to share in the family's grief, sending Amy off safely to the next leg of her journey. Not many knew she was still there, almost more present than she had ever been before.

Amy could never see her, really see Marie. Blinded by her own anguish, Amy couldn't see beauty - any kind of beauty - not for want of trying, but from all colour having been painted black in her world. Sometimes Marie's beauty and light would be too much for her to bear and she would rather hide.

But, now she saw her as clear as daylight. All the things Amy had aspired to, dreamt of, or had wanted in life had eluded her. They seemed to be handed over to her Marie, instead. It was hard to watch sometimes. It were as if Amy weren't there - invisible to the life which had created her - oblivious to her presence here on earth. At times she felt forsaken, cursed even. Why had life favoured Marie and had left Amy barren and stark naked with nothing left to give but pain, anguish and grief?

Life really wasn't fair!

But now, look at her.

She was so beautiful.

What was that she detected?

A tinge of envy, maybe?

She had felt this many times before. She had tried to hide it, as she felt ashamed, and hoped her eldest daughter wouldn't catch her out. But as much as she tried to be happy for her daughter, this feeling reared its head like the green-eyed monster that it was, inhabiting and torturing spirits like hers - raked with guilt and bereft of joy.

What exactly was she envious of?

Almost everything.

It did really seem to Amy that at the time she had inhabited a human body, she was extremely envious of her eldest daughter's youth and carefree manner, her vivaciousness, her honesty, her fearlessness, her vitality, her determination to achieve her dreams, her standing in the local community, her friends, her travels, her clothes, her hair, her smile and the list went on and on and on and could go on and on, forever.

Forever is what she had a lot of at the moment, she gently reminded herself. She would have to revisit this theme some time soon, she was sure, but now her head had began to hurt – or rather the head-space ached and throbbed in pain. She felt dizzy.

There was one thing she didn't envy Marie. It was this one thing she had tried to warn her about some time before she killed herself. But Marie was either too proud, too deeply in love or too naive, to listen.

The Man.

That man wasn't right for her, Amy knew. She felt it in her bones, heart and gut – call it a mother's intuition- call it what you will. She didn't know how she knew, but when you know, you know. It was the little things which convinced her that he would never be able to love her Marie in the way she wanted or needed to be loved. He lived in his head, she through her heart, for a start.

He lacked energy. Apathy – that was it – it summed him up. Apathetic. Very brainy, clever and highly academically gifted, but lacking drive, energy and a zest for life, whereas Marie beamed with life's energy and grace. He would suck it out of her her like a leech leaving her high and dry, taking and not giving anything back in return, for sadly he had not much to give. Maybe, he loved her in his own quirky self-cherishing way, but this wasn't the man who would fulfill her daughter's need for an all-embracing unconditional love which would deepen her understanding of who she was, acknowledge her worth and celebrate her life (as she had done for him).

And what about passion?

Passion was something her daughter oozed in abundance. She was passionate about her job, about children living in poor conditions whom she helped locally and abroad, about the young people in the parish for whom she helped run a youth club, about travelling and seeing the world, about her spirituality, about her physicality. Basically, her Marie was in love with life and passionate about most aspects of it. She didn't do things by half measures. If she put her mind to something she would see it through and see it through, properly. Wasn't it her who had taught Marie that if a job is worth doing, it's worth doing well? And Marie had taken this advice to heart to guide her through her various projects, helping her grow in confidence and in faith that she could and would make her dreams come true.

Did Marie secretly believe that her warm love would melt his ice-cold heart? Did she dream she would be the one who would find a way to reconnect his head back to his heart, bringing him back to life? Would it be one warm tender passionate kiss from her which would wake him up from a seven year slumber imposed upon him, not by an evil witch, but by his own disconnectedness from his soul, from life itself?

Amy's biggest worry was that he was not in love with Marie as she had been with him.

On the other hand, Marie seemed happy enough. But at twenty and not having had any previous boyfriends, she had nothing and nobody to compare him to. Whereas, Amy had known love and passion. She had been erotically embraced and enveloped in love – or was it lust? It was all getting a bit confusing and a bit blurred now.

Anyway, back to the subject that had been playing heavy on her heart.

She had suffered a lot when it came to the matters of the heart and wanted to spare her daughter that same pain, at all costs. This detached, seemingly emotionless man wasn't going to embrace her daughter in passion and envelope her in a love which would make her feel complete, cared for and utterly and totally protected. Even if he could do it in his head, he would not be able to follow it through in his heart and Marie would not be able to relate to that. It were as if Marie and The Man were treading the same path, but at very different trajectories - and never shall the twain meet.

As for her daughter's lust for life, excitement, romance and fun - that would all have to wait. But life was over in the blink of an eye and wasn't being young and in love meant to be fun and exciting, after all? Why did he think that life had to be so serious at only eighteen? Why wouldn't he ever smile? What was the underlying cause of his sadness?

There was a sadness, a bit like a sense of having been cheated out of life about him which had bothered Amy since day one. She couldn't put her finger on it. She often wondered if he had been torn between her Marie and some other girl. Or many other girls, even, pulling him in this and that direction leaving him confused and disappointed in himself for needing so much, yet having so little to give.

It had crossed her mind many, many times in the last few hours whether she had chosen that day of all days for this very reason. It didn't bear thinking about, but as her eyes were wide open, there being no sleep or respite (this where *no rest for the wicked* must come from, she asserted), she was faced with the stark reality of one very important trigger for her decision to end her life on that day in particular.

This man was going to be engaged to her gorgeous Marie – that free-spirited girl, whom no man should enchain, especially not him. Under his auspices, her life-force would be slowly, yet surely, sucked out of her to feed his apathy, lack of enthusiasm, lack of passion, lack of emotion, lack of initiative, lack of drive and motivation and finally - a lack of love.

Marie would never feel passion and love in the way she had, as illicit as it may have been, it was passion and love nonetheless, or this is what she chose to tell herself. Although, she made herself pay for it for the rest of her life, in many ways.

"Better to have love and lost...," she remembered someone had once said. How true this was, she wasn't so sure at the minute.

All this watching and waiting was doing her head in. Where was the Big Pharma's magic poison when she needed it? Was it twelve or fourteen a day she had been prescribed in the last ten years of her life? She consumed them as if they were hard-boiled lollies or soft jellied sweets. How many would it take to numb this throbbing headache from question upon question, plaguing her consciousness? And yet, the more she had tried to numb the brain, the louder and the more incessant it all became, driving her almost insane. Lithium had been her friend and ally too, but its effects wore off in a jiffy. Oh, how she longed for that needle and how she missed her morning, afternoon and evening ritual of pill-popping which served as a distraction from the hell she had been inhabiting.

Hang on, this wasn't hell, was it?

Suddenly her attention was drawn to the priest moving towards the lectern. He was about to start the homily. It was normally done by someone, a priest of course, who had known the deceased quite well. Amongst the three who were con-celebrating her farewell mass, this one was the one she was the least keen on, as he hardly knew her.

Why this priest? Would he know to mention the hours she had spent scrubbing and cleaning the church floor? Would he remember to mention that she had gone to Mass on average twice a day in the last few years and that she had devoutly sat in one of the front pews reserved, almost especially for her? Would this priest know how many times she had prayed the rosary every day? How she had loved St Francis of Assisi and avidly read his life story over and over again? Gone to Medjugorje on a pilgrimage with her daughter and son? Fasted three days a week and ate cereal on most days to atone for her misdemeanours? Did he know her at all?

It hadn't been that she had particularly loved cleaning the inane pews, the floors, the chandeliers, or the candlesticks. It was more that in cleaning the church she had hoped she would cleanse her soul of its *sins*, or iniquities. She had hoped that this penance would purge her and grant her heavenly forgiveness and bliss. But it evidently hadn't procured the desired outcome, so far.

There was one story that neither this particular priest, nor any other for that matter, would know to tell. Only Marie had ever been told and it was only because it had concerned her directly. Surely he wouldn't proclaim it to the whole congregation, even if he had known? Everybody at some point in her life had thought she were mad. This story would have cemented this belief to the many who did, including Mike.

She recalled as bright as day that particular night when Marie almost ten years old, tip-toed towards Amy's bed, declaring that an otherwordly presence was there and urgently wanted to speak with her. "Mum, mum wake up. Mum wake up!" Marie urged. "Jesus is here. He wants to speak with you." Amy recalled this incident as if it were just happening there and then.

As surreal as it seemed, Amy perched herself, sitting up, against her bedstead. And indeed, there at the bottom end of her bed, sat the plainest Jesus she had ever seen - not that she had ever seen him in person before. He was wearing a thick, almost, orange beard, with matching long curly hair which was a cross between orange-ginger and fair. He was tall, tanned and had mesmerising almond-shaped dark deep eyes, accompanied by a somewhat big nose. He sat upright, calm and collected, as his bright eyes bore right into the depths of her soul with an intense love, like not ever experienced by Amy before. It felt as if she were in heaven and for the few moments He was there with her, all her suffering, anguish and pain dissolved in his presence.

As he sat there serenely exuding this divine love, peace and an indescribable joy not of this world, he beheld her whole being in his loving gaze. She felt as if she were floating on cloud nine - everything was perfect. Everything was fine. He had come to tell her, in plain English, that all her transgressions had been forgiven. She need not punish herself any longer, not that she needed to have done in the first place. He reassured her that she need not endure hardship after hardship, as punishment or atonement! Everything had been absolved, wiped away - as if it had never been. It saddened His Father that she should punish herself in this way, every minute of every day. She had been sorry for her transgressions - more than words could convey - and this is all that counted. He reassured her that her repentance had been seen and heard by His loving heavenly Father divine and that His Father always welcomed back a repentant heart. He never turned anyone away. As far as He was concerned, she was back in His sacred heart of love to stay. He wanted to reassure her that she was divinely loved in this way and protected always. He wanted her to trust and to live through this knowing, for the rest of her days.

He had taken the trouble to relay this message to her in person, such a saintly soul was she. He had hoped that His message would be heeded and would change her life, for the better, forever. There was no need for her to carry the blame or the shame - He Himself, The Christ, her Master, her guide, her guru, her healer - was giving her express permission to let it all go, just like that! As if it had never been. She just needed to trust.

She was a great soul, indeed, and she knew it. She had worked hard for Him and His heavenly Farther in many of her previous lifetimes. She got glimpses of this in her dreams at night and her visions, of heaven and her past lives, in the daylight. For His Amy, He would go to the ends of the earth, if needs be. And He had.

He left as swiftly as He had come, leaving the room filled with the fragrance of his peaceful presence. Marie had gone back to bed and slept through all of this. When asked the following morning if she recalled anything from the previous night, Marie maintained she hadn't. And she really hadn't. Marie didn't lie and if she said she didn't remember, then she didn't. But,that didn't stop her from believing her mother's story and endorsing her mum as a very spiritually evolved and gifted soul.

A saint, Marie thought. More of a saint with a past, Amy liked to describe herself as.

If only Amy were able to trust His forgiveness and forgive, love and embrace herself as He had done for her, than all the tragedies which followed could have been avoided, Amy now observed. That's all that had been needed.

Marie firmly believed that this is still one of the main sources of misery in today's world – self-forgiveness and self-love, or sadly, the lack of it. Yet nowadays, self-love got so confused with ego-cherishing, selfishness and self-absorption that people wouldn't know where to start. Now most importantly will Amy have the audacity to forgive herself, as He had so clearly done and had wanted her to do back then, in this present moment?

Oh, saved by the bell, as they say! It was time for the consecration of the bread and the wine. Never was she as relieved as now to hear the knell of this tiny bell interrupting her reverie. She immediately joined in the prayer alongside the rest of the congregation. She couldn't kneel today, of course, but that was OK. The kerfuffle was a welcome break from the deep and intense soul-searching she had just embarked upon.

All this thinking was making her quite ill. But, hadn't she already been allegedly mentally ill since the age of twenty-one? She would have to think a bit more about this one - a tricky one - this theme which she had tried not to think about in her previous life on earth. But why does it keep coming back to haunt me? Amy asked herself. Normally ghosts are known to haunt, not be haunted, she smiled to herself as she momentarily regained some equanimity, and her sense of humour.

She watched amused at all the people walking up the aisle to receive communion. It was strange not being one of them. Just three days earlier she had been sat there, on those very same pews, walking up the very same aisle, taking the bread with everyone else. Every day she would without fail, if not once, then twice a day walk up and say *Amen* as if her life depended on it. How grateful she had been for the new decree the Pope had issued a few years earlier stating that you could receive communion twice a day. So she now consumed copious amounts of bread and sweets to keep her sane!

Sadly, the visit from Jesus himself had lost its impact, so deep had the Catholic church's conditioning run. She still believed she was a sinner who hadn't suffered enough for her sins to be forgiven, or absolved - at least not just yet. What a shame that her encounter with Him seemed to have been in vain. It were as if this institution acting in his name, but so far removed from Him, had much more power over her psyche and soul than He himself had had. And so she continued to carry the burden and the blame. Was there a pride hidden somewhere stopping her from accepting forgiveness from herself to herself and from Him to her, she wondered, or were there other factions at play or at work, to keep forgiveness at bay?

Anyhow, where on earth was He? Hadn't He promised He would come to greet her and tell her if she were worthy of His Father's kingdom, or not? Alas, time was pressing and He still hadn't appeared. Where was He? Indisposed? Otherwise engaged? Busy, perhaps?

Understandably, He hadn't come as yet, as she hadn't been scheduled to see Him not until another twenty, thirty or forty years, perhaps! She had jumped the gun and taken it upon herself to appear here, uninvited. Having taken the law unto her own hands, she honestly believed she should have been on His priority list – an unexpected guest, a visitor, who should be treated as a matter of urgency and with the utmost of respect.

When would He next be free to attend to her? It was all true what He had preached, was it? she asked herself with a tinge of doubt subtly creeping in. "In my Father's house there are many rooms, and I will go and I will prepare you a place, so that where I am so you may be also!" she remembered having read in a book, somewhere.

But for heaven's sake, where was He now, so that she could be there with Him also?

It was partly His fault, she declared, for making His Father's kingdom seem so sublime - a perfect state of peace, tranquility, a safe haven for weary spirits and broken souls – an eternity of bliss. She had had glimpses of it in church sometimes where it seemed she were transported to the heavenly realm itself. She would see angels dancing and singing God's praises and herself, there among them, singing to Him. These were moments of respite and this reprieve brought such needed solace to her soul. It wasn't a blind belief in heaven that she had had. No, she had been transported there on quite a few occasions and seen, heard and felt her Father's love divine. It would have been madness waiting another twenty odd years when she could have it now, as her default state of being. The strong faith in Him, which carried her through life for the last twenty odd years, was beginning to waver in death.

She suddenly felt a jolt. He must be coming, she thought excitedly, sighing a sigh of relief. But sadly, to her utter and sheer disappointment it was only the coffin, her body had been laying in, being moved. It was being lifted up by several men including her beloved hazel-eyed boy and Mike, to be taken into the hurst which would carry her carcass to a cemetery on the other side of the island. She would be buried in a family tomb. These had been the longest three days she had ever known.

Suddenly she knew she'd cracked it.

Of course! Three days, that's it!

Her waiting would be over now before she knew it. Hadn't He had to wait three days after His crucifixion to see His Father in heaven? Why would she have to wait any less?

Hurray, all this waiting would be over before you know it Amy, she reassured herself. As soon as her corpse hit the bottom of the man-made, six feet deep dug hole, her waiting would be over. He would make His appearance.

Wow, will she be pleased to see Him! She couldn't wait.

Chapter 7

She couldn't help but wonder if He would be wearing a long white robe, a thick bushy beard with a shepherds staff in the one hand, ushering her forth with the other. As her body was being lowered into the grave, she felt relieved! Not that at this point in time it mattered whether her corpse was in a coffin, a grave, in the middle of the ocean, in a dump, or in a furnace being burnt to smithereens, to be honest. She was relieved knowing, not hoping - that now her body was being lowered- He would appear. This is the third day and He would come to her, as He had to Mary Magdalene, on the third day.

Hurray!

This nightmare would soon be over and she would be set free. This seeing things she hadn't wanted to see previously, perceiving now more than ever before the impact, possibly irreversible, on all the people she had loved in her lifetime, weighed her down. Thankfully, by now her shame was beginning to feel a bit more like remorse, tinged with compassion. It was an interesting combination and a subtle shift in the right direction.

She had always struggled with the social dimension of *sin* in the past. The term pre-dated Christ, but he came to redefine it - emphasising His Father's love overcame every transgression which was accompanied by contrition. Why hadn't she got this?

What she hadn't understood is, why was it a *sin* to take one's own life? Surely, you only hurt yourself! The term sin related only to damage one did to others, not to oneself, she maintained. At that point she hadn't realised that we are all intertwined in such a way that when one hurts others they are hurting themselves, as well as hurting themselves, they hurt others. She hadn't realised before now, how inter-connected we all are and how springing from the same sacred Creator - we are one.

The Roman universal church (how can it be Roman and Universal or Catholic at the same time, Amy couldn't understand), allegedly representing Him here on earth, weighed the term with blame and shame, as well as the person committing the sin, better known as *sinner*. It made one feel as if they were inherently evil, rather than created perfect, in the image and liking of their perfect sacred Creator divine.

But why was this act deemed unforgivable? Her Master and Teacher had never highlighted any sin as being beyond the forgiveness of His loving benevolent Father. If one decided to top themselves, putting an end to it all as they'd had enough, surely others should understand? If they had loved her as dearly as they had said they did, they would've wanted for her what she so fervently wanted for herself, for so many years of her adult life? Having hurt them whilst living, surely they would be relieved at her dying? Would they condemn her for doing what she had yearned to do for so many years and as harshly as she was condemning herself right now? She remembered His words: "Has nobody condemned you woman? Then neither shall I. Go on your way and *sin* no more." If He wouldn't condemn her, then neither should they and neither should she so vehemently condemn herself!

The deliberate conditioning of His allegedly faithful church of its followers, ran deep. It made people believe that as sinners they were not worthy of divine love, or any kind of love. It kept people subjugated by capitalising on their weakness bound in physicality, rather than empowering them by and through their spiritual strength and divinity. It bound its faithful (for they never questioned), by man-made rules and regulations, the noose of its precepts enslaving, rather than liberating.

He taught that Love was the greatest power and that nobody and nothing was mightier. It was the Law of the Universe - for it was created in love, for love, through love. He preached of the unconditional love of His heavenly Father and of the divine Earthly Mother and how we are not to worry about anything, as it's all being taken care of. As long as we do our best... you know the rest!

It's funny that, isn't it?

She noticed that she did this all the time. She only took on board what suited her, or rather, that which confirmed her deep-seated belief of being an unredeemable *sinner*. A priest, in confession, had hissed that she was headed for hell and that no matter how many tears she shed, or how many candles she lit, or how many masses she went to, the twins she had miscarried at six months were in a place called limbo and would stay there until the end of time, condemned her to this living hell. He sowed the seeds of its inception in her bosom - growing within her - but, not coming from her!

In this mindset she would continue to condemn and punish herself, when He, Marie and even Mike possibly, had all been trying their best to forgive her. Marie had relentlessly tried her best to help her forgive herself. The twins, heaven-bound, were around, wrapping her in their love, wiping away her tears and dispersing her fears with their little light crystalline angel wings.

The urge to suffer was great, but the urge to perpetuate the suffering and self-punishment was even greater. Hadn't her Master suffered? Wasn't that what she was meant to emulate? Isn't this what her Catholic church encouraged? Why hadn't she realised that although He had suffered, He had risen again on the third day transcending suffering, pain, anguish, fear and death itself? This was celebrated once a year, whereas the glory of suffering and the crucifixion were preached daily, deeply inculcated into its faithful's psyche, as if we were born to suffer and die, rather than to live and to resurrect. Why was it called a church and not a cult? And a death cult at that? Amy demanded to know. They say in a cult you cannot leave - but from the teachings of this institution, there was no reprieve. They were meant to be the Easter People - rejoicing in transformation, growth, self- realisation, resurrection - not wearing and bearing crosses. They should be wearing a peace symbol around their neck, for hadn't He always greeted His friends and followers with a "Peace be with you?" Amy asserted. His resurrection was what was meant to be emphasised and Him telling us that what He did, so can we do too, if we have faith and believed in our own inherent God-gifted divinity. Why hadn't **this** been inculcated into its faithful's psyche? Or was this too empowering and would transform the faithful from submissive sheep into powerful lions? Someone benefitted from all these half-truths, misconstructions of truth and misconceptions and it definitely was not *the faithful.* The scales from Amy's eyes were falling fast, as truth revealed itself to her heart and mind. She was ready for it.

She had not always been like this and had not always believed such awful things about herself. She relished lovely childhood memories from when being brought up in a suburban town, in the land Down Under. One story she always loved to tell Marie was of how when a little girl, she had been all dressed up to go to a cousin's holy communion party. She looked absolutely gorgeous in her brand new green dress, black shiny shoes and matching green head band. Green had always been her favourite colour. She remembered feeling so happy and looking ever so pretty. In her excitement and urge to go, she was the first to get ready. Whilst waiting for her three brothers to get themselves sorted, she kept herself amused by closely observing the frogs in the pond at the bottom of their garden. She loved frogs and was always amused by their croaking and frogging about. They always seemed so happy and free. She could not resist the urge to get closer, too close in fact, until finally she found herself wholly inhabiting their world of water.

Whilst her eldest brother ousted her out, soaking wet from head to toe, she heard her dad shouting at the top of his voice that she was grounded. Her new shoes were ruined, as was her new cotton dress. Maybe, this had been a foreboding of what lay ahead – the pattern her life would follow from then onwards. Other people would jump into ponds, dive into rivers, fall flat on their bellies in the sea and everyone else would act as if nothing had happened– they wouldn't be judged or thought any less of. Moreover, it didn't seem to come back to bite them with a vengeance. But she puts one foot wrong and all hell breaks loose, or her whole body gets drenched and she's grounded!

Why was it so different with her?

The consequence or punishment never seemed to fit the crime. Lots of people had affairs with their bosses, with their co-workers, with their neighbours, with their friend's boyfriends, with the milkman, the postman you name it, it's being done. Nothing new under the sun. She has a two-year love affair with her husband's best friend and alas, the consequences follow her to the grave and beyond.

First, there were the twins Matthew and Gloria. Why had he promised her he would leave his wife for her, if he then went and got her pregnant at the same time? Two women, his wife and his illicit lover, pregnant simultaneously! Would she have ever told Mike they weren't his if he hadn't found her and Greg out? Would she have ever told him that these twins were actually conceived in an act of love not in an act of *dutiful* sex?

The twins were conceived in an act of love, is what she chose to believe. But, she often did wonder if it were lust, more than love, on Greg's part. However, she didn't have the gall to go with that. It was much easier to believe he was as much in love with her, as she with him. She would be counting the hours until their next encounter, their next embrace, their next kiss, the next time she would lay her head on his strong, broad, reassuring chest and forget the world.

Having been conceived out of love the twins did not survive. How was it that anything good that had ever happened to her in life had been marred in some way or another? Why was it that if it were bad it stayed, but if it were good it died? Was it that she believed she didn't deserve good things to happen to her? And so they didn't? Or maybe, she was jinxed from birth? Or cursed even? Was it something she did, needed to do, or didn't do? these thoughts assailed her consciousness as she revisited this flurry of heart-breaking events. She never recovered from that tragedy, or never allowed herself to. That miscarriage haunted and daunted her for the rest of her days. She was like a nomad searching for the way back home - but no matter how far and wide she travelled, that home never materialised and her soul never rested in peace. Not then, not now!

It had been an accident, if such a thing exists. Not their conception, neither their birth, but their death. It had been unforeseen. They were going shopping. Mike had been driving. She was the passenger. Nobody knows what was going through Mike's head that day, but he was driving fast, much faster than the speed limit in this quiet suburban area allowed. Most of the roads were being dug up and most only half done. He slammed his foot on the gas pedal like a demented demon, savagely running them into the upcoming deeply dug ditch on the side of the road. The car, badly damaged had to be hoisted out by the recovery services soon after.

The shock from this sudden crash reverberated through the core of Amy's being.

The twins. She was six months pregnant with the twins. Would they survive this? Her back and neck hurt from whiplash, but the twins were well protected within her womb, she told herself and them, as she rubbed her belly lovingly and reassuringly.

A few moments later she felt something trickle down her legs. It wasn't her waters breaking, nor was it an orgasm and neither was she giving birth. The trickle turned into a stream of pure red blood. She panicked. She shrieked. She cried. She fainted. She couldn't remember being rushed into the ambulance as it pulled up at the scene of the crime, after what seemed like a a very long time. She came round in the ambulance to the sight of paramedics contorting their mouths and foreheads in a very peculiar way. She didn't dare ask, as she didn't want to know the answer, but she looked enquiringly at the team who sat staring vacantly at her.

The heartbeat of the babies couldn't be heard nor felt, they declared.

It was twins - a boy and a girl. Matthew and Gloria.

They were confirmed dead on arrival at the hospital.

Still-born. She birthed death - not life.

Little white coffins. Church. Graveyard. Burial. Grief. Guilt.

Had Mike intentionally rammed them into the ditch that day? To some it did seem that way. Or was it an innocent accident? Do accidents happen by accident? Amy wanted to know. Or was this fatality decreed by fate? Or perhaps, destined or predestined by destiny? Or orchestrated by Life or by some other bizarre force, yet to be discovered or not to be named? Whatever it was, it didn't matter as Amy took all the blame and all the shame on herself and sadly never found it in her heart to forgive herself. And although blameless, guilt accompanied her throughout her life, and followed her after her death.

She had hoped she would rest now, and preferably in peace. But thoughts assailed her now, as fervently as they had done when still embodied. Where were they all stemming from? If her head was buried six feet under, and her brain cells were already turning into mush, the nerve endings that connected the spine to the brain as dead as a dodo – then where was this incessant flurry of thoughts flowing from? Where were these feelings flooding from? What was going on? Why hadn't she stopped thinking and feeling? She couldn't stop obsessing when she had been in a human body, but how was she still doing it now after her death? Surely, the main reason she did what she did was to silence the incessant voices in her head which wouldn't allow her a moment's peace. Nothing could shut those thoughts up!

Nothing.

Nothing apart from the tranquilisers. They not only numbed her pain, but also her brain. Presently, thoughts still flowed with the same frequency – and with the same level of loudness and intensity. Taking the drugs had been like dialing the tone down. They made the sound of thinking slightly fainter, as if vibrating in the distance. But that didn't last long and the dose had to be topped up regularly, to keep it to the point where all thought sounded like a faint hum in the background. Increasing the dose was bliss as it meant she spent a lot of the daytime - asleep.

Sleeping was like balm to her spirit. Sleeping was when she was well and truly at peace. That was the only time she would stop thinking. But, as soon as she opened her eyes – lo and behold – the demons returned– sometimes as fearsome fiery flames of fear and at others as ghosts of guilt flying in, from all directions pointing fingers at her, mocking her to the point where she felt deranged. Sometimes screaming or shouting and frothing at the mouth, at others in a gentle hissing whisper reminding her of what she had done, making sure she is never set free from the tyranny of the self-constructed cage of guilt, blame and shame she had locked herself in.

If only she had realised then, that it wasn't the seeing or the hearing of the thoughts themselves that was the trouble. Thoughts as awful as they are, come and go. They hold no value as to being positive or negative, bar the meaning which we attach to them. It is the conditioned self-condemnation, the conditioned sense of shame and blame attached to those thought-forms that beat up the soul and flagellate the spirit within.

Her hope had been that ending it all she would rest in peace. Now shocked to the core, it is beginning to dawn on her that this is an eternal state of being awake. Was this her ever-living, ever-awake conscious aware soul, the one which she had been told never died, which she was experiencing? How is she going to cope with being awake all the time, not being allowed to sleep and get some much needed respite from these thoughts stomping about asking questions? And more pertinently, demanding answers!

Everybody had left the cemetery now and she could tell it was getting late. One by one, they silently and morosely trickled away. Her mum, her dad, her husband, her daughter, her son, her in-laws, her cousins, aunts and uncles and friends were also slowly disappearing into the sunset, until the cemetery was only inhabited by ghosts like her.

He hadn't made an appearance as yet.

So not only was she left waiting, but she was left waiting fully awake and utterly alone. If only she could shut her eyes and sleep for a short while, that would be great, but it seemed very unlikely to happen at this stage.

A sense of despair deeper than the one that had made her commit suicide overcame her and she began to sob gently, until her sobbing turned into crying, and her crying into wailing.

At least, so far there was no gnashing of teeth - luckily she didn't have any!

She can't have gone to hell – that she knew. She had punished herself like no loving God in his right senses would. So where on earth was she? What was she doing here? When was He coming? And when were all these questions going to be answered?

Chapter 8

She didn't know how long she had been waiting for. To begin with she could keep track following her visit to the morgue, followed by her funeral, followed by her burial. She knew that it had all happened within three days – the longest three days of her life. But now after all that, it seemed as if time had blurred into one big blob. She couldn't quite tell what day it was and how long she had been waiting for. It was as frustrating not living in time, as much as it had been living in it.

Time.

She had been thinking about the passage of time, wondering how she could tell how long she had been here for. She knew that as soon as her Marie had tied the knot in this forthcoming union with this melancholic man, she, Amy, would have been waiting for six months. Six full months of being neither here, nor there!

Six months isn't such a long time when you're busy working round the clock. It is a very long time, however, when you have nothing to do, but only to think and to think and to think until you ache all over. She wasn't exactly sure which part of her being ached, for it was unlike when you had a physical body and could easily locate a sensation. Now it was all quite fluid and hard to pin down. It was harder, impossible almost, to tell which part of her ethereal being the pain rested and resided in. It felt like it had been everywhere, as every inch of her being throbbed with the ache of her broken heart which hadn't healed, as yet. And who knows if it ever will? Amy pouted, as she pondered.

There was one person who, she was sure, could help with this conundrum - not the broken heart one, that would have to wait, but that of the passing of time. If she could find out how far off Marie's big day was, she could work it out. It turns out, Marie would be her lifeline now, as she had always been back then.

Marie had always been there for Amy, when her mother had inhabited a physical body. She had been a very doting daughter. Always loving, caring, compassionate and patient, Amy recalled with gratitude. Almost too patient, always very reassuring and ever so kind, Amy asserted with a tinge of guilt.

She was so beautiful and so full of life too. Look at her, Amy marvelled whilst Marie glanced at herself in the mirror before heading out to work. How does she do it? Smiling through the pain, even when tragedy pours down like nails of rain? Marie had endured a lot of suffering inflicted upon her by Amy, but supported her throughout and never stopped loving her, nonetheless. Now she would suffer no more, Amy reassured herself with a sigh of relief, as Marie in her simplicity hid any sign of grief.

Hang on a minute, how did Amy know Marie wouldn't suffer anymore? Did she put this idea out there to quell her conscience? Were this indeed true or was it wishful thinking on Amy's part? She didn't have any way of knowing, whether Marie were better off without her. How dare she so rudely assume?

The grace of this place or state of being seemed to be that she could tell if and how much a person were suffering, especially if it had been pain caused by her own doing. It was a blessing, as much as a curse. It seemed as if now her and the person she had caused to suffer were one. The pain she had inflicted on others, she felt herself in its full force. When she came close to Marie, what she could see and feel was unbearable emotional anguish. She could now experience the pain she had inflicted upon her daughter first-hand. How is it possible that she had never been able to perceive the impact of her behaviour on her Marie like this before?

She hoped that her actions would be excused, as they had always been up until now. Hailing the *mentally ill* label got her out of taking any responsibility for her own thoughts, intentions and actions on the earthly plane for many years. But here, there were no labels, no badges, nor any certificates to exonerate or excuse her hard-headedness, ego, pride or willful ignorance. Here there was no excuse for having eyes and choosing not to see or having ears and choosing not to hear.

The shrivelling of her inner world, the tightness in her chest, the inner brokenness which had caused her to shut down completely to protect herself –unable to love herself or anyone else- stared back at Amy as large as life. The reflection made her feel uncomfortable as it bore right into her soul. Alas, she had nowhere else to rest her gaze and as sod's law would have it, she couldn't shut her eyes, either. Mirrors didn't lie.

She looked and saw how loveless her life had been.

The acts of love she performed were always through such an effort - everything in the daytime, on the earthly plane, had been very much like hard work - she recalled. Maybe, not so much the church cleaning and the praying which she incessantly did on her knees as penance for her sins. But everything else from preparing meals, to cleaning the house, ironing clothes, shopping, having sex, were all chores which required a tremendous amount of effort on her part. Amy had never kept this fact hidden from Marie, as she constantly reminded her that she did all she did, for her. Marie would understand, Amy believed. But, in actual fact Marie hadn't understood and didn't understand.

No.

She wanted to, but couldn't.

In Marie's world, love - true love, was effortless and spontaneous – something which flowed straight from the heart, spilling over and filling everyone and everywhere with joy, peace, laughter and fun. At times effort were required if tired, or too busy, but it wasn't the order of the day.

Watching her mother plod on, day in day out, dragging herself out of bed as if she were carrying the Colosseum around her neck, was beyond Marie's comprehension and caused her much anguish, suffering and pain. But perhaps this is true love? Doing things for others when the will isn't there? Doing things for others when the burden is too much to bear?

Marie couldn't bear to watch her mother so weary and downtrodden. Worse still, she saw her mother's plight, in plain sight, knowing that there was nothing she could do about it. Amy had made that very clear. This reality was of her own doing, or her own making. She didn't want it changed. If she had, she would have changed it herself!

But she hadn't, and she didn't.

It grieved Marie to watch her mum struggle - merely existing rather than living. It made her often wonder whether, at times, she suffered more than Amy herself. Her mum took tranquilisers to take the edge off all her pain, but Marie would have nothing to quell her mother's pain within her.

Like most of us, Marie had her highs and lows, but she seemed to weather them fairly well. The highs gave her wings to fly. The lows stirred a strength latent within, to surface. She always managed to come back up whether it was crawling on her belly or crouching on all fours, landing at times on her bottom, at others on her feet.

Marie tried in every way possible to help Amy carry her heavy load, vehemently wishing it upon herself more times than she cared to remember or than Amy ever knew. But when she did, it didn't take any weight off Amy's shoulders. So, instead of having one woman buckling under the pressure and pain, you had the twain. Marie had loved her. Her Marie had loved her with all her heart! Marie woke up every single day with the hope that her mother would be happy and healed. On the days when Amy did perk up, Marie's face would light up and her soul would sing for joy. When Amy smiled, Marie would sigh a huge sigh of relief and smile to herself in the mirror reassuring herself that life wasn't that bad after all, and that all would be well.

On the other hand, Marie detested anyone who would use the cliche' *all will be well, all manner of things will be well.* How dare they be so presumptuous and make such reckless assumptions? They hadn't lived through what she had, for sure, otherwise they would know. And no, it hadn't all ended well and all manner of things hadn't been well, were not well and wouldn't be well for many, many years to come. What a liberty, what a f**king liberty to make such an assertion when you yourself hadn't endured a loved one's suicide, transforming your *all manner of things shall be well,* into *all manner of things shall be a nightmare!*

Amy could detect the anger, possibly rage, underlying Marie's strong response to that cliche' and wondered whether this was due to the trauma she herself had caused her. There was a lot of hurt and free fleeting feelings of fear and anxiety floating about. But, hadn't she understood? In all those years, didn't Marie know that the only thing Amy had wanted to do in life was to die?

Marie knew only too well.

To have lived with a mother who detested a *good morning* as it meant she hadn't been taken during the night, caused suffering in itself. Amy would then explain to Marie that the only reason she was still around was because she wanted to make her daughter's life easier. With Amy gone, Marie would have to cook, clean, wash, shop, iron and do loads of chores herself, for her dad and younger brother which would have made getting a good education, going to University and landing a fulfilling career in teaching much more difficult. It had been Marie's dream to become a teacher, from even before she went to school. Grandma Jo was the one who had taught Marie how to read and write - it was so cute watching the two play schools - Grandma Jo pretending to be the teacher and Marie the pupil, accompanied by all of Marie's dolls and teddies, to make up a complete classroom.

Amy hadn't been that selfish and had hung around much longer than she had ever thought possible, for Marie's sake. She would reassure Marie that she would wait till Marie finished secondary school. Then Marie would plead for more time, so Amy would extend it to when Marie finished Sixth

Form, then it was Uni before Amy would do anything stupid, as they used to refer to Amy's death wish, moving the goalposts to suit Marie, to the detriment of Amy. It was a shame that she had to remind Marie almost daily the sacrifice she was undertaking for her daughter, as if she, Amy, were the sacrificial lamb.

But, she couldn't help herself. She was scared Marie would not realise the magnitude of her sacrifice and the depth of her love. And to be honest, Marie did struggle sometimes to understand, but still managed to find love and hope in this entanglement of fear, ego, pride, hurt, abuse, and sheer and utter brokenness. Whereas many people her age thrived in lush terrain, enlivened by sunshine and satiated by rain, Marie was trying to survive and thrive in a parched dry arid desert.

At times Amy would ask Marie if, indeed, she needed to wait that long, hoping Marie would let her off the hook sooner, as if she were her keeper. Marie would answer, in the affirmative with a mixture of compassion, fear and self-doubt; almost feeling guilty for wanting her mother to hang around any longer than necessary, for her sake! Amy would wander off resigned to her fate, figuring that the right time would come and that she'd know when that would be. She just had to wait and see.

Marie's graduation, as much as signifying Amy's carte blanche for seeking her long-awaited liberation, brought with it the feeling that it had come at a great personal cost to her. All in all, Amy couldn't bear to attend Marie's graduation when it came to it. At least she had hung around long enough for her daughter to have graduated - an opportunity much greater than she had ever been given - to see her through life. Soon Marie's graduation would be followed by her wedding day. It was only a matter of time. And sooner, rather than later, Amy would have to make a decision - to live or to die. This time it won't be a *cry for help* as the many failed suicide attempts in the past had been called. No, this time she would make sure she concocted a foolproof plan and stop messing about, wasting her and everyone else's time.

As for Marie, she had to live with a constant state of uncertainty and insecurity. This was all through her childhood, teenage and young adult years, causing her excessive anxiety. She would go home after school, or after work, or after a day out, wondering if her mum would still be there upon her return. She lived anticipating the worst, and when it didn't happen, she would be so grateful for life proving to be more powerful than death. But how long would this last?

Marie lived with this fragmented state of affairs for far too many years to remember. It was hard holding your head up high when you were constantly treading on eggshells, making sure they didn't crack. Most of the time Marie managed it with alacrity, poise and peace. At others she did not - her head drooped and the eggshells cracked.

If Amy happened to be out on Marie's return home, Marie would be thrown into a sea of insecurity. She wouldn't know if her mum had decided to pack her bags and go - abandoning the family, or gone - to end it all. Marie clearly recalled being physically sick with worry at the prospect of coming home one day after school, finding her mother not there and not knowing where she was. She waited with bated breath, her body frozen in fear and her mind numb with terror at the prospect that the day is now here - her mum had fulfilled her promise - or threat, rather. She remembered the sigh of relief tinged with irritation and anger when the front door opened and her mother, all cheery and happy, waltzed through with a big bag full of freshly cut meat from the local butcher's.

Oh how she squeezed and hugged her mum on her return home that day, as anger and fear melted into a joyous celebration. At thirteen, this was just the tip of the iceberg, as much worse was in store for this young girl. Her patience, love, fortitude, faith, strength and courage would be tried and tested beyond belief, yet she would come out the other side, in one piece - she would not just grow and survive, but she would thrive. And one day, in the long distant future, this would all just seem like a really bad dream.

If only she knew this at the time. They say that life is like a box of chocolates – you never know what you're going to get, or something like that. But, what if she got the same box of chocolates as her mum? Marie often wondered, as she rested her head on her pillow at night. What would she do then? She would lay awake praying to her Creator that it would never be allowed for her to end up like her mother. Marie went to bed every night terrified that as she grew older, she too would suffer depression and being unable to cope with life, would curse the dawning of each new day and the setting of each dusk. With each setting of the sun she would hope for the end, not just of the day but of her own dreary dreadful drab existence. When these seemingly sleeping dragons reared their heads spitting out the fiery fire of fear and self-doubt, as often happened at night, Marie didn't know whom to turn to. Life was terribly lonely at times such as these and she was often scared. Very scared.

At the time there were not many people to talk to. Her brother had been too young, her father too busy, too rough, too angry and too hurt. Her mother was too self-absorbed, too resentful and too depressed. She had her own crosses to bear and someone else's might just tip her over the edge, literally and symbolically, Marie wisely observed.

Grandma Jo sometimes lent Marie her ear, but Amy was her daughter and Marie didn't want to worry or burden her too much. Grandma Jo had loved Marie with an unconditional love only grandmothers know. Her heart would burst for love of this little girl, with big dark brown eyes and black curly hair, who very suddenly and savagely had got taken away from her when they all lived together in the land Down Under. It was many years later that grandmother and granddaughter were reunited on the small island in the middle of the Med, to everyone's sheer and utter delight. There were angels' trumpets blowing at full throttle that day, their music being heard by those who had ears and chose to listen. The connection that these two women enjoyed transcended space and time. The love between the two continued to grow, and only they did know the intensity of their connection and the depths of their bond.

She had felt responsible for the welfare and well-being of her beloved mother since she had been six years old. Marie remembered that day very well and so did Amy. It had been etched into her memory and stayed there for as long as she could remember.

Amy, on the other hand, hadn't wanted her little innocent daughter, whom she had devoted her life to, to see her in such a state. She sat kneeling on the floor, her hands cupped, covering her bloodshot eyes, hoping Marie wouldn't catch a glimpse of what Amy had been doing. The initial gentle sobbing turned into crying and with tears streaming down her face, she didn't dare allow her hands to drop to her side, just in case her face were uncovered and her daughter see her mother's vulnerability.

But it was too late for that now. Marie's wisdom was beyond her years and before Amy knew it, she felt the patter of tiny hands resting on and rubbing her back in a gentle and light circular reassuring movement. Those hands flooded Amy with love. Amy felt them filling her heart with an inexplicable warmth and a sweet sense of peace. It felt as if she were being soothed and looked after by a host of heavenly beings, and one could say that Marie was like an angel that day. And perhaps on many more days to follow.

Her daughter's genuinely loving touch made her cry even more.

She realised how unable to take care of this vulnerable child she had been and how unnatural for a daughter to comfort her mother at such a tender age. She, Amy, had brought this innocent, beautiful child into the world to love and to cherish and love and cherish she did try, to the best of her ability. Now it was this little girl's lot in life, not just to love and to cherish her own mother, but also to protect and save her, from an unrelenting world and from her own harsh judgement full of condemnation.

But who would protect Marie? This was a poignant question to which there was no straightforward answer. Marie loved Grandma Jo almost, if not more than Grandma Jo loved her. This wasn't a competition of who loved whom the most, but the connection and the love which flowed between these two women gave mutual strength and a sense of purpose and protection to both in equal measure. Grandma Jo was a rock to Marie - and this Marie felt, knew and could see. Sometimes the deepest conversations are the silent ones, and this is how these two great women communicated most of the time.

Now Grandma Jo only got to know about her daughter's love affair a few years after it had taken place, and was shocked at the news when she found out. Amy had sent her a tape-recording a couple of years after having left Oz, confessing the truth, the whole truth and nothing but the truth. It explained many things for Grandma Jo who had been left on the brink of despair, her heart broken beyond repair at having lost both her daughter, but mostly her grand-daughter, so abruptly. Amy's disclosure filled in a few missing pieces of Grandma Jo's puzzle, but left Grandma Jo nonplussed!

When they had left the land Down Under unexpectedly, in such a sudden rush, she did suspect something had been amiss, but didn't want to pry and didn't see why there should be something Amy hadn't been telling her. Amy always seemed so calm and happy. After their sudden disappearance Grandma Jo was beside herself with grief. This loss was like a death. She missed that little girl - *her sunshine, her only sunshine* - more than she could ever express in words or in silence. She used to hallucinate and see *Marie* when out shopping, walking through the park or looking out at the path Marie used to come running down, to come to her house. She was losing her mind and needed to get a grip. And she had. But it had been the most brutal separation Grandma Jo had ever experienced in her life up until then. Other ones were to follow, but not for a while, yet.

Things between Amy and Grandma Jo were strained for quite some time after all had been revealed. Now that Grandma Jo had learnt of the affair and how Amy had married Mike not out of love, but out of a desperate need to get away from her father, she felt betrayed. Betrayed by the fact that her own daughter hadn't loved and trusted her enough to confide in her. Why hadn't Amy turned to her own mother for help? Had Grandma Jo known of her daughter's predicament, she may have been able to help. But she had not been in the know. And so, there's nothing she could do now. The tape -recording which Amy had sent her detailing the happenings of back then, had landed on Grandma Jo's heart like a ton of bricks shattering her life-view and all that she thought she knew.

Up until then, Grandma Jo had secretly blamed Mike for their sudden disappearance and return to the Med. She had been told that he was missing the sea, as they had also told Marie for many years following their departure. Now she wanted to exonerate her daughter and chose to believe that had Mike shown Amy more tender loving care and attention, she wouldn't have so easily fallen into the arms of another - whether it was his best-mate or not.

Alas, it was neither here nor there whose fault it was as at this stage. It might be fairer to say that it was mostly six of one and half a dozen of the other. And pointing fingers served no real purpose. What was done, was done. The losers in all of this were mostly her and her god-daughter and grand-daughter Marie - Amy, and the rest of the family.

Grandma Jo had responded to the tape-recording, sending Amy one back. It wasn't the condemnation that Amy had been expecting which set her off - rather, it was the unconditional love her mother had gifted her, which had made her burst into tears. Grandma Jo apologised for how she never realised all this had been going on right under her nose. She had wondered why Amy still sent Marie over to hers when she had stopped working at the office as a teleprinter operator, but apart from that she loved having Marie so much that she didn't question. A part of her felt like she had been taken for a ride - but her motherly instinct wanted her daughter to know that she did not condemn her. Her biggest regret had been that she hadn't known and so couldn't help! And if she had, things may have turned out differently! Perhaps, Amy would've been able to have stayed in Oz with Marie, after all. Alas, what was done was done.

That day, falling on the floor like an empty sack of potatoes crying, Amy had been touched by her mother's love which was filled with compassion rather than condemnation. It were almost as if this love was beyond her comprehension and condemning herself, she couldn't or wouldn't be able to accept her mother's unconditional love.

But why was Amy thinking these things now and going right back in time? She had hoped Marie would show her the passage of time going forwards, not backwards! She didn't care in going backwards, she wanted to go forwards to stop this watching- and unbearable waiting. She detested this state of being, where she was totally and utterly powerless to do anything or go anywhere apart from where her time-travelling conscious awareness chose to take her. A fleeting thought suggested to her that she may have been playing the victim card, but at the moment she wasn't in a position to ascertain with clarity how much of it was victimhood, falsehood or truthhood. She hated seeing things now and not being able to change them or do anything about them. What had been done, had been done, full stop. If she couldn't change it, what was the point of dwelling on it? What was the point of dredging up all these painful memories? What was the point of all of this thinking, watching and waiting, anyway? It was making her ethereal head spin.

Going backwards wasn't going to get her anywhere. The more she time-travelled backwards, the more powerless she felt and the more helpless she seemed to become. Powerlessness and helplessness. Hadn't that been the story of her life? Why had she revisited these themes with a vengeance in her death? Was there no end to her suffering and pain? Or was this some kind of cosmic joke? Or God's idea of an experiment or a game? Or an optical illusion, even? She narrowed her eyes to think deeply, as she looked into the mirror for the nth time today.

Hadn't her Marie mirrored those states of being too? Is that why she was going back in time - the time when it was evident that her and her Marie, would share a similar destiny, in so many ways. She hoped and prayed that it would be more in the process, than in outcome.

Wasn't the six year old Marie also feeling powerless and helpless in the midst of her mother's misery and vulnerability? As what could Marie have done more than she did, at barely six? That's when the psychic link between the two had been forged. Amy realised that that's why she had been taken back there, back then. That link was still there and very strong. It seemed to become stronger, the longer she had been away on the other side.

This psychic link would enable Amy to see, through Marie, the passage of time. Marie would be the connection between Amy's ethereal existence in her disembodied state of being and the physical world of the embodied she had just vacated, making way for more to come, completing the cycle of life.

Now not only had He not appeared (and it was approaching the wedding, so it must be approaching six months since she had popped), but she was more alive than ever before. A part of her continued to live through the pain she'd caused those she'd claimed to have loved. She hoped that one day it would be through joy, that her and Marie would live and connect, but it was far too early for that.

She lived through Marie's pain as if it had been her own just as Marie had lived through Amy's pain as if it had been her own. How the tables had turned. She had hurt her Marie, sometimes intentionally and at others unintentionally. Sometimes it was hard to watch her own unfulfilled dreams being fulfilled in her daughter. Sometimes resentment seeped in. Only a mother on the brink of despair and in a state beyond repair would feel this. It took courage to see and acknowledge it now. So in some way she was moving forwards, although there was still a lot of looking back to do.

Amy would make incessant demands on her daughter's love, attention and time. Her daughter would kindly and lovingly oblige, with a lot of compassion and love as she cared deeply for this woman and loved her dearly, this mother of hers.

As she grew older the demands grew bigger, whilst her mother grew needier. No matter how much Marie gave, it was never enough, Amy always wanted or needed more. And Marie would then give more and more and more until her mother's needs or wants would consume her. There were no boundaries. So enmeshed had their realities become, that when Amy died, Marie did not know where Amy ended and she started.

After Amy's death, Marie did not have a clue as to who she was, what she believed in and why all the love she had lavished upon Amy had been thrown back at her face in one single act of defiance, of pride, of despair!

If true love never dies, then Marie would be OK and so would Amy, but whether this tenet was true or not was to be seen by both women on either side of the veil.

Chapter 9

She woke up with a start.

Finally, it seemed as if her eyes had gently shut and she was allowed some sleep. She felt relieved and rejuvenated by a renewed strength. She hoped that many years had passed with each breath as she slumbered. Alas, it was only for a few moments that she had been allowed to lightly nod off. She recognised the music, but not the place. She recognised the people, but not the priest. She recognised the readings and the readers, but not the people in the choir.

She had rather slept through Marie's wedding day, if truth be told. But the playing of the organ and the choir singing, jolted her back to being fully conscious and wide awake. This respite came in very small doses. It had seemed that when she just couldn't take any more suffering or when what she saw was too painful, she would be allowed to be unconscious for a short while until she regained enough inner strength to deal with the next set of memories or experiences which came up for healing. This state of being resembled fainting in this realm.

He still hadn't appeared. She had only been waiting for six months and four days, not that she was counting! Amy had never been daunted by the idea of infinity before, an infinity of bliss in His kingdom. But this waiting with nothing to do and nowhere to go was a different kettle of fish. It was a very difficult state to endure.

She hadn't bargained for this - an infinity of waiting and watching and thinking and dissecting and judging and analysing accompanied by feelings of guilt, anguish, blame and shame. It drained the life out of her - of course, what was she thinking - that had already happened, she was already dead.

She felt tired of it all. Before, she would pop pills to sleep through days and endless days of meaninglessness. She would pop more when thoughts of what she had done in the past, whom she had hurt, what she would do differently next time, pressed for attention. The pills took the edge off all these pertinent questions clamouring for her attention, demanding answers. Now with no pills to pop she was going out of her mind. They would quell the discomfort in her body and calm the turbulence in her soul. Albeit, she now had no body, her soul yearned for some substance to dissipate the storm of thought thundering through her conscious awareness. Here, there is no escape. No escape, whatsoever. What she had run away from, followed her into infinity and beyond!

So, it was true.

Marie was going to go ahead in spite of everything.

The stubbornness of that child. Unbelievable!

She was as stubborn as herself, if not more. In that respect, they had been so similar. Physically they were like two peas in a pod, but their likeness did not end there. Both very generous to a fault with energy, time and money, hard-working and kind. Both very hard-headed, sticking to their guns even if it killed them, when it came to defending principles they believed were ethical and honourable. They were both loyal and faithful friends and would fight for family or friends till death.

That's why they always clashed. That's why they had antagonised each other so vehemently. In many ways, they had been so alike, yet in so many others they were poles apart. One was for life, the other for death; one for joy, the other for sorrow; one for forgiveness, the other for self-punishment and self-abasement; one for self-acceptance, the other for self-condemnation and self-hatred; one for love, the other for fear; one for change, the other for stagnation; one for moving forward, the other for going back; one for dancing, the other for lying down; one for being awake, the other for falling asleep; one for choosing to see, the other for choosing to have her eyes wide shut; one for hope, the other for despair.

Today she did not envy Marie at all. In fact, today Amy pitied Marie.

She wholeheartedly wished that due to her death Marie would postpone, even cancel the wedding. In that way, her death would have benefitted Marie in a practical way. It would have served more than one purpose. But, that stubborn girl of hers, had always believed she could change the world. She believed she could open and soften this man's heart which like a citadel was surrounded by a thick brick wall, which became higher and thicker as the years rolled by. Was it the folly of youth? If only her daughter hadn't been so naïve, so trusting and so full of hope, so much heart-ache could have been spared!

Why had Marie believed that this is only as much love as she deserved from a man? Why had Marie settled for what was like breadcrumbs falling off someone else's lavishly laid table, when there were other men offering her sumptuous dishes to feast off? Amy tried to work this out, but her head space ached. There was a lot to unravel, but with the wedding ceremony unfolding before her eyes- it wasn't the right place or the right time.

There had been lots of young, handsome and kind-hearted men chasing after her Marie, seeing in her the goodness that this man would try his best to destroy. Lots of generous, fun-loving, open-hearted men who would have loved to have fallen into the arms of her Marie. She could have had a man who would truly love her, who would set her heart on fire, take care of her and protect her. And what does she do?

She gives her heart away to a man who would lust after many other numerous women. She gives her heart away to a man who sees her goodness not as something to be cherished, but as a threat to his own selfishness, ego-cherishing and self-indulgence. She gives her heart and her life away to a man who needs constant reassurance of how handsome, good looking and intelligent he is – and not from her Marie only, sadly. It didn't even bear thinking his name in her head, that is, in her conscious thinking mind, not even now, so she referred to him as The Man.

The Man himself had hoped that Marie would be his redemptress. She would save him from himself and from his own ego-cherishing, selfishness and weakness. She would do it for him, as he had seen her do for her mum. Perhaps, he hoped she might take full responsibility for his salvation and appear in his place when being judged on the day?

She had hoped that his need for constant validation from beautiful women would subside after they got married. He had hoped that the love Marie lavished on him would save him from his insatiable lust. He prayed and hoped he wouldn't need to feed his ego as much, as her love would dissolve it. He hoped she would help him preserve his goodness, overcoming or even melting away his coldness, shielding him from his own iniquity, restoring his dignity. In that way, he would have to do none of the inner hard work himself. He would not have to take responsibility for any of his misdemeanours or misconduct – she would do it all for him. He went as far as to assert to her that he hoped she would suffer enough for both of them in life, so that he, The Man, would not have to suffer at all. The gall of that Man made Amy want to throttle him. It was a good job she had no arms with which to wring his neck, she grinned.

Marie had secretly hoped she would be the one who would save him from himself, with the same intensity he had wished it. She too, had hoped to dissolve his narcissism, egoism and vainglory. Yet he flirted with fire and got burnt many more times than he cared to admit to himself or to Marie.

It seemed as if he couldn't help it. But we always have a choice, Amy chimed in.

He wished he didn't capitalise on the status his position, in his highly regarded profession, offered him. But he did, Amy observed now, more clearly than ever before. Arrogance and pride smirked across his face, cutting through his cold vacant eyes, beholding a secret only they thought they knew.

Amy had always told Marie she would make a much better mother once she had *crossed over to the other side,* as she put it. She imagined that she would be much closer to Him and that her prayers would be answered more readily. Her prayers would have been answered, had she been with Him, in His kingdom. But, He still hadn't appeared and her prayers were far from being heard, let alone answered. All she could do at this stage, was to watch, and to wait and see. That's all she had been able to do in the last six months or so. Not much help to anyone, really. This was the first time she had actually regretted not being there, on the other side, in a physical body. Perhaps, if she had physically stayed on earth, she would have been able to actually do something practical to stop her demented daughter from procuring her own life sentence. But hindsight is a beautiful thing, as Amy had heard it often said before.

What would or could she have done had she still been there or here, rather?

She wouldn't have had the courage to *accidentally* stain the wedding dress, surely? Or to hide the brand new white wedding shoes? Or fake a fainting fit? Or demand to be taken back to hospital on the day? Perhaps, she would go missing and hope that they would have to spend the whole day looking for her? Or would she find the gall to speak out during the service and proclaim the unsuitability of the match?

She smiled mischievously at herself as she imagined having gone for the last option. It would have been hilarious, as his side of the family would have fully agreed with her for different reasons and on different grounds, but they would have supported her. They had believed that Marie was unsuitable for The Man, but did not ever dare entertain the thought of saying it out loud. They would have welcomed Amy's outburst in church, but it would have been for another reason entirely. Social status. They believed he was marrying beneath him. It was true Marie had procured a degree – a four year degree, at that –but anyone could get themselves a degree these days. Besides, Marie had very humble beginnings and came from a very working class background. The daughter of a local fisherman and truck driver – what would she be able to offer The Man?

Why hadn't he gone for that lovely long-legged brunette whose dad had been a very wealthy renowned jeweller? Or for the other brunette, who lived in the same prestigious village as them, in a massive villa, whose father earned lots of money and whose mother always looked as if she had just come out of the beauty parlour? He liked her and she liked him. Or perhaps, the other dark-skinned girl with long, straight, jet black hair who had been their second daughter's best friend for a while? All these lovely girls had come from high standing backgrounds, well-to-do families and lived in reputable areas of the island. Any one of these would have done superbly for their blue-eyed boy.

They could see Marie had a heart of gold and a very kind smile, but would that be enough to make a good doctor's wife? It's true she had spent all her teenage years and early twenties doing voluntary work with children and young people locally and abroad, but the long and short of it was her parents did not come from a professional background, as they had. They had wanted to believe that social standing did not matter to them; that they would accept whoever their son chose because they loved him and since he was happy, so would they be too. In their heart of hearts, however, they always blamed her social standing or lack of it for the irreconcilable differences which set them on different paths later on in their marital life. Only time could tell what the final outcome would be. Everybody just had to wait and see.

They didn't know the mettle her daughter was made of, Amy thought indignantly. And although Amy would put her own daughter down, or criticise her, she wouldn't have anybody else, especially *his* family put her down and think any less of her loving, caring, compassionate Marie. She would fight tooth and nail, not that she had either at the moment, to prove that actually it was the other way around. She would give her life to say this to her Marie. But she had already given her life!

Now she had no life to fight with on this side of the picket line.

Chapter 10

Amy looked on awe-struck as the wedding rings were being exchanged. Her jaw dropped - as it were - as the vows rang unequivocally throughout the church.

This is it. The deed is done -it's a fiat accompli.

She couldn't cry over spilt milk now, could she? She sadly, couldn't cry at all.

But what happens to this sudden sadness, a bit like a grief which was taking hold of her? Where does it originate and abide? And where does it go when it subsides? She had no idea, but it did feel similar to something she had experienced in her previous existence. Her heart was being wrung like an orange - on one of those modern-day electric squeezers she had seen Marie use in her kitchen - pressed harder and harder down, until all of its juice got squeezed out. If she had blood, it would've been drained from her in the same way. She felt crushed. Suffocated. Finally, she passed out.

When she came round she was accosted with more of the same. It was a shame, but such was life - or death, rather. She couldn't bear to watch the joy on her Marie's face. Not that she was jealous.

No.

It was a feeling of impending doom drowning any joy she

could have felt. In her heart of hearts, she hoped she were wrong, but her gut feeling or mother's intuition - call it what you will - remained as steadfast now as it had been years earlier. The Man wasn't right for her Marie and his pious act to win her daughter's heart over won't last long, Amy was convinced. He would sooner or later expose himself for who he truly was and show his true colours. In their mother tongue there is a saying which roughly translates as: *oil always rises to the surface when mixed with water*. She'd wished truth had surfaced sooner. Or had it and Marie ignored it?

Amy had *accidentally* eavesdropped on a conversation the two of them were having in the car, parked outside Mike's house one evening, a couple of months before the big day. She held her breath, hardly daring to move just in case any movement from her interrupted the flow. She fought hard to suppress a sneeze or two when she caught a whiff of his cheap perfume. He had just confessed to Marie of having had a crush on someone else - someone who wasn't her Marie - and who didn't mind his taste in perfume, luckily!

When she heard Marie wanting to postpone or cancel the wedding by a year, Amy was deliriously happy. Amy hoped her Marie would see this sensible decision through, as it was the right thing to do. Phew! What a great idea - reason at last - our silent witness rejoiced raucously.

"Hip Hip Hooray!" she shouted, glad that nobody could see or hear her jubilant spirit soaring high and higher and then low and lower in a roller-coaster celebratory space dance. She hoped nobody would get a whiff of the wind her being, flitting gleefully through space, caused. This was the first and only moment of happiness she'd had since being in this state – in this no-man's-land - this limbo. She edged Marie on, "Go girl, go girl, tell 'im." But no sound came out. She was lucky that her intention was as powerful as her action (intended action), and emboldened her Marie subliminally.

Sadly, her rejoicing was short-lived. She couldn't believe the power The Man held over Marie. She couldn't comprehend how her daughter, a strong-willed, intelligent young woman who knows her own mind and soul, could be so gullible. So was it true love? Was it fear? Was it manipulation? Was it naivety? Foolishness? Absurdity? on the part of her Marie.

How on earth had he convinced her that postponing the wedding by a year was a silly idea and that regardless of his crush on a colleague they should forge ahead? Was her Marie out of her mind?

"Marie," she shouted, "you're going to regret this for the rest of your life. Walk away. Now is your chance. You are on the right track. Listen to your heart, gut and me telling you to not go down this path, with this man. If he has such a powerful crush on a girl now, before he marries you, what is ever going to stop him having other crushes on other women? And how can he guarantee that he will not ever act upon these crushes? Can you live with this fear constantly hanging over your head like the Sword of Damocles?" Amy whispered under her breath, subtly yet audibly.

"How can you be so naïve, so gullible, so trusting, so believing? Why are you choosing to go for much less than you deserve? Are you settling for stability?" Amy refused to acknowledge the possile futility of her interjections, but continued nonetheless to urge her daughter to see reason. "He can't or he won't love you. He lusts after other women, Marie. M-A-R-I-E!" she now screamed like a demented woman losing her mind. Her words didn't fall on deaf ears, as Marie heard, but The Man's arguments won him her mind. She had already given him her heart. Sadly, the loudest voice was victorious.

The battle was lost.

The Man had won.

As time went by, sadly his heart hardened even further and showed no signs of softening. And he did act on his crushes. He would come home with lust shining right through his visage, that smirk still adorning his, seemingly, nonchalant countenance. Marie felt it through, let's call it her female or wife's intuition and knew it through the physical signs he exhibited. She felt isolated, unloved, and used and abused. It is said that there's no loneliness worse than that of being unloved or unseen within a marriage, or any other kind of relationship.

Amy had feared this to be her daughter's plight in years to come. In the meantime, all she could do was to watch in silence as everybody ate, drank and made merry at the sumptuous, yet modest wedding reception. She was proud of Mike. He had done the right thing by Marie and paid for all the food and drink. He wasn't well off, but loved his only daughter and wanted to give her a proper send off. Besides, he had a lot he had to make up for and now was his chance!

The Man's family looked happy enough. They hadn't actually done much apart from turning up, all very well turned out on the day, looking the part. Everything had been down to Marie. The Man would collaborate to a degree. He was still at the stage where he wanted to make a good impression just in case she had had another last minute change of heart, perhaps not turning up on the day. And that wasn't far from Marie's mind, shall we say.

His powers of persuasion had taken Marie right from under

Amy's nose and there was nothing Amy could do about it. Amy had constantly previously promised Marie that she would be a much better mother on the other side than on the earth plane, Amy reminded herself. But she wasn't, was she? Amy had failed Marie and couldn't see how she could make it up to her. She couldn't stop Marie from making the biggest blunder of her life, not when embodied, let alone now. Not only did she feel an overwhelming sense of frustration, but also a deep sense of responsibility and what was that again? Guilt. Had she, Amy, in any way in her lifetime contributed to Marie finding herself in this perilous predicament? Or through her death, perhaps?

Through her death - the inception of an interesting new notion was taking place. Before, when thoughts of taking responsibility for something came, she would promptly put herself to sleep. She couldn't face the feelings of guilt, anger, frustration or self-condemnation which accompanied such an inner inquiry. Unfortunately, she couldn't put herself to sleep now and the question was pressing.

The thing is that it was hard and hurtful to watch. This looking was meant to be dispassionate, but instead it was accompanied by a deep sense of self-deprecation and an anger at herself for having failed Marie as a mother in so many ways. This was not objective, dissociated looking. This was not non-judgemental and was not accompanied by a love and compassion towards oneself, as Amy had learnt it should be, through Marie's Buddhist meditation techniques, yoga teaching and daily practice throughout the years.

This was very subjective looking, coupled with judgement and a growing awareness of the part she played in her daughter's lack of self-love, self-esteem and self-belief. Amy had unintentionally contributed to this, although, as we know she hadn't been the only guilty party.

For the first time she began to hear her own words spoken to Marie in disdain, reverberate throughout the ether, as if they were being spoken there and then. They were more like a condemnation, accusing Marie: "You are so selfish... you can think of no-one but yourself, you can't love anyone, but yourself... don't ever say that you are my daughter." These words often spoken in anger, especially when Amy hadn't got her way, left an indelible mark on Marie's sensitive heart. Amy wanted Marie to obey at all costs - even if it went against Marie's own common sense, or sense of right and wrong, or a sense of what she herself needed to do, for her own survival.

Did that behaviour have a particular name? It was beginning to dawn on Amy that it might have done, but for the life of her, she couldn't remember it. It was a term that had gained tremendous popularity in recent years and many behaving in this way were being born and bred throughout society. But, how convenient that at this moment the band began to play and The Man and her Marie - well his, not hers anymore - opened the dancing on the dance-floor.

Oh my goodness, Amy smiled. She did look stunning. Her make-up had been professionally applied and her longish, black, curly hair had been beautifully set. She had help getting into her hand-made, made-to-measure, satin pearl-studded wedding gown earlier that morning, from a kind neighbour and friend and her skilled sister who had sewn the dress from start to finish. She did look stunning, indeed. Amy looked on with great admiration at the daughter she had ushered into this vale of tears.

If only he knew how lucky he was!

He knew, of course, but would never appreciate neither her outer nor her inner beauty. And mind you, neither had she, to be honest. Amy on the other hand, remembered how she had envied Marie her beauty – believing it was deeper and much more genuine than hers. She wasn't as good a person as she had thought she had been in the last twenty years, was she? Yet, she had suffered as her Master had done - on behalf of everyone - and that should count for something.

Suddenly, her spirit gave a loud anguished cry and hollered, "My Lord, my Lord, why have you forsaken me? Please come now and save me, if You will!" She couldn't bear herself any longer. She was the perfect portrayal of a woman who had lost all hope - pulling at her invisible hair, gnashing her non-existent teeth and waiting for a redemption that was a figment of her imagination.

Nobody came.

Her desperate plea had fallen on deaf ears. She needed some respite and she needed it quick. Just a couple of minutes. A siesta. A mini-siesta, fainting, even. If only the music would stop blaring, then maybe she would be able to shut her eyes and just be still for a few moments. But, the band played on and her spirit hovered in a state of anguished agony. All she could do was watch, wait and feel remorse at how badly she had treated this beautiful, innocent, loving creature. She had poured so much fear and insecurity into her throughout her young and formative years. The thought that Marie might never be made whole and forgive her, weighed heavy on her heart.

Indeed, would it be Marie's forgiveness that would one day set Amy free? Would that be necessary? Could it be that her Marie held the key to Amy's future happiness, or lack of it.

But for how much longer must she suffer for her *sins,* for want of a better word? How long will it take Marie to forgive her? She had no way of knowing. Is this why He hadn't made an appearance as yet? And what if Marie did not want to forgive her and never will? What will become of her then?

What if Amy herself managed to stop judging herself, criticizing herself, hating herself and had the audacity to forgive herself would that set her free, instead of her Marie? Or would she still have to wait for Marie to do the same for her? Perhaps she would have to wait for both these conditions to be present simultaneously as if decreed by some divine synchronicity? These were questions the catechism book, she remembered reading on the loo, hadn't answered!

That night was the first night since she'd been here, she wished she hadn't done what she'd done! That night for the first time she came to realise that her *sins* weren't the masses she'd missed on Sundays. Her *sins* hadn't been the not fasting on Good Friday. Her *sins* weren't having had an affair with her husband's best friend for two years. These were just decisions she'd made. They may not have been the best decisions, but they led to a life experience one way or the other, which she had to live through.

Her *sins,* for want of a better word, pertained to states of being. Her living in a state of constant fear, a lack of self-love, a lack of self-forgiveness, constant self-criticism, harsh self-judgement, self-hate, an inability to let go of her culpability on the one hand, and the forfeiting of any kind of responsibility for her thoughts, words, deeds and actions, on the other - were her *sins.* She had created a deeply dark negative world-view of herself and of her own world as if she were beyond redemption on the one hand, and not worthy of it, on the other.

She found it almost impossible to look without breaking down and diving into a sense of shame and deep despair.

Eventually the guests, tired from dancing the whole night through, dispersed and went home. The music stopped and the newly-weds were chauffeured to their new abode. They would consummate their marriage, but it wouldn't change the crush The Man still had on his colleague and friend. Who could tell if he hadn't been thinking of her whilst making love to Marie, for the first time, that night? Could that be called *making love*? Amy asked herself heart-broken. And did it count as consummating the marriage?

Marie perceived deep down in her own heart, what her mother had also picked upon. So why hadn't she listened to her heart, mind, body and soul which hadn't stopped warning her about the precariousness of this situation, before the big day?

The Man had told Marie, in no uncertain terms, in the car that day, that if he didn't settle down with her, he wouldn't find another like her to settle down with. So he would flit from woman to woman, forever. And so he may have done, but that wouldn't have been Marie's problem, Amy remonstrated. These were his problems which he should take responsibility for and solve himself not, use Marie to solve them for him, or even worse, use Marie as the solution. There were no proclamations of an undying love for Marie. There was no protestations as to how he would struggle, first thing in the morning, to wake up without her loving smile or going to bed, at night, without her heart-warming embrace, Amy remembered observing, overflowing with sadness

He would not let anyone see how he much he depended on her steadfastness, faithfulness and strong moral compass.

Nobody must know, not even Marie - especially not Marie. For many years to come, Marie was beguiled into believing that she was the weak one in need of him; that without him she was a nobody; she will have nothing and go nowhere. He perpetuated his position of power by deliberately feeding her words, attitudes and actions which would leave her doubting herself, her sound judgement and her very own sanity, even though they were spot on - in fact, because they were spot on. He would keep her bound to him, at all costs. He would make her think he was right all the time and that any mistrust she had shown over his conduct or misconduct would be just a figment of her wild, jealous imagination. And no they weren't, Amy asserted jumping in. She could vouch for that - she knows what she's seen.

He would invalidate all her emotional, spiritual and physical needs. He would smirk at her claims of his infidelity, because it suited him and because he felt he could. Marie would doubt herself, despite having picked up upon concrete signs he had been playing around. He continued to feed his ego with manipulative power trips and thrived on this for many years. Her oil lit his lamp, whilst her own light and life vanquished.

Having tied the knot now, would Marie find the strength within her one day to set herself free from his tyranny? Nobody, at this point in time could guess what would happen twenty or thirty years down the line, neither Marie, nor Amy and neither could The Man. For now, a happy picture of domestic bliss is what caught an outsider's eye apart from Amy's who could see beyond the happy façade right into the two newly-weds' heart of hearts.

Chapter 11

Time was ticking, but she couldn't hear it. By now she had completely lost track of how long she had been here. She turned back to Marie for illumination, as her own imagination failed her. Perhaps Marie could give her a clue as to how long she had been hovering in this nondescript place, suspended between heaven and earth.

Marie had just given birth.

The Man and Marie beheld a beautiful baby. Marie fell in love with him as soon as she lay eyes on him and cuddled him affectionately. A warm whoosh washed all over her as she held him close to her breast trying to latch him on for his first feed. It had been a secret lifelong dream of hers to become a mother, ever since she had been a child. And it had been fulfilled in mothering Amy to begin with. But now even better, she was holding her very own son. She would be the best mother she could be, she reassured herself and this tiny-in-size, yet not so tiny of a miracle - Mark.

Mark was a good name, Amy observed. A Mark had written some holy script, if her memory served her right. A good name for the most gorgeous new-born baby boy she had ever beheld, not that she was biased, of course!

She couldn't believe Marie would ever give birth, as she

had always had an over-the-top needle and blood phobia, and everybody teased her when younger about her future ineptness at having children. And although Marie's phobias were still going strong, her desire to bear new life was even stronger. Amy too was truly grateful for the gift of this new creation. It made her grandmother Amy or *nanna* (in Maltese) Amy, as Marie would often allude to her. And although not there in body to coo over the beautiful baby, she is still entitled to be called grandma, granny or nanna, she asserted to herself.

Amy watched engrossed as this tiny bundle of joy achieved his first milestones. She jumped for joy, or so it felt like, when he smiled his first smile, uttered his first word, took his first step, and all the many other firsts this first-born achieved. Looking on at him brought her so much solace and joy. These were the most joyous times for Marie, and The Man seemed happy. Moreover, unbeknownst to Marie, Amy was ecstatic.

Marie was besotted with this son of hers. She had truly found her calling in life. She would lavish on him all the love, affection, time, energy and attention she never had been given herself from her own mother. And most importantly, she would love him unconditionally. She spent many joyous hours playing with him, reading to him, looking for bugs, going to zoos, cafes, parks, swings, mother and toddler groups and relished wholeheartedly every moment they spent together. There was a special bond between Marie and Mark, a bond which only a first-born son and his mum could possibly know. It was such an exalting experience for both Mark and Marie, and lovely for Amy to see.

Amy, on the other hand, was gutted she couldn't be there in person to share in these moments of bliss. Her gorgeous new grandson would never see her and will never know her. Well that could be a blessing, she thought to herself. Hadn't she ruined all the lives of the people she loved and who loved her? At least from here, going forward, she cannot ruin anyone's -summed up her sentiments, on second thoughts.

As she watched, she felt remorseful at how things had played out and for her part in that performance. Remorse was not damaging like guilt - it implied taking some responsibility, which is what this place or state of being is about, she reckoned. She was making progress. Little by little she was moving forward even if she seemed to be standing, or rather, being still. She was silently moved to tears as she marvelled with a mixture of joy and sorrow, at this miracle, Mark, which could be traced back to her. She may have messed up, that's true. But you wouldn't be able to tell, when you looked at this angelic boy full of so much love and joy.

The Man had yearned for a daughter, but got given a son.

He had loved his son in his early years more than he had ever been able to love anyone. Mark opened The Man's heart, feeling something stir deep within his being. It was love. The Man didn't recognise it, so it scared the life out of him. We are often scared of things we don't recognise or don't comprehend. Yet, he looked at his son and felt proud of the fruit of his loins. He couldn't believe that a being so perfect and so pure could have come from him and neither could Amy, for that matter.

The Man hadn't been anything special to look at, but had a charm which appealed to women. A quiet charm. Introverted, dark and mysterious he made you want to delve deep into what lay hidden within. Living in his head, nobody was ever allowed into the deepest recesses of his heart, not even Marie - especially not Marie.

Marie longed to be the one who would enable the Man's

heart to soften, open and be able to love and be loved. She hoped she would be able to activate his innate latent light buried deep within, for his own happiness and that of others. Alas, in her mother-tongue there is a saying which goes something like: those who live in hope, die condemned! And Amy had, but had no way of knowing if Marie would follow in her footsteps or not.

Amy also hoped that the love Marie lavished on The Man would one day magically transform him. At times she glimpsed a dismantling of the great cold thick wall which *protected* his heart, but it would only be a glimpse and the wall would come back up as quickly as it went down. It was unbearable to watch, as she was completely and utterly powerless to do anything about anything. It drove her mad, not just for his own sake, but for the fact that his aloofness and emotional unavailability had an undesirable impact on both Mark and Marie.

How do you stand by watching your own child suffer and do nothing? When a mere mortal, it was fine. She had been oblivious to all the suffering Marie had endured most of the time. What she couldn't see, didn't hurt. This seeing brought a lot of uncomfortable feelings with it, so that sometimes she wished she were blind or ignorant of what she now perceived. Ignorance is bliss, she remembered and couldn't agree more at this point in time - or in this seemingly eternal present.

Amy reflected on how Marie had always been trying to help others activate their innate, inner light - for it to shine through - for their highest good and the highest good of all. She was always reassuring, affirming and enveloping others in love, so that they would, through her love and compassion, come to realise their own. Marie had firmly believed that this had been an integral part of her life-purpose, whatever that meant! It would take her many years to discover and learn that unless she did that for herself first and unless the other person wanted for themselves, the freedom, the love, the peace, and the joy which she wanted for them - then all her efforts would be in vain.

Amy wondered if all the love Marie lavished on The Man would be in vain, the same it had been in her case. But was love lavished on others ever in vain? Didn't it, for some time, alleviate Amy's pain and enlarge Marie's heart? Perhaps, Marie's love would not transform The Man himself, but would alchemise her, into a more loving, a more compassionate being? Amy inquired, hoping some good would come out of this entangled web of different people's non-actions, actions and intentions.

In Amy's case, Marie had totally failed - or so she believed. Whilst Marie had wanted her mother to be fully whole, fully human, fully alive, happy, at peace, forgiving herself, loving herself – healed and made whole - Amy had been hell-bent on punishing herself, persecuting herself, flagellating herself, so that she would never allow herself to forget her transgressions or, heaven forbid, let them go! Whereas Marie had believed her mother deserved a clean slate, Amy believed she deserved, at a very deep level, severe recrimination and punishment. And so she punished herself like no loving God sacred or divine would ever punish her.

This way of thinking was inculcated into Amy by that god-forsaken institution she had started to frequent more often when in the Med. That institution, posing as a holy one, depicted all beings as *sinners* and *sinners* as beings who needed to burn in hell, whether it was the one in the after-life, or the one created here for souls such as hers. All in all, no matter how hard Marie tried to help her mother love and forgive herself, Amy's contrived sense of unworthiness, undeservedness, unlovableness and guilt, constantly undermined Marie's efforts. Amy's dark deep-seated beliefs about herself created insufferable suffering for Amy who lived it and for Marie who watched it.

What Amy really wanted to know was whether Marie would keep hoping against hope that her love would soften and open The Man's heart to love? Or will her hope one day give way to despair? There will come a time, Amy felt in her loins, or where her loins had been, when Marie would touch despair the same as her. Despair would be Marie's companion time and again, coming to teach her a lesson or two about herself, about others and about life. It would bring her to a point where she would not just realise, but know that nobody can change anybody else. People changed all the time – their world-view shifted with knowledge, their behaviour transformed through wisdom accumulated throughout the years, their inner life evolved and expanded with life-experience or lessons learnt – only if and when they desired it to be so. Each created their inherent reality according to their own self-created inner trajectory. The outside was not always a reflection of what lay on the inside, as many chose to teach and believe. More often than not, the outside offered a relentless testing ground for what lay inside to be healed, purified and solidified, Amy observed.

Often Amy pleaded with Marie: "Please, Marie don't try to change me. It won't work. I know what I have got to do to be happy and make myself better, but I can't do it. I know where all my unhappiness and mental illness stems from, but I can't and won't change it. Furthermore, I do not want to and cannot do anything which makes me happy, fulfilled or healed. I don't deserve it."

Marie silently watched and prayed brokenhearted, as her mother continued to hate and condemn herself - killing her soul whilst living - powerless to do or change anything, apart from loving her as unconditionally as she could and being on constant red alert, doing her best to avoid the unavoidable.

Marie was thirteen the first time Amy had tried to commit suicide. On this particular occasion Marie had come home very excited to fill her mum in, on what had gone on at school that day. She loved doing this for two reasons: one was that she simply loved chatting to her mother and the other, more important one, was that whilst her mother was actively engaged in listening to her stories, being transported momentarily to Marie's world, she was distracted from her own inner inflamed inferno.

By now Marie knew that there were two things and two things only on her mother's mind: leaving her husband and dying.

Every day had been a chore since the unfortunate passionate love affair with Greg, or rather, the bitter end of it. Picking up the pieces, she had shards of glass in her body everywhere. Fresh blood of disappointment, disillusionment and despair still oozed out of the open wound from that time, which sometimes seemed so remote and at others ever-so-present. Marie's body also had cuts, bruises and bleeding caused by random bits of sharp-edged glass from the debris she helped her mother gather.

As Marie rushed through the front door that day, Amy hadn't been busily buzzing about the house, but was tucked up in bed. The bedroom door was shut and there was no sound of Amy hustling and bustling about, or getting up and out of bed. It was getting later and later in the afternoon and still no sign of Amy budging from her bedroom. At around six o'clock, Marie was getting really anxious and worried. Concerned that her mother had still shown no sign of moving as she normally had done by then, Marie began to pace up and down outside Amy's bedroom door, trying to listen out for any movement. It had been unlike Amy to sleep in later than five. It was usually half four when she dragged herself out of being ensconced in her tomb-like cocoon of a bed to get on with the motions of the rest of her day - some days mechanically, at others excitedly - depending on whether her mind had taken her to heaven, which she had often been shown in visions, or to the hell on earth she inhabited. At around six, Amy could sustain her apprehension and fear no longer.

At the risk of being badly told off by Amy, Marie tiptoed into the bedroom and peered over Amy's peacefully sleeping body. Anxious and scared, expecting to be shouted at, Marie nudged Amy to wake up. But Amy wouldn't budge. Marie nudged further, but still no movement and worse still - no shouting.

Amy lay in her bed, inanimate and very unconscious. No matter how hard Marie shook her lifeless body, and how loud she begged her mum to wake up, Amy lay there motionless and speechless. Marie yearned for a scolding, but it was a deadly stillness and a deafening silence that confronted her that evening.

Marie panicked.

Her heart beating fast, she raced to the neighbour's house even faster. It was the neighbour who had been her mum's best friend for years, many years earlier. In shock Marie described how her mum lay motionless, despite her efforts to wake her up from her, much longer than usual, siesta. The kind-hearted neighbour Rosie, who had loved Marie as if she had been her own daughter, rushed back to the house with her. They were accosted by an unconscious Amy ready and about to die.

Rosie ordered Marie to rush to the doctor's surgery just round the corner to explain, once again, to him as she had to her, what had happened.

This is it, Marie thought.

She's dead!

She has died!

At thirteen Marie still didn't comprehend how it had happened, but knew that on that day she could have lost her mother, forever. After what seemed like aeons, an ambulance pulled up outside the house. Amy was ushered to hospital where she was washed out and sent back home emptied, the very next day. End of - or so Marie had hoped.

Marie's life was never the same after that. The ghost of the remains of that day haunted her for the rest of her life. She lived with the constant fear, of going home one day after school to find, that the same thing had happened. It filled Marie with a lot of anxiety, feeling as if her heart were being crushed within her chest. She'd beg life to let her breathe as she lay down with her mouth wide open waiting for the next in breath to enter her being. It couldn't come in, not until the tightness in her chest subsided. With the release came a monumental sense of ease, as life flowed back through Marie.

It saddened Marie that Amy hadn't been grateful for being brought back. A sense of great disappointment accompanied her growing sense of despair. She'll have to do it right the next time, Amy promised herself. She would put herself out of this anguish and end Marie's days of fear, apprehension and anxiety, before it all got too much for everybody. No pain whilst committing suicide would supersede the hell she was living in at this moment in time and the hell she was creating for others around her, she concluded.

It all stemmed from many years earlier, Amy later explained to Marie, as the two spent some quiet quality time together, as they often did. Amy confessed to Marie that although she had married Mike through her own volition, she had never really loved him. She was determined to get rid of her authoritarian father who had strictly forbade a relationship with a boyfriend - a foreigner, yet native to their now new homeland in the land Down Under -whom Amy had fallen madly in love with. At the age of fifteen Amy believed that you only fell in love once in a lifetime and that this forbidden teenage love was the one and only true love - ever. At fifteen, she believed her life was over. She was doomed. It seemed like a fatalistic view of life, but this is what she believed to be true.

She knew she had to get away from her father. He had been driving her mad. Every morning without fail he would follow her to the bus stop, while she waited for the school bus. He wanted to make sure she stayed away from this guy whose only fault was - and please, don't laugh - Amy could see the absurdity of it now, but definitely not then - was to flick his hair sideways, glancing in the mirror every time he passed the inviting looking glass in the hallway, as he did so. Her father detested this flippant teenage act of vanity and loathed the person who executed it and what he stood for, in her dad's eyes. So he was constantly on her case, lest she met up with her illicit love behind his back. She could not go anywhere without her dad stalking her. Amy found her father's overbearing protection suffocating and gasped for life, just as her Marie had just been doing. She had to do something, so that she could breathe freely again.

She hatched a plan. She would tell no-one, not even her mother.

Her mother, had endured wars, and had suffered a lot in life. Yet, the worse was yet to come. For many years she had to put up with a demented husband, father to her four children. He hadn't always been so. As lifelong friends and neighbours back in their home-country in the Med, Grandma Jo had admired his carefree lifestyle - flitting from woman to woman, amassing nine engagements - but no wedding bells ever being rung. He would confide in Grandma Jo and tell her all about his girlfriends, engagements and break-ups. Finally, he hit the jackpot when he proposed to Grandma Jo herself, after having procured her father's blessing, of course. They married soon after.

Soon after the wedding, the couple decided to relocate, together with thousands of others from their tiny island, to the land Down Under in search of work and better living conditions, as the war had left great devastation on their tiny island. George Cross or no George Cross the situation was dire, and many sought and found refuge emigrating to Oz. The husband left sooner than Grandma Jo to find himself a job and set up shop, ready for when his beautiful wife of three, including Amy, would go and join him.

A fresh new start. A brand new life. A new beginning.

The war had ended. When Word War II broke out, it broke him too. He had been an open-gunner. His sensitive psyche couldn't cope with the atrocities he had witnessed and the horror he had lived through. His body beaten, his mind tortured - his soul couldn't find rest. He suffered severe survivor's guilt and post-traumatic stress disorder. There was no PTSD diagnosis back in the day, let alone therapies to alleviate the trauma living and playing out in one's mind, day after day. He relived that hell every single day and night - there was no respite - until it drove him insane.

Yet, he had to get on with life and couldn't afford to break-down, having had a family of six to support and in a foreign country, at that. They had their youngest there, a while after Grandma Jo had joined him. This little boy's presence was a blessing to the family, bringing much joy and solace to all. They all loved his carefree ways, and he brought a lot of love and laughter to their days.

But sadly as time went by, the dad's condition grew worse. The whole family suffered from his bouts of physical and verbal aggression, violence and abuse. The whole family, including Grandma Jo, lived in utter and sheer fear of upsetting him. It was like constantly treading on eggshells. Nobody dared stand up to him. He raged about always ready to shout, or to strike in anger, at the slightest sign of any indiscretion no matter how small or insignificant. Nothing escaped his hawk-eyed vision. It's like he was still at war where he had to see and hear everything, and miss nothing, as if his life depended on it. And it had. But that war had ended and in its place another war raged - his own inner war - was breaking him and the whole family apart.

So was it an act of defiance? An urge to run away? A not being able to stay and live under the same roof as her deranged dad? Was there something which needed realising? Or a world-view which demanded revising? that made Amy decide to marry Mike. For the first time, Amy declared to Marie that day - that whatever it was - it wasn't love.

He, on the other hand, had been madly in love with her and would never love another woman the same way he had loved her. Over the years, Amy would tell Marie this story repeatedly, lest either of them forget. She stayed because of the children, and because back in the day most women did, Amy revealed. She hoped Mike would never find out. He mustn't. She swore Marie to secrecy. She deliberately refrained from telling Marie about her passionate love affair with Mike's best friend Greg. This she kept to herself, terrified of her daughter's judgement. Funnily enough, Marie always felt that there was something Amy had hid, but it wasn't until many years later that she plucked up the courage to ask. And it wasn't Amy who answered. She couldn't.

Amy did elucidate that she was a saint with a past and that she couldn't or wouldn't let go of that past. If only she would! But how? All this lying by omission or commission didn't do her any favours. You can fool some of the people, some of the time, but not all the people all the time, Amy remembered someone saying. The truth has a habit of catching up with you when you least expected it to, sometimes to shock, at others to surprise. A bit like oil always rising above water, Amy recalled her native saying which expressed this very same sentiment. Lies come to life assuming their own unique shape and form to haunt and taunt the person lying and the person (in and through ignorance of the truth) being lied to. The phantom of Amy's lies haunted and taunted, not so much Marie, as much as Amy herself.

A few years after this first incident there were a couple more tries or cries for help, as some would call them. They weren't really. According to Amy they were just failed attempts. It was always Marie who came to the rescue in the nick of time. Whilst Amy struggled to stay alive, Marie struggled watching her want to die. It was poignant to watch her mother being terrified to live, rather than being scared to die.

On another evening, Amy had had a cocktail of pills and alcohol hoping not to wake up the following morning. In the meantime, Marie had heard her fumble and faff in the kitchen. She had a gut feeling that something was amiss. Marie, the ever-vigilant one, the responsible one, the one who bore the brunt of all the lying and conniving, of all the sadness, brokenness and misery, was in a state of constant high alert. Her fight, flight or freeze response was activated the whole time wherever she happened to be, whatever she happened to be doing.

In this case, Marie's ears pricked up for more clues as she lay motionless and frozen in bed. What was her mother doing, up this late, in the kitchen? Marie pleaded with God praying that this wouldn't be another trip to A&E, in the dead of night. The fear of her mum's death faithfully followed Marie everywhere, at all times, as she lay in bed at night and religiously greeting her upon waking up every morning. It was an unbearable burden for a child of her age to bear. Sometimes, like her mum, she longed to be taken away from this mayhem and mess. Yet, she didn't dare utter a word to anyone, lest by so saying she would procure, for herself, the same fate as her mum.

So, whilst most struggled to stave off the dread of death, Amy strived to lure herself away from the lustre of life. In death she envisioned her soul flying heavenward, as soon as, or if, she had the courage to end it all. She had it all sussed out. The gain would, by far, outweigh the loss. He, her Creator would come to judge her, floating on white clouds in his silken white robe and long white beard, emitting a radiant warm golden light shining bright. He would perhaps judge her harshly and she would have to go to a place she had learnt had been called purgatory. Purgatory would be where she would be purged of all her *sin* like gold being purified by fire, the catechism book had claimed. When all was complete and she had been burnt to smithereens by her *loving, all-embracing Creator* she would then fly heavenward to rest in peace, forever.

Marie, on the other hand did wonder and ponder what to do that night.

It wasn't as straightforward as one would think.

Whilst her gut urged her to check up on Amy - call it a daughter's intuition - her mind and body were urging her to quell her over-active imagination and stay cosily tucked up in bed. 'Anyway, why would I want to stop mum from committing suicide, if all she wants to do is die?' she asked herself as the two conflicting fatal factions fought a bitter battle over Amy's soul that night.

It wasn't that she endorsed euthanasia; although at this point she didn't know what she endorsed and what not. She believed that she had all the answers to everything in life – the arrogance of youth, perhaps - but, to this question there was no answer forthcoming from anywhere.

Who was she to stand in between her mum and her mum's deepest desire as deathly as that might be? Who was she, Marie, to decide whether her mum lives or dies? Are the efforts to keep her alive coming from a place of ego-cherishing and self-preservation rather than from a place of freedom and true love? Who was she, Marie, to say whether it was best for her mum to stay embodied on earth, when without a shadow of a doubt, the only thing which Amy wanted, was to die? What gave Marie the right to play God? It was as if by stopping Amy, Marie were asserting that she knew more than her mother herself what would make her happy. And did she? Did she? Did she? thoughts such as these flooded her conscious awareness mocking her gut feeling, whilst taunting her sanity.

It pained Marie to live with and take care of a mother whose deepest desire in the whole wide world, was to die. On the other hand, it gave her the impetus to embrace life to its fullest, to relish each breath, to be filled with joy at the dawn of each new day and with gratitude for the respite of each night - despite fear lurking in the background trying to gate-crash her party, which it sometimes did - she mostly stayed joyous and at peace.

Marie believed she had been put on this earth, here and now, for a reason. Would one of those reasons be to save Amy from herself and stop her in time, every time? Her mum brought so much richness to life and the world would be a much poorer place without her. On the other hand, would her reason for being here be to allow her to follow through, on what she wanted to do?

No child or teenager should ever be faced with such a dilemma. It was terrifying for Marie. And yet, Marie learnt later on in life, that hundreds, if not thousands of children and teenagers faced the same dilemma as her that night, every day and night. It tore her to pieces to realise this. She would do everything in her power, as the years rolled on, to alleviate the pain of people in situations such as these and prayed that night that whatever the outcome - if through this suffering and pain she would be able to help one person, just one other person in the future - then all of this anguish would not have been in vain. This she prayed, again and again.

She suddenly heard footsteps approaching her closed bedroom door. Amy's voice interrupted her wildly racing thoughts, weighing heavily with a responsibility which should have never been hers to shoulder. Amy asked if she could come in. Marie sighed a sigh of relief, as Amy had come in, in one piece, sane and fully conscious just wanting to chat.

Phew! What a relief.

It must have just been Marie's tired and overactive imagination conjuring images which don't even bear thinking about.

However Marie knew otherwise, when Amy opened her mouth to speak.

"I love you, Marie. You know that, don't you? You know, don't you that whatever happens, I love you? I want you to know that and to remember this, Marie."

These words were being spoken with utter sincerity, lots of love and humility, but Marie's heart stopped beating. Her gut had been right. These words had confirmed her deepest fear and worst nightmare. To the untrained eye, these were professions of love - to Marie, these were words boding a farewell.

"Have you just done something stupid, Mum? Is this what all the sneaking and rustling in the kitchen is about? Mum, please tell me the truth," Marie pleaded. At this stage, Marie had made up her mind. She had to interfere. As much as she had wanted to respect Amy's free will and desire to die, she had to do her best to keep her dearest mother alive - the mother she loved not as much as herself - but, much much more.

Silence is consent, she remembered Amy taught her. She wouldn't have killed her herself, but in not stopping her she would bear responsibility, especially now that her eyes had been opened. Not doing anything now would make her complicit in the act, an accessory, as it were. She had to do something and quick.

But not so quick!

For another soft, subtle voice whispered it wasn't her shout. It was Amy's call. Who was Marie to get in the way of the plan her mum had underway? Couldn't Marie respect her mother's wishes? Was she wanting her mum around for a bit longer so that she could sit her GCE's and 'A' levels? Now wasn't a good time - but, was there ever a good time to commit suicide? And for whom wasn't it a good time?

For Amy, any time was a good time!

But wasn't Amy also playing God, deciding when to die? It was like being trapped between a rock and a hard place with feeling selfish for wanting her mum to hang around for a bit longer and preserve her life, as where there is life, there is hope, whilst letting her go, which is what Marie knew Amy wanted. Marie's mind was in a tizzy and she was feeling dizzy.

Suddenly Marie jumped to her feet.

Out of nowhere, something had kicked in.

Marie woke Mike up, calmly and deliberately, and lo and behold before anybody could say boo to a goose, they were at the accident and emergency trying to save Amy's life, yet again. The instinct to preserve her mother's life had prevailed against all odds and against all thoughts, theories or idealogies to the contrary.

At the hospital, Marie could feel her mother's pain and anguish intermingled with her own. In fact, it never seemed clear to Marie where Amy finished and she started. A dagger of deep sorrow cut through the daughter's heart, for she had been damn'd if she did, and damn'd if she didn't. She didn't know whether Amy would bless or curse her when she came round, but that was a risk she had been willing to take.

Marie watched patiently as her mother regained consciousness. She felt sick in the stomach and wanted to throw up. She couldn't bear to watch her mother suffer in silence and she, Marie, not being able to do anything to change that, not for want of trying, but more for want of failing. Marie had believed herself to be a failure for many years to come, for not having been able to heal and save her mum. Amy, on the other hand, was very disappointed that her attempt to end her life had failed. She couldn't believe she had woken up back on this earth plane - back for more of the same.

A loud shriek cut through Amy's ruminating, abruptly bringing her back to the present moment. It wasn't exactly a shriek, but more like a scream or rather, lots of screaming. As she peered on she perceived Marie's legs wide open, astride, on a white cold metal bed, with bleached white sheets surrounded by many people dressed in stiff starched white costumes. Her screams were loud enough to wake the dead. And had done! Amy smiled to herself.

What on earth was going on? Amy moved her spirit a bit closer, to get a better view.

Marie was giving birth. The head had crowned. It was the last few pushes that were the most painful. Marie was almost there. The newborn was almost there, too. This time the little son she bore, she named David.

David, the fruit of his loins (although he swears having no recollection of his conception) and her love, was another adorable baby, younger brother to Mark. As Amy cooed all over him, she felt the same joy she had felt when Mark had been born return with a vengeance. Babies bring so much joy, Amy asserted surprised she could enjoy Mark and David so much, from the other side.

Marie huddled the bonnie new-born close to her chest as he latched onto her breast feeding slowly and steadily, for the first time. A deep-seated sweet peace descended upon mother and son in the stillness of that silent night, holy night.

They were living abroad now in the land of highland cattle and haggis. It was the land of The Man's dreams. However, changing countries had changed The Man too, almost beyond recognition. His heart was like the walled city of his homeland – cold, imposing and impenetrable. Marie didn't know the whys, the whats and the wherefores but, nonetheless, felt the shift. He was completely out of reach of her love for him and the closeness she dreamed would be wrought on those crisp, cold winter nights eluded her.

Marie had changed too. Motherhood, Amy observed. It multiplied the love in her heart a thousand-fold, so that there was plenty for anybody who wanted it. The Man didn't, but grew restless and quite jealous of the mother-and-son bond between Mark and Marie. He resented the joy that Mark's bedtime routine of story-telling or reading, singing and chatting, brought both Mark and Marie in equal measure. Marie would keep Mark company until his eyes grew heavy, and he would suddenly sleep serenely, with a contented smile upon his face.

The Man would sit downstairs in front of the tellie waiting for Marie to join him, his voice betraying the resentment he felt at how much love his wife so generously lavished onto their eldest son and newborn baby. She would lavish it onto him too, if he had let her. He didn't believe how much she had loved him. It suited him not to. That way he could justify his misdemeanours and misconduct and rationally and callously blame it all on her.

Amy watched in complete silence as the chasm between Marie and The Man continued to grow. She continued to watch as the Man turned to other women for affirmation, reassurance and pleasure coming from a place of lust, not love. As she watched, she wanted to reassure Marie that her gut was right and that her suppositions and suspicions were not unfounded. But she couldn't. She could only watch and wait, and wait and watch, in a surreptitious silence.

Chapter 12

Marie couldn't believe what she saw as she peered at her reflection in the mirror that morning. She narrowed her eyes, squinting, examining even more closely what the looking-glass reflected back at her. Her eyes must have deceived her. No, maybe it was the light. You can't ever be sure of what you see, in this dark and dreary god-forsaken country. One day you looked fine. Then the sun came out and all the blemishes and facial hair you had happily been oblivious to up until then, smiled at you as if to say, they hadn't gone away! It's not that it hadn't been there previously, of course, but ignorance can be bliss and what you can't see, can't hurt you, Marie mused, not believing a word of what she was telling herself. She wasn't happy with the mirror that day and she wasn't amused.

It was a long white bristled hair springing forth from the front of her forehead. It leapt out forwards like an antenna reaching out and up into space. It refused to blend in unobtrusively with the rest of her black hair. It was conspicuous and like a radar attracted attention, in her eyes, at least.

Wasn't she too young for white hair?

There wasn't an answer to her rhetorical question, not from her physical self nor from her virtual reflection staring blankly back at her. She realised they are called greys in this country and not white as back home. Why? she wondered. Probably to match the constant murky grey sky, the grey moods she had been sinking quite deeply into lately, the grey thick clouds which had a habit of conspiring against her, hiding her dearly beloved sun. She could think of many more reasons why grey and not white, but she had to attend to the matter at hand with a great sense of urgency, acting with great alacrity as it was time to go to work shortly.

The appearance of greys is no biggie for most people these days. A bottle of hair dye bought cheaply at the chemist or supermarket can make them magically disappear in an instant and one could easily pretend they never were, or had been. So why the big deal this morning? Marie asked herself. It wasn't that she was barely over thirty and nowhere near prepared for the onset of ageing. It wasn't that she was scared that The Man would mind - he had gone grey since eighteen, anyway! It wasn't that she would have to dye her hair for decades to come.

So what was it? Amy's curiosity was piqued as she looked on, perplexed.

Marie was convinced that morning that she had been jinxed! The evil eye was something quite hot in her homeland and widely accepted. People would wear a cross or crucifix to ward off any negative energy. Alternatively, to stave off any curse, they would wear an eye on a gold or silver chain. Evil eyes (to ward off back luck - why they weren't called good luck eyes, beat Amy!) were stuck on traditional fishing boats, put on the old colourful traditional buses, on brass doorknobs and other places, to deflect evil spirits and to protect the boat or bus or whatever else from the much dreaded evil eye, which people believed procured evil, as the name suggests.

Marie had never actually been into these things herself although she had been very aware of how people from all walks of life went about life believing in such, shall we say, tales. But, today to poor Marie first thing in the morning, this didn't appear as a tale at all. It was happening for real. Mirrors didn't lie!

Was it a hex? Had she been jinxed? Why did Marie feel like it had something to do with Amy? Why would she think that, Amy wondered. Amy half smiled and half cried as she eventually worked out what was going on. Although she was totally powerless to help Marie in any way, she was able to hold the space lovingly, sending Marie all her motherly love, abundantly.

This took Amy back.

She had to force herself to go back to the days when her spirit roamed the earth in a physical body. Amy hadn't been a fitness fanatic like Marie - it hadn't been in their culture back in the day. Most of the time she had been too dosed up on clomipramine hydro chloride and lithium to be able to walk, let alone keep herself fit and trim. But, she tried her best at all times to look her best. And she did. She would buy nice new clothes for Sunday mass and to go out in on Saturday nights. She had fond memories of her and Marie going clothes shopping and walking along the promenade on Saturday evenings in their newly acquired outfits.

She would have her hair cut every six weeks without fail. And although she wouldn't normally wear make-up, she would occasionally wear some lipstick and nail varnish, which would really suit her, when going out. She looked stunning during her youngest son's First Holy Communion in her pink pleated dress (as was the fashion in those days), a delicate pink feathered fascinator in her hair, and red lipstick accentuating her beautiful brown tan.

There was one thing she hadn't been into and that was hair-dye. She was adamant she would not dye her hair. And to be honest, until that fatal day, at the tender age of forty-three, she hardly had any greys, apart from a few sparse ones occasionally craning their long threadbare necks over her hairline. She hadn't realised how lucky she had been.

Amy herself did have an issue with the couple of greys or rather white ones that did sprout up unexpectedly, every now and then. When Amy caught a glimpse of one she would want it removed immediately, but because of very poor hand-eye coordination she wouldn't be able to pluck it out effectively.

Now, as for plucking greys we are told time and again that for every single one plucked, seven others get growing in its place, or so the old wives' tale goes. Amy didn't care for such tales. She would hold a pair of tweezers in one hand, promptly accosting Marie with the other on her entry through the front door, pointing at her hair whilst waving a pair of tweezers around in mid-air making sure she caught Marie's attention, signalling to what it was she was hoping to get - a good plucking!

Marie would try to dart past or pretend she hadn't seen the shiny lethal weapon that would cause an argument between the two women time and again. Marie would remind Amy that seven would grow for each one plucked. Amy would maintain that she absolutely did not care, she just wasn't having them there! It wasn't the fact that Marie really believed seven would grow for each one plucked; it was more a matter of principle. Marie fought for her freedom to do what she needed to do, say what needed to be said and to go where she needed to go, throughout her teenage years and in her twenties. Amy would always guilt-trip Marie if she were doing something not involving her, chiming that charity begins at home, sometimes begrudging Marie the voluntary work she did with children in their local village, or in other parts of the island and abroad.

Marie had to pick her battles. Some battles were just not worth the aggro. At times such as these it was easier to appear weak and give into her mother's wild wiles and whims, than to pick a fight. Arguments involving Marie trying to assert herself and perhaps saying *no* to Amy's seemingly unreasonable demands, almost always ended in tears and with words like: "after all that I do for you," taking Marie on a guilt-trip, she'd rather not go on. To the untrained eye, or to the odd observer of such scenes, this would seem like a very innocent flippant comment, possibly even justified. To Marie it was loaded with deep meaning and felt very unfair.

Amy guilt-tripped Marie every time she didn't get her own way. She reminded Marie that if it hadn't been for her, she would have stayed Down Under when Mike had wanted to leave, taking Marie with him. She would remind Marie of how she missed the rolling green hills, the fields filled with wild flowers, the creek water flowing freely, and fresh air filling her lungs. She had never wanted Marie to forget that it was for her sake that she has found herself on this dry, arid, dusty rock. She hadn't realised at that time, that Marie was just the victim, for want of a better word, of a series of unfortunate events, which were not of her making. It's not that she saw herself as one - she chose not to.

Amy reiterated time and again that plucking a few greys or whites was a piece of cake and a slight price to pay for Amy's continued presence, not having as yet, followed through with her threat to take her own life. This sent Marie into a frenzy. Her mother was a very determined woman. Surely, despite poor hand-eye coordination, she could find the patience and the capacity to pluck a few greys and refrain from making Marie feel so bad for not doing so?

There was more to this than meets the eye, as far as Marie was concerned. Amy wanted more and more of Marie's time, attention and energy. It seemed to Marie that no matter how much she gave, Amy needed or wanted more. Sometimes, Marie felt she had to draw a line somewhere, and that the plucking of greys seemed a reasonable one, the least harmful if left undone.

Amy would never tire of Marie's company and relished every moment she got with her daughter, whom she loved more than she loved herself. It often seemed to Amy that Marie wasn't around enough for her during her dreary days and lonely long nights. Her daughter had a healing energy which Amy loved to bask in. It brought her solace, and filled her with a calm and tranquility. It made a nice change from the sense of dread which often inhabited her reality.

On the other hand, as much as she loved spending time with her mother shopping, walking, chatting, dancing in the rain and having little tete-a-tetes, Marie ran a very busy schedule. She had spent her teenage years as a member of the local parish centre teaching catechism to children of various ages every evening, and that included weekends, which Marie hadn't been too keen on herself, to be honest. It wasn't an easy life - it required hard work and commitment.

Whereas, all of Marie's peers were going to the cinema or out drinking and dancing, Marie would be at the centre -

teaching and learning catechism. Marie had to split her time and energy between the centre, her mother, her studies, her part-time work, going to private tuition and later on her full-time school teaching job and voluntary work running the local youth centre. There was hardly ever any time for Marie to just be. She would spend time with some very close friends and neighbours, and sometimes go for walks - she loved walking and talking - but that was all the socialising Marie had time for.

Amy hated the catechism centre, which Marie attended religiously between the ages of fourteen and twenty, with a passion, and took every opportunity to have a dig at Marie for spending so much time there. It was a shame, as ironically the fact that Marie attended this centre meant that she could support Amy in the way she needed it the most. And what did that look like, exactly? It wasn't by plucking grey hairs, that's for sure. To answer this question we would need to go back a bit.

Over the years Amy's guilt, caused by her misdemeanors when young and innocent, instead of resting in peace as she atoned for her *sins*, became evermore present, prevalent and persistent. The obsession with what had transpired clung to her as a limpet to a rock and would not release its hold on her. The suction was so great that Amy could not contain any state of being other than that of guilt. Most of Amy's embodiment was filled with guilt, so much so that there was no space for anything else, such as love, peace, joy and compassion for herself or anyone else.

It was her inability to let the past go - and absolve herself of the guilt which accompanied it, which made her mentally ill. She knew this and tried to explain it to Marie a trillion times. She knew what she had to do, but felt unable to. It was marring her present and destroying her future. She had given her power completely over to this spineless man - Greg, Mike's best friend - twenty odd years before, and hadn't been able to reclaim it since. She had let him walk off with her heart, mind, body and soul leaving her stark naked with nothing. Nothing. Nothing at all. She had lost the twins. She had lost the country she grew up in and loved, she had lost him and in the end she ultimately lost herself. Bereft of all, she grieved the *what was*, resented the *what is*, and feared the *what will be* - in fact, the future filled her with a sombre sense of dread.

So, she would turn to Marie in her hour of need not once, not twice but many times during the day asking Marie about the nature of her thoughts and whether they were *sin*. Were they *sin* if they just appeared out of nowhere and she didn't want them? What if they appeared out of nowhere, she didn't want them but would enjoy them, would that constitute *sinning*? Plagued by self-doubt and fuelled by fear, the questions seemed pressing and never-ending.

It continued to make Marie feel very responsible not so much for her mother's physical well-being, now that Mike hadn't lashed out for many years and the fear of going home finding her mother murdered had subsided. It was more her mother's mental, psychological, emotional and spiritual well-being that was cause for concern.

Marie would reiterate day in, day out to her mum that whatever the scenario, for Marie wasn't privy to the full details, it wasn't a *sin*. "A thought is a thought, how could it be a *sin?*" Marie would repeatedly reassure Amy, like a mother would reassure a child who was scared of her shadow in the depths of a dark night. It took a lot out of Marie, this constant need to hold and reassure Amy, but she did it wholeheartedly, with all the love her tender compassionate heart could muster.

She would go as far as telling Amy, that even if it were *sin,* she, Marie would take that upon herself and add it to her own karmic debt. This idea, this insight of taking on responsibility for Amy's *sins* - which were not *sin* at all - came from Marie's spiritual teacher at the centre. The guidance Victor gave her then was invaluable now. Marie still feels him around her sometimes, although he passed many years ago. So the centre, unbeknownst to Amy had been the greatest blessing, for both women, not just for her dear Marie, but also for Amy.

Marie hated watching her mum suffer endless bouts of a panicked fear of living in *sin,* having committed *sin,* or committing future *sin.* To Marie *sin* was a completely different notion to Amy's. To Marie *sin* was when people closed their hearts to love and to be loved; when people were not kind, caring, lacked empathy and compassion; when people deliberately and with intent hurt themselves or others; when people hated themselves or others; when people were fearful, jealous, resentful, judgmental, arrogant and proud. Amy needed love, empathy and compassion, not being labelled and condemned a *sinner.* Marie would help her the best she could with the knowledge she had at the time. And she did a damned good job too, Amy reflected gratefully.

If only Marie knew then, what she knew now through her in-depth yoga training and practice, then things could have worked out differently, perhaps. What Marie learnt, practised and experienced regarding the nature and the workings of the mind and thought, through eastern philosophy and Christian 'lost' and found sacred texts transformed Marie, and would have transformed Amy, maybe.

Yet, Marie did the best she could, with the tools she had at the time, and that was, and would always be greatly appreciated by Amy. What Marie learnt wouldn't go to waste, as one day it would help Marie, who in turn - for reasons different to those of Amy - would have despair knocking at her own door.

Marie's presence brought Amy solace and healing mostly by her just being there. Marie didn't have a clue that she had this effect on her mum, although she knew that her mum loved her company and could never get enough of it. Amy maintained that Marie's company alleviated her anguish and pain - sometimes by her silent presence - at others, by her reassuring words. Amy needed to be reassured constantly that she was not a sinner and that her thoughts were not sin, sending her to hell. And if this isn't hell, I don't know what is, Marie would assert to herself. Poor Amy! Marie always obliged patiently, with a lot of love and compassion which quelled Amy's inner turmoil, until the next bout of self-doubt hit and the cycle started all over again.

It was a good job Marie did attend the centre, after all. It was there that she discovered That which is in everything and within which everything exists. It was at the centre that she discovered that innate sacred life-love-light divine reverberating through sacred cosmic sound and experienced Its presence as her essence and as the essence of creation. There she experienced a sacred love beyond words, an unconditional, all-accepting, all-embracing love which she believed loved her beyond measure, even if she felt nobody else did. Some would say she found God, others that God found her or that she found herself or within herself all that is sacred and divine. The long and short of it is, that both women benefitted from the mystical episodes Marie experienced -Amy not any less than Marie.

She also found a guardian angel - a rock, a fort, a citadel - in the form of her spiritual teacher, who had loved Marie and believed in her, when not many did at that time. Like a surrogate father he supported her in many ways. It was thanks to him that Marie's faith in a sacred and divine loving consciousness that transcends time and space was discovered and experienced by her, first hand. It was this that saw Marie through many of life's travesties, present and future. Her strong faith would be the rock upon which she would build her house and her faith would be unshakable, in the eye of many a storm.

Alas, in spite of all of this Marie still kicked up a fuss every time Amy accosted her with tweezers in hand as she sauntered or sneaked in, depending on her mood that day, into the house of an evening. Surely, plucking her mother's greys was beyond the call of duty, and there should be a manual somewhere stating this, Marie asserted. Although she obliged a couple of times sometimes through the fear of being rejected, at others through an *I can't be asked* to argue kind of mood, in the end she put her foot down and refused to have anything to do with any plucking, of any greys.

Marie had hoped that after all these years of wherever Amy had ended up, she would have forgiven Marie for this and for many other things she had done which Amy had seen as transgressions or a lack of love, respect and consideration. Most of the time, it was nothing personal. It was Marie just trying to live her own life and assert her independence, as a healthy teenager should. By now it had began to dawn on Amy that she, herself, was meant to have taken more responsibility for her own well-being and should not have depended totally on Big Pharma or on Marie for her emotional and psychological well-being.

Amy had forgiven Marie for trips abroad doing voluntary work and leaving her to fend for herself, in her dark depths of despair. She had forgiven Marie for having gone to the centre daily to take care of other people's children, when she had believed Marie should have been at home taking care of her, instead. Amy now realised that there had been nothing to forgive, in actual fact. Marie was just trying to live her life - following her path and pursuing her dreams. The more pressing question was – had Marie forgiven her?

Six years after her mother's passing Marie stood baffled at what accosted her that morning. Something within her had been triggered. She time-travelled to a time gone by, almost wishing it were here again. In a way, in her imagination it was - in her memory, it lived on. It had taken her on a journey, but now she was back in the room staring vacuously at the mirror in front of her, wondering what to do!

She looked enquiringly, almost asking her reflection if she should or shouldn't pluck the hair. How the wheel of life had turned! It seemed as if it were only just now that Amy was waving tweezers in hand, and the argument about the plucking or unplucking of greys was taking place. Oh life, so wasn't fair! Marie pouted indignantly .

As Marie gazed intently at her image in the mirror, her eyes reflected back the sadness in her heart. Had she always had such a sad smile? Perhaps, her heart hadn't healed as much as she thought it had. Maybe at this point in time she hadn't forgiven Amy as much as she wished she had, either. But what was it that needed forgiveness? Was it what Amy did in her lifetime or was it more what she did through her death?

In the meantime, Marie's heart was still numb from the pain of Amy's act of recklessness or release depending on which way you looked at it. The peace she used to know had been torn away from her on that fateful day. Her life, her world-view, her own being had been shattered too. What she had known, or thought she had known about life had been decimated. In killing herself, it felt as if Amy had killed a part of Marie too. It took many years for Marie to see it differently and to come to terms with how things transpired in Amy's life, and in her death. But for now, she had to grapple with the tantamount inconvenience of greys - or a grey - as if it were the biggest problem she had ever encountered in life. "What a conundrum," Marie sighed, as she hustled and bustled getting ready for work.

Chapter 13

It was seven years since that fatal day today. It had seemed like the seven years of famine, a seven-year itch, or a seven-year dark night of the soul, robbing her of the inner joy, contentment and peace she had always known before. The taste of years of inner sweetness were now a distant memory, replaced by a much less palatable bitter after-taste threatening to taint everything she consumed.

The number seven had been very significant in Amy's religion, perhaps still is. Amy remembered reading about some seven years of abundance and seven years of famine, Seven Years in Tibet - no, that was a film actually! Then there was an exhortation to forgive not seven times, but seventy times seven or something like that. There were seven days in the week, seven acts of mercy, seven deadly sins, seven gifts of the Holy Spirit, seven loaves, seven demons, seven foolish brides and seven wise ones, seven chakras, seven wonders of the world and the list went on and on. Seven seemed to be a very significant number. Amy perked up believing He would soon come, it being her seventh birthday in this place of timeless tiresome watching and waiting. Seven years, and He still hadn't made an appearance. "What a liberty! What a f**king liberty," as Marie's favourite British comedienne would say, leaving her here in a state of limbo for all that time!

If she had known it was going to turn out this way, she would have hung on to her human embodiment for much, much longer. But how could she have known that this was going to be the case? The catechism book hadn't covered this bit and she had religiously read it from cover to cover, many times over. Seven years of doing nothing, saying nothing, just watching and waiting, and waiting and watching - was a very long time indeed!

Marie had left the house in a huff that morning. She had pleaded with Amy to hang on in there. She hadn't fancied a trip back to that dreaded mental hospital the night before. It was the most painful place and state to be in. *Mount Mar Elias* - where you had the odour of hospital disinfectant in exchange for the freshly smelling mountain air and trees; the spaciousness and freedom on the mount replaced by tiny white cells for people's containment and confinement; replacing the snow on the mount, were pure white clinical coats, ice-cold, dotted everywhere. Mt. Mar Alias, indeed!

Marie's engagement was in a couple of days and Christmas the day after. A trip to that callous and calculated place would ruin everything! Etched in their DNA, in every iota of their being was this day, for both these women, I have to say. It was the day that changed the course of their lives - forever.

Had she really done the deed on this particular day to spite Marie? Had the tiff which had ensued between the two, just a few hours earlier been the impetus she had needed to go all out? Questions such as these tortured Amy's consciousness which continued to sway in a sea of doubt and despair, which at times she couldn't bear.

For the last seven years she had engaged in this soul-searching practice, but in some ways she was none the wiser. She was able to release things she had taken full responsibility for and that did lighten the load. However, there was always more to look at, evaluate and question, to get to the heart of the matter, for that's where the truth lies - at the heart of the matter, in her own heart - that sometimes Amy got disheartened. The sole scope of being in this place is to recognise, acknowledge, accept and embrace truth even if it hurt like hell, or maybe this was hell? Amy's brow contorted, confuddled.

She wanted to run, but from here there was no escape. She wanted to skulk, but here there was nothing and nobody behind whom to hide. She wanted to turn back time, but she wasn't in time. If only she could go back across the veil, she would definitely do it differently this time.

This time she would stand on top of the city's historic bastion's wide wall, shouting for joy, celebrating being embodied and alive. She would refrain from free-falling without a parachute! Alas, now it was too late. Hindsight is a wonderful thing - she didn't think she would get it where she was - but it seemed to be the most prevalent, pressing and present sentiment.

She mostly missed being able to sleep. She hadn't had a proper good night's sleep for seven years. This constant state of wakefulness was driving her insane. It was enough to drive anybody mad. Here there was no Marie to reassure her that all is well, and will be well. There was no sweet Marie to take full responsibility for her well-being, thoughts, decisions, actions and intentions. Here she had to be fully present in each moment, in spite and despite her seeming inability or unwillingness to do so. Even worse, she had to do it for herself and by herself.

Having been mentally ill when embodied exonerated her from so much. It was like a free pass which would absolve her from her self-centredness, self-absorption and ego-cherishing. Here, on the other hand, she would have to recognise what she had done, accept it and take full responsibility for it. After that, with eyes wide shut (for she was dead, remember), she would have to forgive herself - which involved letting it all go - so that it could be released and she could be set free. Simples.

Forgiving herself was something she had not been able to do so far. She hadn't forgiven herself all her life, so how could she forgive herself in death? How would she be able to forgive herself, after having recognised the full magnitude of the damage her thoughts, mindset, attitudes, actions and intentions had caused?

She wondered if Marie would ever forgive her. Ah, how apt to be thinking about forgiveness just as Marie was pulling up into the car park of the old Benedictine Abbey in the quiet rural village of Woolhampton. What a weird coincidence. But, was anything a coincidence? She had been exploring this notion in the watching and waiting state for many years now. She hadn't come to a definitive conclusion yet, but was beginning to perceive things as being, what she would call, divinely orchestrated, in some way.

Anyway, back to more pressing matters.

What was Marie doing here? Wasn't she working today?

Amy felt a sudden urge to pray, as she followed Marie into the abbey. She prayed for the forgiveness of her *sins* to the God she had so devoutly prayed to every single minute, of every single day of her embodied existence. She still hadn't forgiven herself for choosing death over life, fear over love, dis-ease over well-being, sadness over gladness; sorrow over joy; anger and resentment over forgiveness. Sad. So sad. It meant that she would have to wait a while longer until she came to her inner Promised Land, where love lavishly fell like manna from heaven and forgiveness flowed like a river of sweet honey, throughout her being and beyond.

She did pray for Marie too. She prayed that Marie would forgive her everything from beginning to end. But Marie wasn't at the abbey trying to forgive Amy, on this crisp cold sunny winter's morning. Today Marie was desperate to begin to forgive herself and to let go of her own sense of culpability which weighed her down. Guilt had festered inside her being like a demented demon who sumptuously feasted off it day and night, robbing her of the life-force, the joie de vivre and inner peace she had known seven years earlier.

Marie felt as if she were going mad. Life was becoming unbearable. She didn't want to follow in her late mother's footsteps, but she felt she was close. "Seven years of drought," she said out loud to anyone who would listen. But, there was nobody in the car with her to hear what she had just said, or so she thought. It was no use that all her loved ones reassured her it hadn't been her fault; she couldn't have known, she couldn't have guessed; that there was a bigger picture of which Marie had been unaware of; that there must have been a good reason. That all passed her by. None of it sank in.

It was no use that the people who loved her tried to reassure her time and again that Amy would have done it anyway, if not on that day, then on another day soon after. The Man himself had been very good at helping in this respect, especially to begin with. But then he ceased caring, partly thinking Marie had it all sorted and partly not giving a toss, either way, of what Marie thought or felt.

Marie had not had it sorted.

She had come here today to ask forgiveness of herself and of Amy. She believed, at the time, that Amy had committed suicide on that day, of all days, to make Marie feel guilty for not having heeded Amy's plea, the night before, to be taken to the mental hospital, *Mt. Mar Elias*. This notion made it hard for Marie to forgive herself and, moreover, to forgive Amy.

It left Marie feeling as if she had been played like a fiddle. It was one thing manipulating someone whilst alive, Marie maintained, but manipulating someone in death, being unable to fight back, or get closure - was another. Marie had put up with mental, emotional and psychological manipulation whilst Amy had been alive on earth. And that was OK. Well it wasn't, but it was what it was. She handled that well, and learnt a lot from it. It taught her a thing or two about herself, her mum and life. The two would argue, they would fight, but invariably in the end they would always make up. Heartfelt hugs, kisses, tears and professions of how much they loved each other would be exchanged. It would be as if nothing had ever happened, as the love between the two overcame all and everything. And that was what kept both going as long as they had. That was love, true love.

However, this was a game changer. As how do you argue a point, discuss an event or an idea, speak your truth or communicate your fears, anger, dreams or guilt to a phantom from the past? And furthermore, how do you make up with a being beyond the grave? Haunted by Amy's essence somewhere in the ether, she still found it hard to know where Amy ended and she started. She did not know who she was and what she believed about life, death, or about anything else, anymore. She had lost direction and in the kerfuffle had lost a part of herself too. It felt as if when Amy left, she took a part of Marie with her.

The terrible longing to forgive herself and be forgiven by Amy, was eating at Marie and not being able to make up with Amy physically, was driving her insane. She perceived it as if there were a thick brickwall in between herself and her beloved mother, not allowing her to move forward from this unforgiving place of guilt.

Amy had hoped that Marie would eat her own words and heed her own advice - she had had enough practice trying to have got Amy to forgive herself, now she just needed to use what she knew on herself. On the other hand, Amy, in this state of limbo, was waiting desperately to be forgiven by Marie. She believed that apart from her own self-forgiveness, she needed Marie's to turn the key opening the portal which led to Amy's next realm in the after-life, or more aptly, the after-death. The fact that Marie was still holding on to a lot of grief and guilt wasn't helping either of them. Marie needed to set herself free, trusting that that's how Amy would want her to be. Free.

Father Nicholas was a very kind-hearted man. Marie was touched by his wisdom and healing presence one Sunday morning. So here she was, today, on her way into Douai Abbey, being greeted cheerily by this old and holy monk who had been eagerly expecting her. He was a godsend and would help her, Amy had been sure of this. It was the beginning of Marie's healing journey, ushering in the seven years of abundance. Marie hoped and prayed for an abundance of life within her, of love surrounding her, and of light shining in and through her.

It didn't take him long to ascertain that Marie's late mother had had a hold on her for the last seven years. A psychic link, he called it. It needs severed. The sooner, the better - the quicker will Marie be set free and hopefully, Amy. This was the turning of the key - the beginning of the whole process, you see.

Two women waiting, not knowing exactly for whom or for what. One on the earth- plane doing everything in her power to let go and set herself free from the tyranny of grief, guilt and fear, whilst the other on the other side, also needing to absolve herself from guilt and needing to take responsibility for her past life. Both being much harder on themselves than the other had been on them. Both yearning to envelope each other in a loving and compassionate embrace, hugging, kissing and making up, like they used to back in the day, but unable to.

A simple hug would have solved this conundrum almost instantly, and healed both simultaneously, but Amy not being physically present made that somewhat harder for Marie. How we underestimate the healing power of a simple hug! People don't hug as often as they should, Amy concurred. The power of physical human touch to heal, is vastly underestimated and not as highly valued as it should be. Everybody seemed to be living more and more in their own bubble, and less and less inclined to burst through, connecting to others.

Father Nicholas' presence brought Marie a lot of healing. But who would Amy be able to enrol for her healing and evolution, on her side of the veil? Amy would have to think outside the box on that one! Even if she took full responsibility, in full awareness of what she had done, how would she go about extricating herself from this state of being with no guidance bar the silence and the sound of its stillness whispering in her ear, things she didn't want to hear?

Marie began to bare her soul to this holy priest who thought it necessary Marie confide in him from her earliest memories. He believed that once these memories were acknowledged, accepted and embraced they would be healed and once healed they would not hold any more power over Marie. This is the process which would set her free. This was the theory.

Amy watched and listened in suspense as *her* sins were being unveiled and all truth uncovered. It was their truth, being told through Marie's eyes and first-hand experience. But they were Amy's words, attitudes, behaviours and decisions affecting Marie, as the lives of both were always so intricately enmeshed and interwoven like in a plait. There was many a story in which Amy's comportment had affected Marie negatively and this is what Marie was here to acknowledge and release or transmute into love. The hold monk wanted to know everything and made sure she hid nothing. And so Marie started to pour her heart out to him, freeing her soul from decades of holding on to distant memories which bound her by their timeless traumatic presence.

Amy listened intently.

Oh my God! Marie wasn't going to tell Father Nicholas what Amy had done to her Freddie the Teddy, was she? Had Marie still been carrying that with her from all that time ago? Anyway, hadn't Amy taught Marie that these things were not to be divulged to strangers and to people to whom this was none of their business?

It was as if Amy's eyes began to widen and water (Amy was perplexed as to where the tears were coming from) as Marie recounted the incident of when her Freddie the Teddy met his own unexpected sudden death. Marie recounted to Fr Nicholas how that precious teddy, one of the few remaining remnants of her homeland Down Under, was brutally and violently dismembered by an angry Amy one random sunny afternoon. His pure white insides drifted like soft clouds of snow strewn across the pavement for all to see, neighbours, friends and family. Marie watched horrified, not believing her eyes, as Amy thrust knife wound after knife wound into his inanimate body. Marie's heart was butchered with each stab wound to Freddie, on that fatal day.

Who did Amy think she was stabbing at the time? the question begged to be asked.

Marie, gasping for breath between the sobbing and shrieking, asked her mother to have mercy and stop, as the pure white wadding from the teddy meandered into the gutter, turning black.

Would Amy wake up from this nightmare to find out she was only dreaming? Will there be a change of scene soon? Sadly, her eyes opened wider still, beholding this obscene scene. She heard Marie wail loudly, "STOP! STOP! STOP! PLEASE STOP!" but her pleas fell on deafened ears and a demented mother. It is still not known how and by whom Amy had been possessed to do such a thing, that day, but something had taken hold of her being - something dark and sinister making her see this brutal murder till its bitter end. "I'll be good. I'll share him with Susie, please mum, please stop, please," a little Marie bleated, blue in the face. In her fit of frenzy Amy couldn't or wouldn't stop until Freddie the teddy was utterly decimated. Everybody looked on in a stunned silence.

Had Amy in a moment of madness been mutilating Greg

and his memory, instead? Amy now reflected she may very well have been. She felt a subtle sense of shame slide over her. It was a fleeting feeling. Shame was senseless. Remorse had its place, but shame was shameless! It was all too hard to handle, from where she was standing (not literally). Amy had to have a break. She needed some respite, and she needed it quick. So she glided through the small gap in the window and wandered into the picturesque abbey gardens.

On the other hand, this incident taught Marie a thing or two about actions, reactions (responses she learnt later on in life were much more fruitful) and consequences. Marie was only eight and had only wanted to play with her teddy. Why was that such a crime? Why was it that everything she loved got brutally and suddenly taken away from her? And this continued till this very day, she explained to Father Nicholas. Was it such a crime that as a child of eight she had not wanted to share her teddy with Susie who was insistent on having it? The punishment did not fit the *crime* - and Marie wasn't fine for a very long time after this incident. In fact, it took a good forty years or so of inner work to come to a place of recognising her true value and that she deserved love as much as the next person. She had to work very hard and for a very long time to come to that recognition, so she relished and appreciated it with her whole heart.

Susie had carried a secret guilt for many years at having hassled Marie for her teddy, that god-forsaken day. She had been insistent on wanting to play with it and remembered hustling it out of Marie's hands. Marie held tight onto her Freddie the Teddy with all her might and a fight broke out between the two little girls. That's how it all started. Now Susie had been given a beautiful purse from Down Under, by an aunt who had come to visit, which she gifted to Marie under the shade of the palm tree at the water-park, by the sea.

Susie and Marie now both grown women hugged and cried recalling the incident under a clear blue sky, as their offspring jumped up and down water slides together that hot, sunny summer's afternoon. Over the course of their lives the women stayed friends and saw each other through many of life's ups and downs. There is a bonding in trauma that seems to bind beings in love and compassion as these two children-cum-women had just found out. They lived in different countries, but travelled in each other's hearts for many years to come.

Amy began to comprehend some of the damage she had caused this daughter of hers, whom she had actually loved with all her heart, albeit a broken and shattered one. She began to sob silently. She couldn't believe now looking back, how she could have done that. What had possessed her to do this? she asked herself feeling very remorseful.

She had truly traumatised Marie. She silently prayed that today Marie would forgive her and that her tears would wash both of them clean. Little did she know that Marie had long since forgiven her the wound, although the scar remained. Marie had never wished her mother ill because of this incident. In fact, it had hurt so much only because Marie had loved Amy so much. Marie loved Amy with all the love the heart of a little eight-year-old could muster, and longed to be loved by her mum in the same way. Amy realised now, how short of this she had fallen.

Remorse hit her hard in the heart space and it seemed to make her whole ethereal body ache, writhe and contort in a way a human body would when in the agony of childbirth. Perhaps, this was the beginning of Amy's new birth? Or

Marie's? Or both?

There were many other memories Father Nicholas would encourage Marie to uncover. He would help her release any remnants of trauma that were preventing her from being whole, united in heart, mind, body and soul. He would bring her to a point where she would be able to confront the nature of her guilt, and to see the futility of it. He would help her come to a place where she would recognise, acknowledge, accept and embrace what had transpired so that she would be able to let it dissolve into the ether and be transmuted into love. She could already see herself walking with a twinkle in her eye and a song in her heart, but most of all the pure contentment of a clear conscience which she had known before, was returning. It was time to celebrate the beginning of her home-coming.

Amy did not know how long it would take her to be able to forgive herself. Now, that she was directly confronted by the trauma, pain and suffering she had caused, it seemed harder to do. She knew her God loved her beyond imagining and if she wished it hard enough, prayed for it hard enough and trusted hard enough liberation would be given her – one day when the time was right and she was ready, it would all be made right!

One day the scars would heal, hers and Marie's and they would all seem like a distant memory. Amy longed for this day and so did Marie. Marie sometimes wondered if she would be so lucky for all of this to happen while she were still in her human embodiment or would she have to wait until she crossed onto the other side, for total and utter healing to take place?

Marie didn't want the traits that went back generations to spill over into the next one – the generation of her beloved boys. She would do anything to stop this abuse, misery and manipulation. She would make sure that the buck stopped with her. She was willing to pay the price. In a way she did pay already. She had chosen exile in a freezing cold country, to break the ancestral cycle she had found herself at the end of. In the name of putting a stop to what had happened before, she chose to forgo the love of her family and friends in this foreign land.

Marie would do all within her power not repeat the same pattern. She would start her own new one. It would be a vibrant, benevolent and loving one - one in which patterns symmetrical and asymmetrical together weaved a warm, soft blanket for cold climates and hard hearts. This brand new colourful blanket incorporated only ancestral patterns of thought and behaviour which served everyone's own highest good.

It was thanks to Father Nicholas that Marie's heart began to throb with life, once again. Whilst Marie did all the inner work of recognising, acknowledging, accepting, embracing, and transmuting or releasing the trauma, he provided a safe, non-judgemental space for this to happen. The sense of peace, joy and contentment that had accompanied Marie in her previous existence – the one before her mum's suicide – was returning like a long lost friend, ready to accompany her once more on her journey ahead.

Chapter 14

The church bells were ringing their hearts out, their knells loud enough to wake the dead.

And so they had.

She woke with a start.

She had briefly nodded off, but was now brought back to the present with a vengeance. It took her a while to get her bearings and to ascertain what was going on. Amy was duly entertained as she watched people gather in front of the statue of The Lady of Lourdes. She recognised that statue. She knew it well.

The choir was singing its heart out. The church was lit up, as one can only imagine heaven to be - warmly lit, emanating a bright golden light - bathing the ceiling and the floor, and all those who came through the church door. It was packed. Thank God this wasn't her funeral, that was long gone! Well thank God all you want, Amy mused. He still hadn't made an appearance and goodness itself only knows, if or when, He ever will!

The bells rang louder. The crowd cheered as the statue left the niche in the church, and began to be moved slowly and deliberately, by some very strongly-built men, out onto the courtyard. It would make a rendezvous around the village with some devout people following, whilst others would be staggering home stone drunk in the dead of night, after gathering in all the local bars brimming with custom.

Amy had loved the village festa. She abhorred the outer trimmings. She couldn't see the point in flags, loud brass bands and expensive street decorations all over the village streets and back roads accompanied by booming bombs fired throughout the day. The Catherine wheels in the village square she loved, however, and the colourful fireworks she enjoyed. But ultimately she preferred the *inner* celebrations where people gathered in the church building to pray and sing together. She loved the sense of community and coming together that it elicited, although she was always oblivious to who else was in church or who she was sat next to, so absorbed in her own prayer she would be.

She sat on the end of the third pew from the front, on the right hand side of the altar, all dressed in white and would pray, and pray and pray for forgiveness, for world peace, for an easy way out -but most of all, she would pray to die. She would pray for that every single day without fail. And every morning as she woke up her faith would be shaken, as her prayers would not have been answered. She had often wondered if He had actually heard any of her prayers, at all.

What was wrong with her prayers? Why hadn't they ever been heard and more importantly, answered? she used to wonder very often intensifying her intention, with no apparent successful outcome.

In fact, the more she had prayed to die, the stronger and the healthier she seemed to be, physically at least. She was much healthier than her contemporaries. She had no asthma, eczema, arthritis, rheumatism, menopause or menopausal symptoms, physical aches or pains; no glasses, no high blood pressure, and no stress. She didn't suffer from lung disease, liver disease, heart disease or any other dis-ease, no matter how much she had hoped and prayed she would. The only problem, if one could refer to it as such, were the few grey hairs which would rear their heads every so often. Apart from that, she had a completely clear bill of health.

She yearned to go to the doctor's and be told she had a terminal illness which only gave her a few days to live. She longed for one of those local monstrous trucks to crush her to pieces as they did, every so often, to unsuspecting pedestrians pottering on pavements. She prayed for a bolt of lightning to strike and stop her in her tracks. She wished an escaped convict would appear out of nowhere and shoot or stab her as sometimes happened. She dreamt that the people who were producing illegal fireworks, whom she had shown up to the law, would pursue her and after torturing her (that would purge her of her sins and make her justified before she enters the Kingdom), would throw her already badly mutilated body over some cliffs.

Why hadn't any of this ever happened to her?

Why was she so alive and well, when all she had ever wanted to do was to die?

She now began to realise that the grass always seemed greener on the other side, but even here it wasn't all it was cut out to be. Or hadn't been up until now.

In her many years here she had taken a good look at her herself and her previous life and little by little had begun to recognise and acknowledge quite a lot of what she had previously, very conveniently, ignored. She was well on the way to accepting and embracing what was and how things were and are, up until now.

She was suddenly touched to see her Marie at the village festa. She didn't think Marie had ever been into festas. But, alas there she was with her two good-looking teenage sons. Would she have made a good grand-mother? Amy's conscious awareness posed the question as she watched her two grandsons with adoring eyes and a loving heart, so to say.

The answer was left hanging as Amy caught sight of Marie looking all radiant and holy. Her gaze was transfixed on the statue's face as if in a deep meditation (and she probably had been), whilst the boys were making signs (at least not rude ones, as was characteristic of boys that age) to one of the statue bearers.

How silly! How could she have missed that? It was nobody other than her hazel-green eyed dearly beloved son. He hadn't been into the village festa either, if her memory had served her right. And her memory at this point in time had been the best it had ever been, to her detriment, of course, as all the things she had been so keen to forget kept coming back alive and kicking.

He had been offered this prestigious position of front statue bearer by his then business partner, who had strong connections with the institution of the church. Not necessarily with the Creator or the Christ himself, but he knew people, who knew people in the right places who could procure one, not anyone, such an honour. And there he was in honour and remembrance of his beloved mother who had already been dead for more than seven years. He recalled how devout she had been to the village saint in the shape and form of The Lady of Lourdes and wanted to honour that memory. If only his mother were there to see him then, he mused. "If only you knew," Amy whispered in his ears "that I'm the closest to you I've ever been, son." He felt a gentle breeze tease his ears, but sadly he didn't have a clue who or what it was.

Marie hadn't stopped loving her brother like a son and although he was a grown man, she still couldn't help feeling partially responsible for his happiness. She felt guilty that she had got married just six months after Amy's passing, leaving him and her beloved dad to fend for themselves. Not that they had not been capable of being independent. Mike had made it seem like he wouldn't cope at all, but he did just fine and took care of her hazel-green eyed son as much as she would have done. And although this son of theirs was now a grown man, Mike would still cook for him, clean after him and even iron for him, supporting him as best he could, in all his endeavours. They were a right pair, those two! A right pair! Rarely seeing eye to eye, turning every conversation into an argument, yet they loved each other dearly.

The son, however, as much as he loved his father held a bitterness which tainted the love between them for some years to come. It took a while for him to release the experience of Mike's dark side which had tormented the brother as a child. It had been hidden from the rest of the world - known only by him and Marie - a side people would speculate was there, but which only a few were ever able to see first-hand.

The son, for some time, could not let go of the terrifying images of Mike coming home drunk, swearing and tearing furniture apart. It wasn't just the chattels that were being decimated into a million pieces, but each and every member in that family. Amy, having been a super-sensitive soul would want to run for the hills when outbursts such as these shook their house to its foundations. But there were no places to run to, nor anyone to turn to.

What neither Marie, nor her brother knew at the time was that Mike himself, as cool as he seemed on the outside, was battling demons which came relentlessly to sumptuously feast off his anger and hurt. Red-hot ambers of anger fuelled the fire of that hellish furnace which burnt within his being day and night. His fiery frenzies made both children freeze in terror. They would be in fear for their own life as well as that of their mother, never knowing whether they were going to make it out alive by the time the outburst was over.

Yet, he was a good man deep down and would regret such episodes when the wrath subsided. At times he would get himself dead drunk to silence his conscience and numb the memory. Fear terrorised him day and night – the fear of it happening again - danced a sordid dance around and inside him, casting its long dark shadow on all he did and on all he thought. It was hard to reconcile the two warring factions constantly at each other's throats within his soul - but alcohol, or spirit would quell the phenomenal force of fear and confuddle his mind, so that nothing was clear.

In all that was going on, not once had he spoken ill of Amy to anybody. Not once did he mention to either Marie or to her brother what had happened in the land Down Under. Not once did he make the children think any less of her. There was never any talk of any affair, to be fair. He had always asserted that they had left because he had missed the sea!

He loved her. In fact, he adored her.

This is what Amy saw at her funeral, not that she hadn't suspected.

She had such deep regard and a great respect for this man who had suffered innocently at her hand. They were all victims in some way or another, or so it seemed. He never referred to himself as one, and didn't see himself as one - for this was the bed he made for himself - and now he must lay in it! Any pain or trauma he just brushed under the carpet, and just kept going.

A fresh situation was triggering his unhealed, undealt with pain from previously. It was driving him insane. He could cope with the idea of Amy having made a mistake in the past, and was willing to let it rest. But, the idea that she might be falling in love with his new best friend, on the tiny island shaped like a fish in the middle of the Med, was too much for him to bear. The way she looked at him and the way she flirted with him gave Mike cause for concern.

Uncle Don had been the husband of her own best friend Rosie and the father of little Susie, not so little now. There was Susie, in a very elegant new dress she had bought especially for the village festa, talking to Marie. Now Amy could just watch them, unhindered. She had a great view. How those two had still remained friends after all the family history, Amy did not know. It was heart-warming to watch them hug and greet each other with so much love. They stood on the street corner where Susie's family lived and happily chatted away oblivious to time and space.

Nobody had ever found out whether Amy had actually had an affair the second time around with uncle Don himself. Flirt she did. Even Marie at only ten years of age noticed how Amy's eyes glistened every time he entered the house, when him and his wife Rosie visited Amy and Mike on many a winter's eve. Amy's face would burst into something like a cross between a genuine smile and an awkward grin. She couldn't help herself. Rosie was vigilant and super-alert, and also noticed the light that uncle Don emitted every time him and Rosie were around Amy's.

Marie as a little child had often wondered if uncle Don had lit something back up, the spark of love, within her mum. She was secretly pleased to get glimpses of her mother coming back to life. There was no judgement coming from Marie - she just wanted her mum to feel alive and be happy. Even if Amy had feelings for uncle Don, she had learnt many lessons by now and, she wasn't going to repeat the same mistake twice. But neither her, nor uncle Don could help their hearts missing a beat every time they did meet.

But, poor Mike was losing his mind at the mere possibility that Amy might be having another love affair. If she weren't, the thought that she might want to, was enough to send him off his rocker. He didn't have the gall to ask whether she actually did love him still, as the answer might destroy him and the truth rather than set him free, might send him into a demented frenzy. He didn't know, and he didn't want to know. To him ignorance was bliss, and he wanted to keep it so.

He tried to escape from this pain, but often it was in vain. He tried alcohol and being drunk; having two jobs - a day job driving a truck and a night job - swordfish and tuna fishing. He'd be tired even before the day's work had begun, which meant he didn't have much time to ponder or speculate. It suited him better this way. Besides, when out fishing, the sea water and air soothed his wounded spirit and troubled soul.

Amy wondered whether her son and Marie were at the festa to remember her. Neither of them seemed to have bothered before. Alas, things change and people change. People change, really? Do they? Had she ever changed? Amy looked back, deep in thought. She was as stubborn as a mule and as unforgiving as the freezing cold weather in Antarctica. She wouldn't change or allow herself to be changed, even if it cost her, her life - which sadly, it had done.

In a way it was her obstinate nature, tinged with pride or ego which perpetuated her mental illness. She wouldn't let go of the hurt, the pain, the memories, so scared had she been of what that change would do to her. But, she was changing now, little by little, somehow. But what use was it changing now? Did it count for anything or anyone? Was this what all this watching and waiting was meant to be about?

Change.

The thing she had resisted the most and was adamant would not happen to her no matter what, had caught up with her beyond the grave. Had she changed enough to be fully justified to be in the presence of her loving sacred heavenly Father divine? This was the most pressing of questions, at this point. Obviously not, as otherwise she would have done. But how far off was she?

Well, how long is a piece of string? I can't answer a question with a question, Amy debated within herself, but she had no choice. She had made progress. But there were still hurdles to overcome and realisations to be realised. Once they came, she would have to recognise, acknowledge, accept, and embrace (we know the drill by now) what comes to light, before allowing it to be released or dissolved into the ether to be transmuted into love. She figured out the drill, but wasn't sure what would come up next to be stirred into the melting pot. She would have to wait for it all to unfold organically. It wasn't looking as if she were going to be released from her perch in the watching and waiting place any time soon. This isn't something that can be hurried and besides she had all the time in the world! she mused.

The truth shall set you free, rang and reverberated throughout her whole being. She could only process the truth a bit at a time. When she bit more than she could chew she would choke, as it were, and panic. There was still so much more to mull over, as other truths about herself came to light. For hadn't a philosopher once said that one needed to *Know Thyself*? And knowing yourself, mustn't you have the audacity to love yourself? And didn't loving yourself entail being true to yourself? And how can you love and be true to yourself if you didn't know yourself? It was dizzying going round this circular maze in the trails of her mind.

This process was not for the faint-hearted, that's for sure. Amy needed a lot of courage and a strong will to unfurl layer upon layer of what had come to constitute the bed she made herself lay in. But hadn't Marie been doing all of this already in some shape or form, on the other side? She had to give Marie much more credit than she had ever done. Marie had much more courage, strength and faith than Amy herself had ever had. She had underestimated her eldest daughter's capacity for honesty, authenticity and search for truth.

Marie was on the right track and headed in the right direction, but she wasn't quite there just yet. Amy was emboldened by this observation and happy on her own daughter's behalf of her daughter's progress. It seemed as if by some sacred alchemy that when one healed, the other felt more at ease, and when one let go, the other felt lighter. Amy often wondered whether it was Marie who turned the key which opened the door to the next dimension for her, setting her free from this onerous watching and waiting state of being.

Marie oblivious to Amy's imminent presence, continued to follow the statue, with her two tanned, tall, dark and handsome sons who were the apple of her eye. She looked up at the statue of the Mother - Mother Mary - almost in supplication. Her eyes shone with a love and faith in something much more real and powerful than a papier-mache' statue, Amy observed as she caught a glimmer of it shining in her line of vision.

Marie too would one day, sooner or later, have to face some home truths, in spite and despite her faith, Amy surmised as she watched her daughter grapple with challenging life situations which didn't bring her joy. Marie would need to look at herself consistently, making sure she listened to her heart, mind, body (gut) and soul, when making decisions, ensuring each decision brought her closer to wholeness. But this was a minefield - one she wasn't ready to tread today. Marie was having too much fun meeting friends whom she hadn't seen in ages. This annual five week stint back home in the hot Mediterranean sun, clear blue sea and sky, and warm golden sand - her homeland - with her boys, brought her so much strength, solace and was a source of great joy.

At the right time, Marie would continue to look and search at what needs reviewing and possibly changing as she had been doing, Amy had great faith in this notion. She wondered what Marie would do, if she didn't like what she found. Would she have the courage to face it and change it, or would she opt for the *easy* way out as she had done? Amy hoped and prayed it would be the first one.

Amy joined Marie in her supplications to the representation of this most holy Mother made of papier mache', knowing it was just an image, a reminder of the Mother's presence as she walks with her children, just as Amy walked with Marie.

And as Marie looked straight into Mother Mary's eyes and prayed for the soul of her dearly departed mother and for the spiritual awakening of her beloved sons, Amy prayed that Marie would be true to her own heart, more than anything else. She ardently prayed that her daughter would have the courage to live according to her original purpose and divine plan. She would require a lot of courage to do that. But she believed that Marie had what it took and would get there in the end.

One day Marie would be faced with a choice - to move closer to where her heart wanted or needed her to be - or to drive herself onto the path of self-doubt, darkness, destruction and despair. Those would be questions only Marie would be able to answer and decisions only Marie would be at liberty to make.

What was certain was that Marie's heart didn't want her to suffer anymore at the hand of an abusive spouse. It didn't want Marie and her needs ignored, her presence deplored, her being not seen, heard or felt by a man who had sworn to love, nourish and cherish her throughout their sojourn together on this earth. Marie's heart wanted her to be somewhere and with someone who accepted, cherished, appreciated, valued and moreover, celebrated her.

In the meantime, Amy would have to continue to watch and wait tirelessly, until Marie found her own way back home to herself and to her own heart, mind, body and soul. In the end, Marie would come back to rest in her own divine being accepting, cherishing, appreciating, valuing and celebrating herself before anybody else can. But it wasn't the end, not yet.

Chapter 15

Today it was Marie's birthday. Amy realised that what had seemed like an eternity, had only been nine human years in total. It wasn't the candles on Marie's birthday cake which had given it away. They wouldn't have fitted on the cake, Amy smiled, full of admiration for the daughter she had given birth to, on that day, many many lifetimes ago, or so it seemed. It was more the myriad of cards which Marie had got given telling her age which relayed the passing of time.

Both of Marie's sons had been happily settled in their respective primary schools. She had secured herself a school teacher's job in one of the boy's schools, and to all intents and purposes was getting on with life, with a business-as-usual kind of approach. She always seemed so happy and so upbeat, as if she hadn't ever had a care in the world - nobody would have ever guessed the life she'd had - and they weren't supposed to, Marie would tell you, in no uncertain terms. She felt she had to spread the joy - especially since her life and the world were devoid of it. She had managed to access it from a source deep within, some would say through her soul-searching and finding that which lies hidden within the depths of each human soul, some others that it was divinely bestowed upon her - a spiritual gift - others, that it was a bit of both, whilst some others that it was neither.

Despite everything, Marie had preserved what is called her *inner child*. You would often see her dancing in the playground with the kids she taught, swirling and twirling them around, whilst joining in their role-play as if she were a child herself. Inside she felt as if she were nine or ten years old - joyful, lively, free and full of energy.

She had preserved her child-like sense of awe and wonder and had not been embittered by what life had thrown at her. This blessing was probably procured through her simplicity of spirit and great humility. Moreover, she loved children and years of teaching older and younger children and being within the confines of their pure, innocent energy must have helped preserve her own. The children felt this in her heart too - the ones she taught, as well as her own two sons - and knew beyond a shadow of a doubt that this woman loved them wholeheartedly and always would. They loved her back with the innocent pure love that only children and some child-like adults, the same as her, can give. Children's love is a blessing, as it is pure and unconditional - a gift to be cherished and respected, not to be used and abused, as was rampant in this day and age, Amy observed. Her child-like innocence and joy won Marie the love of many, in heaven and on earth.

On the other hand, a latent guilt tormented her spirit and ravaged her soul with every waking breath. She had set herself responsible for her mother's death, as if she were the all-knowing and the all-seeing, and beat herself up for not pre-empting what was going to happen on that fateful day.

If only she could see that she was only human after all!

It seemed she couldn't forgive herself Amy's death, just as Amy couldn't forgive herself the affair and the twins' death -

the fruit of her love and Greg's - who had died -through no fault of her own. These two women travelling along parallel lines traversed very similar terrain, much more than Amy realised, and than Marie dared to admit.

How could she have not predicted such an atrocious outcome on that one very particular winter's morn? Marie's head could rationalise it, but her heart couldn't and wouldn't let go of the self-blaming she carried with her twenty-four -seven, sometimes at a conscious and at others at an unconscious level.

Would her heart and head ever be reconciled? A long and arduous journey with lots of twists and turns and some major changes in direction still lay ahead of her. Would it bring her to a state of oneness within herself or would it serve to further fragment her already shattered world and world-view? You can never tell how suffering is going to effect someone, Amy pondered. For some, the victim mentality takes over, and they cannot move past identifying with the trauma allowing it to define who they are. For others, it is swept under the carpet as if nothing had ever happened, hoping it will just go away, blissfully unaware that the crumbs which had gathered had become mouldy and smelly. And yet for others who faced the truth of their predicament and made a decision not to be embittered by it, through self-awareness and lots of courage and faith, come out transformed, reformed and healed, Amy analysed and realised, perhaps a tad too late.

Or was it ever too late?

The past whispered its lessons incessantly, until Marie had no choice but to lend it her ear. This listening was as significant as it was subtle. And yes, she did have a choice. The voice in silence told of the times Marie had saved Amy's life and how Marie had been Amy's life-line from the tender age of six and now beyond the grave. It reassured Marie she was blameless over and over again. It reiterated that Amy had made that decision also through choice, exercising her God-given right of free will.

But had she really had a choice? Do we always have a choice? Amy contemplated. To her, at the time, it seemed as if suicide had been her only option. And maybe it was - but, maybe it wasn't. Amy was still working this one out. She didn't want to get her knickers in a twist, not on the morning of her daughter's birthday - this would have to wait.

In a way Marie was luckier, for she had options she could explore and was spoilt for choice. Times had changed drastically when it came to marriage and divorce. People were much less inclined to stay in unhappy or abusive marriages just because an institution says so, as they did back in Amy's day and age. Moreover, women who wanted to set themselves free from the tyranny of a loveless, soulless or abusive marriage now had the financial help of the state as well as that of society at large, Amy reflected.

Little by little, step by step, small and seemingly insignificant changes started to shift and change Marie's perspective about herself, her mother, her mother's death, her mother's life and her own life, finding some wriggle room in the dark cocoon she had constructed for herself. She moved slowly, but surely, albeit in a dark and confined space. Something inside her knew that all she needed to do was to trust the process and that everything would unfold effortlessly, and ultimately be as it should be when the time was right.

But when dark nights of the soul came, sometimes unexpectedly and for longer than Marie anticipated, she doubted she would ever transmute from chrysalis to butterfly. One day, her dark night in the cocoon would metamorphise into the light freedom of a beautiful butterfly fluttering its newly formed wings - it was a cycle - and she had to learn to enjoy the ride. She had faith that a higher power was holding the space in unconditional love and compassion, although at times she felt that her faith was tested to the limit. She had to use her eyes to see and her ears to listen to what she knew internally and to the signs she was given externally.

She was sent signs.

She was given dreams.

Sometimes the signs were butterflies, dragonflies, bees, spiders, deer, feathers and many other nature-related phenomena. At others it would be meeting people who would give her seemingly insignificant messages, which meant something to her or held a missing piece of the puzzle of her life. At times it was a book, at others a film. Whilst at others, it was her own inner knowing she had to listen to, trust and follow. This was the hardest, but Marie was growing ever more confident and proficient in recognising her own inner voice, in and amongst all the others clamouring for her attention. As she grew older she accessed, from deep within her, the courage to trust and to follow its bidding.

This seeing, listening and trusting what she saw, heard, felt and knew- reminded Amy of what had been happening to her presently, in this state of being. Transformation may have been subtle and slow, but the impact of change, no matter how small, can never be underestimated, for its ripple effect reaches into the infinite realms and beyond, Amy observed from her higher perspective, floating on the other side. Little by little Marie began to absolve herself of a crime she hadn't committed, enabling the noose around her neck to loosen, allowing her to breathe. Would Marie go all the way in setting herself free? And in so doing, would she release and unleash Amy from this static state of being?

Humans on the whole found change difficult, Amy observed. Nature gives us infinite examples of such cycles of change and the importance of the dark times as much of those that are light. Each stage requires a death, followed by a resurrection, followed by a death and the cycle continued. It required courage to go with the flow of this cycle and not resist it, but the new life after each death created new neural pathways in the brain, bringing one to higher perspectives and to lighter states of being - as if being newly-born - seeing the world with a renewed sense of awe and wonder, as if for the first time.

Marie began to forgive herself for *not having been psychic* and *not having had the foresight* that Amy would act on her all life-time wish, on that particular day. Little by little she began to realise that she had done all she could for her dearly beloved mother. She began to see that there had been a bigger picture, which she had not previously been privy to, which pushed her mother over the edge physically as well as figuratively speaking.

In the process, it began to dawn on her that in a funny weird sort of way, although seemingly manipulative, contriving and controlling, her mother had loved her with all her heart. Amy had tried to put her daughter first in all her major life choices, starting with when she had left the land Down Under, which she did solely for Marie. Luckily, Marie was able to see this now. It had taken her some time, that's true - but better late than never, as they say.

Day in, day out, Amy reminded Marie, lest she forgot, that

she had left her life in the land Down Under for her sake. She had done it out of a pure love for this being she had given birth to four years previously, but deep down wanted some recognition and appreciation for this act. It made Marie feel beholden to her in many ways. Is this what Amy had wanted? she did wonder.

In reality, Amy would not have been able to live life without Marie, as much as Marie would not have been able to live without Amy and had found it near impossible to do so, even now. To Amy, Marie had been the light at the end of her tunnel - shining bright in her endless days of a seemingly forever dark night of the body and soul - stuck in the dark confines of the cocoon she created to protect her. Alas, she hadn't burst forth into a free flying beautiful butterfly. But would Marie?

As she began to forgive herself, Marie also began to grow in compassion towards herself and towards her dearly departed mother. Being a mother of two herself, made it easier to walk in her own mother's shoes. Thoughts of Amy, filled Marie's heart with joy today, on her birthday, as she celebrated not just the day she was ushered into this world, but the day her mother birthed her, almost dying in the process. It had been a miracle that both women survived, relatively intact - something definitely worth remembering and celebrating.

Marie continued to feel lighter inside. The more she released of that dark matter which had settled insidiously into various parts of her body and mind, the more light shone in and through her, lighting her eyes and illuminating her face. The peace she had known in her youth continued to come back to her in steadier and longer bouts. The more she trusted, the more she was blessed with the courage to hear and to follow the truth within her. She found the strength to look inside.

"They are so conditioned to look outside," Amy said out loud, although nobody could hear, "that to look inside, one needs the courage of a bastion," (a translation of an idiom from Amy's mother tongue), Amy continued to tell herself.

Marie's faith in the whole process, believing that things were unfolding as they were meant to, was tested to the limit. The unconditional love of her sacred Creator divine, and the sustenance of the divine Earthly mother continued to sustain her when her abundance of love, peace and joy dried up and it all seemed to fall apart. The Son's light illuminated her path during her most anguished, darkest hours. She turned to Him to help her activate her own Christ-consciousness within her as she connected completely to her sacred heavenly Father and divine Earthly mother in and through the Son, so that they were all one.

And so it was. As Marie continued to heal inside, as if by some ethereal synchronicity (or was it so decreed by some divine universal law, maybe?), so did Amy. Amy too, was able to judge herself less harshly and to view herself much more compassionately, releasing a lot of shame and blame. As her daughter forgave her, so was she able to forgive herself in little bouts of self-love and compassion. In baby steps, requiring patience and perseverance, as Marie healed, so did she. It felt as if it would be Marie who would set Amy free – as if Marie held the key to the place where Amy needed to go and be, after this one.

Both women continued to journey together. Amy breathed in the same air as Marie, feeling the same exhilaration at being alive, as well as the pain she endured during her dark nights of the soul. Who would have guessed that their paths would be much more intricately interwoven now, more than ever before? Connected through sacred love and compassion knowing no boundaries, rather than by a psychic-link fuelled by fear and control, both women held hands as they traversed the same path, albeit in different dimensions, in different realms, at different vibrations.

Today, on her birthday, Marie seemed particularly despondent. Amy picked up that something was amiss. Marie sat solo, silently on a bench watching the ebb and flow of the Thames and the comings and the goings of the ducks, swans and geese. The kingfisher heralded its presence, as it always does, with its shrill sharp whistling sound, falling lightly on Marie's heavy heart. She sat on the grass deep in thought, praying and meditating on life's little ironies and its dark sense of humour. Sometimes she was able to laugh with life, at others she wished she weren't the butt of its jokes, so that she could laugh even louder. It was true she always made lemonade out of the lemons she was given, but she was quite tired of drinking lemonade and yearned for something a bit more exotic and pleasing to the palate.

Nothing escaped Amy's keen eyes as she watched and waited with razor-sharp vision everything unfolding before her. It was becoming more and more obvious to her that something wasn't right between The Man and Marie. They had been growing apart for quite some time now. It was becoming much more apparent to her, to Marie and to the boys as the cracks in their marriage began to become more visible to the naked eye. Their constant arguing left no doubt as to the direction they were headed in. The Man seemed to be completely oblivious to the cognitive dissonance which jarred and marred any potential symphonic vibration between the two. Unless he wasn't really that unaware, but preferred to dig his head in the sand and play the *ignorance is bliss* game! He was very good at playing games.

A deep dark gulf separated these two souls who had once promised to live as one. Nothing Marie would do or say could thaw The Man's heart or open his mind. He was as stubborn as a mule and believed that he was a perfect specimen of the male species. Marie often felt powerless in procuring any positive change and in narrowing the ever-growing chasm that engulfed them. She often wondered whether the sense of togetherness that was once, would ever be again.

The pang of pain in Amy's chest matched that of Marie. She could not only see, but feel her daughter's suffering as if it were her own. It was all exacerbated by a sense of powerlessness which overwhelmed her at times such as this. She wouldn't dream of telling Marie those dreaded words *I told you so,* as perhaps she would have done were she still here, on this side of the veil.

Instead she would now wonder if things would have turned out differently had she still been here, on this side, before the wedding. Would she have been able to help Marie, not walk into the travesty of this defunct formal union? This is a question Amy asked herself time and again. She also wondered over the years whether Marie would have gone ahead with the wedding, hadn't she been weakened and made somewhat vulnerable by Amy's suicide. This question confused her mind and contorted her brow in thought for many years to come, as there didn't seem to be a clear-cut answer.

The Man had been so hell-bent on marrying Marie that it would have been hard to have stopped the union, had she still been there. Grandma Jo had believed it had been entrapment. It wasn't meant to have happened. But somehow it had. Now

Marie had to stand on her own two feet and set herself free - independently.

As harsh as it sounds, Marie's shackles sang a sad birthday song today.

The ache in Marie's heart grew stronger. She could not deny its presence any longer. Every heartbeat, a painful throb reminding her of the truth of her reality. But what was her reality, really?

Once again Marie listened. Marie always found it much harder to listen when it came to matters of the heart - her own heart. There always seemed to be too many voices subtle and almost imperceptible wanting to be heard. How was Marie to know the one which spoke the truth? Only in the deep silence of meditation can the one true voice coming from the heart, rather than from the conditioned mind, be known, Marie learnt over the years.

In the cocophony of all sound The Man's voice shouted the loudest, convincing Marie (or trying to convince Marie) that everything that was wrong with their marriage was her fault. He hissed that if she changed they would have the perfect union. On the other hand, he also constantly cooed that it was all in her head. Then there was the voice of her church screaming in her ears that the *bond* (a human bond?) of marriage is forever and that there are NO exceptions to the rule, so that mental and emotional bullying and abuse had to be endured, just because! Compounding this were voices of family and some *friends* questioning her judgement, as well as her conditioned mind inundating her psyche with more rules, regulations and rationalisations.

Marie's tiny inner voice of truth - the one which always said the same thing - was muffled amongst all the other louder ones. Yet, Marie heard it, although all the others would come in to promptly discredit and silence it.

In spite or despite all of this, Marie continued to teach in various schools, various classes, various children of various ages. She continued cooking various food everyday for The Man, the boys and for anyone who cared to pop in for a Sunday lunch or a weekday brunch. She continued to take the boys to various after-school activities, at various places, on various days, at various times and continued to make new friends and go to various yoga and meditation classes and events, dance classes, attending various academic and spiritual courses and doing various voluntary-work activities.

So life went on and to an outsider it seemed like a bed of roses. This beautiful woman, with a handsome husband, two healthy boys in a small, but cosy house (which Marie lovingly turned into a home), in a small picturesque village, seemed picture perfect.

But not to Amy. Amy knew better. She watched as tears came strolling down Marie's face every time The Man came home late, giving her not just the cold shoulder, but a cold, unrelenting heart. It was a dynamic of give and take – she gave, he took. What he ever did give was measured and very limited. It felt to Marie as if she were constantly being fed crumbs off someone else's sumptuous supper. Marie's own needs were not recognised, acknowledged or accepted by The Man, let alone met. Would Marie continue to put up with this? Amy worried herself sick, as she watched it all unfold.

All she could do was to watch and pray, and to pray and watch hoping her daughter would sooner, rather than later, do what she hadn't had the courage to do, leading to her untimely death. As Amy felt her daughter's desperation, she hoped against hope her daughter would not follow in her footsteps, but would find an alternative life-affirming way forward.

Marie would never be able to comprehend the extent to which The Man had actually damaged and hurt her. Many things between them had been left unsaid. Perhaps, this was a blessing as it made it easier for Marie to forgive him what she thought she knew, remaining oblivious to what she did not know. 'What she doesn't know, won't hurt her', Amy whispered to herself. The Man smirked an evil smirk at getting a whiff of this sentiment traversing the ether. It was his thoughts exactly. Would Marie one day be able to set herself free from his tyranny and procure her own liberation?

Amy longed to see the day. She longed to see her daughter set herself free, as she could never have done herself. She had taken the shorter route, or rather a long-term loss for a short-term gain. Marie had taken the long-winding narrow route, which required copious patience and perseverance. But would she get there in the end - a liberated, truth-seeking and truth-finding woman? Amy asked, hoping against hope she would.

Amy's heart created and conjured a picture of Marie, totally free. She ardently hoped her hope would make it come to be. For a few moments there, Amy was concerned solely for her daughter's well-being, healing and liberation and not her own. She forgot her own predicament and spent days on end in her daughter's shoes, as the expression goes. This earned her many *brownie points* in this state of watching and waiting. She suddenly jumped a few rungs ahead. She felt lighter and freer. Compassion was rewarded not just in this realm, but is the cornerstone of many others too, Amy now knew.

Suddenly from the corner of her eye Amy caught a glimpse

of a figure approaching her. This was a rare occurrence and took her by surprise. She got excited and wondered who it could be. Maybe her time to be judged had come? Or was this her mum?

Grandma Jo's being, like a mysterious mist on an early clear cold crispy winter's day, settled in a mass in the ether close by and was visible to Amy.

What an unexpected surprise!

She had stopped expecting anything to happen in this limbo, as she would call it, only because nothing ever did. Yet, this morning the spirit of her own mum had come. Her essence exuded the most exquisite sweet-smelling scent. It reminded Amy of the David Austin roses Marie had in her garden, as the perfume wafted through Amy's nostrils, so to say. Amy uplifted by her mother's presence, smiled. She hadn't smiled in a while.

Jo was a source of strength and supported Marie through many a crises within the family. It seemed as if Grandma Jo had succeeded where Amy had failed in loving, accepting and celebrating Marie and Marie's presence and essence on earth. The bond between grand-mother and grand-daughter brought solace to both, especially after Amy's suicide when it was sealed, one could almost say, by blood.

Grandma Jo hadn't been one for much affection whilst on earth, but since on the other side, the softer side of her flowed effortlessly and embraced Amy in a heartfelt hug filling her with a deep forgiveness and unconditional acceptance. Amy allowed her mum's love to flow freely right through her, making her feel restored and renewed.

It was the pure love that hugged Amy through Grandma Jo's heartfelt embrace that moved Amy to tears. She hadn't cried whilst on the other side for a while but tears of joy, releasing all the self-blame and shame, came flooding forth. The two women looked into each other's eyes, communicating telepathically through the language of sacred love divine. It is a silent language which speaks through the presence of all That which surpasses words and understanding, and can only be known through first-hand experience.

Things were shifting. Energies were moving. Amy was healing. There is so much power in the love of a mother. Just as Grandma Jo had done for Amy, so would Amy do for Marie and Marie for Amy.

Chapter 16

Marie woke up early that morning ready to repeat the ritual she annually held on the anniversary of her mother's death. It was fourteen years this year. Fourteen years in a state of limbo for Amy and fourteen years of having gone to hell and back, for Marie. They say time flies when you're having fun - but, this state of being wasn't fun for neither, if truth be told. Marie had come a long way in evolving into a more authentic version of herself and the peace she had known before Amy slid onto the other side, settled into her heart once more, Amy was pleased to see. She, on the other hand, had come a long way, too.

Both women were the most healed they had ever been. Marie had addressed and taken responsibility for who she was and where she was in life, thus far, with an honesty and authenticity that warrants copious amounts of accolade, Amy pondered proudly. Marie recognised, acknowledged, accepted and embraced many aspects of her life past and present, some on her own while others with some help or guidance from others. Following this process Marie had managed to let a lot of the trauma and guilt go - lightening her heavy burden.

By some kind of osmosis, it made Amy feel lighter too.

There were copious scientific explanations for all of this,

but neither was bothered by such. They were much happier trusting what they themselves experienced over what others explained, in terms they couldn't understand. They trusted the process - their process, their journey, their reflections, their experiences which they had faith in - over anything coming from someone else's experiences, hypotheses or theories. This needed a lot of faith in oneself and self-assurance which both now had in abundance.

It had been a cold crisp sunny winter's day – the winter solstice. The energies on the winter solstice are always very strong, Amy noticed, becoming much more sensitive to them since on the other side. One wonders, had there been any other reason, why Amy had chosen that day fourteen years earlier to do what she had done. Perhaps not consciously, but subliminally the solstice energy had helped in some way to push Amy over the edge.

Both felt that today was going to be a very significant day, although neither of the two knew in what way. Would Marie's greys miraculously turn back to black? Would she suddenly lose the weight she had wanted to shed for a while now? Or perhaps, win the lottery? Or would there be a sudden change to her challenging life situation? Life, in actual fact, had been one big miracle so far, and Marie would count her blessings incessantly day and night, despite the hardship she had been facing, mostly brought about by her married life.

The Man gave her grief with the death of affection and lack of emotion - her suffering, in this respect, had been tantamount. Yet, her mother's death had given her a new take on life all those years earlier. Nothing good was left unnoticed and everything beautiful, no matter how small, was intensely appreciated. She seemed to always want to counteract the unpleasantness of her life with an equal, if not greater degree of love, laughter and fun. It was how she coped. She smiled through the tears and the pain, not to deceive anyone, nor to deceive herself, but to keep herself vibrating at a high level which would help her traverse and transcend this dark, dense terrain.

On the other hand, there were times when Amy well and truly feared for her daughter's life. On days such as these, Amy would watch with trepidation the unfolding of her daughter's life, lest she would go down the same slippery slope as her. It's very easily done, as she and many others can testify. And sometimes the signs were there, Amy reflected, signaling despair. However, unlike her, Marie always found a way to heal and repair. She trusted that if she were to seek, she would find. Her search was relentless and no matter what, she would never give up. All the right people and opportunities appeared at the right time, to further cement her faith in her Masters words: "Seek and you shall find."

Today, Amy hoped her anniversary would bring something better to her daughter's life, a special kind of blessing, as it were. Perhaps today would be one of those miraculous days which come bearing gifts, surprising us when we least expect it, Amy hoped, as she knew a day- any day - could go either way.

What Amy had hoped hadn't been beyond the realms of possibility as miracles do happen all the time, it's not as if they didn't. Marie encountered them constantly and would often declare herself as living proof that miracles do happen - herself being the miracle! But many, blinded by the drudgery of their daily lives, either failed to notice them or took them for granted and failed to see the magic as it unfolded before their very eyes.

It began to dawn on Amy, as she was learning from Marie, that life itself is a miracle which begs celebration every single moment of every single day, not just on special occasions like birthdays, anniversaries or Christmas. Every single breath was cause for celebration and a miracle in its own right. Marie believed that the air we breathe isn't just a concoction of chemicals, but our life-force, intricately interlinked with all that is sacred and divine. There is such a fine line between life and death, between having a heartbeat the one minute and suddenly having none the next, that each breath and each heartbeat is cause for rejoicing in and of itself.

It's funny how many people profess not to believe in miracles. Alas, they are faced by new birth, human or otherwise, every second of every day and accosted with a new sunrise with each dawn and that of a sunset at dusk - but failed to see them as miraculous phenomena, or to see them at all. The miracle of life accompanies our every living breath - until death. At the point of death we surrender all life within us, sometimes reluctantly, at others willingly and at others, too willingly as in the case of Amy, to continue our travels through the many mansions in the Father's house.

Amy promised herself that if she were ever allowed to come back, she would celebrate each and every day as if it were her last. She had wasted enough time moping about the past, anxious in the present and fretting about the future, that the next time round she would, she vowed to herself, continuously live in the present moment joyously and make the most of every living breath. End of.

What else would she do differently? Amy asked herself.

She would make sure she showed and told the people she

loved, how much she loved them. She would embrace and joyfully accept any love bestowed upon her, knowing she is deserving of it and equally allowing her love to flow forth freely to all. She would sing at the top of her voice in the shower and dance stark naked in total abandon in her living room. She would eat, drink and be merry. She would make love on snow-capped mountains, writhe in passion and ecstasy on sandy desert dunes and languidly lay on long deserted beaches, embracing the joy of doing nothing - or what is perfectly described by the Italians as *dolce far niente*. She would silently watch the sea, listen to its sweet symphony touching her soul, moving her to tears. She would watch the sky burn at sunrise and shimmer at sunset, wherever she may be - as she would travel and see the world. She would be active, pro-active and make her dreams come true with a fervent passion and a stalwart determination. She wouldn't settle for second best, but would make sure she honoured her heart's deepest desires, as long as nobody else got hurt, of course.

If she were ever to come back, that is. She was not sure she would have to or would wish to. But who knows, life is full of surprises and that included life in the after-life, as she has just found out.

She definitely wouldn't smoke as it had made her breath stink. Besides, Marie used to get very upset when all the curtains, clothes and the whole house stank of cigarettes and was stained with nicotine. She would make friends and not keep herself to herself, living as a recluse, as she had done. Friendships bring so much joy if we allow them to. Besides, special moments shared with a good, loving friend nurture heart, mind, body and soul. She would be a good friend the next time round given the chance, and wouldn't sleep with her best friends' husbands, no matter how hard they seduced her! That's one lesson she shall carry with her into wherever or whichever realm or dimension she might be in next.

On the other hand, she would allow herself to make mistakes as that's how we all learn and grow. Besides, it's only those who do nothing at all, who don't make mistakes. She would allow herself the blessing of learning from her mistakes and not condemn herself, judge herself or punish herself as harshly as she had done. She would smile, accept her *mis-take* or *error*, call it what you will and move on. She would smile a lot, just like her Marie. Smiling was such great medicine and spread so much love, cheer and joy.

She would not call her misdeamours or mistakes - *sin* – that word with its ugly connotations, did her no favours in the earthly lifetime she had not long ago left. Because of it, she saw herself as evil, almost to the point of being unforgivable, unlovable and unredeemable by herself and by her most loving Creator. Amy saw today, for the first time, the error of her ways in this respect. The next time round she would want to be free from the tyranny of cold-blooded, stone-hearted institutions which controlled people's hearts and psyche through fear and coercion. If she were to come back she definitely would not belong to any church, universal or not.

Mother Earth sacred and divine would be her church; her own heart would be her temple and the word of her sacred loving Father creator divine written in her DNA, would be her bible. She would listen to her heart and trust its dictates. She would breathe in tandem with a light- image (not beaten to a pulp under a cross) of the Christ before her, surrounding her within and without, His breath activating her own Christ-consciousness whilst she bathes in their united presence, within His sacred essence. This would be her sacred holy communion.

She had loved His message then, and would still adhere to it the next time round. She loved how He taught His listeners how to connect to the divine Earthly mother, how to love and respect her and how to be one with her. These teachings were claimed to have been lost, sadly, but Amy believed that they were kept hidden from humanity for a reason. He taught that His Father's Kingdom was within each and every one of us, so that we are all Christs - as He - sacred and divine. We must allow our light to shine out into the world, as He had done, so that in and through Him, and in and through the Father and Mother, we would all be one.

He had promised His disciples the Solar Logos - or more familiarly - the Holy Spirit. The Holy Spirit - the most sacred and divine shard of the Father's presence and essence - made to measure, one could almost say, to what a human being could contain within themselves - would be allowed to fill her entirely with Its grace. This presence would sustain her physicality and her divinity, making her more able to live in community, as she unites in and through this sacred presence, with all that is, was and shall be. Basically, she would create a heaven on earth within her, the next time round, Amy promised herself.

It took a whole fourteen years on the other side for her to realise that she could only love, accept and forgive others when she had done those things for herself, first and foremost.

Did things take longer to process from where she was? Amy wasn't sure whether or not being immersed in the physical world was a help or a hindrance, but veered towards the former rather than the latter, as Marie seemed to be making steadier progress than her.

She definitely would do more of the things she enjoyed doing, rather than just those which she believed she ought to do. She would shed the exaggerated sense of obligation and the unrealistic sense of duty which she dragged around like a heavy leaden load around her neck. She'd spend much more time dancing, singing, eating out, socialising, walking, scaling mountains, fishing in rivers, snorkeling in oceans, climbing trees, breathing in pure rain-forest air -leaving no stone unturned, in her quest to make the most of her every waking hour. "I'll sleep when I'm dead," she would say, even though she knew she wouldn't be allowed to sleep a wink when she crossed over.

She would have oodles and oodles of fun and travel the world, rather than spend her whole life on her knees church-cleaning, attending mass twice daily, praying the rosary four times a day and reading the Bible from cover to cover, many times around. And to what end? He still hadn't come and neither had His mum!

The next time around she would make sure she was spiritual, but not religious. 'I would want live in a constant state of joyous celebration of life and creation', she promised herself. 'I would take my life into my own hands, but not in the same way as I did, the last time. No, next time I'll make sure I live my life to the max and live it a bit more light-heartedly, too - I don't need to take myself or life so seriously,' Amy declared making a pact with herself, should she ever return.

'I wouldn't want to hide behind rituals, rules and regulations which claim to protect me, yet stop me from living life fully, from feeling pain and ecstasy, from taking full responsibility for my actions', Amy reassured herself. Rules and regulations may have a place, but she vaguely recalled someone saying that rules and regulations did not sanctify one, neither did they set one free. Rather, they ensnare and enslave all who serve their dictates. It may have been The Christ who had said something along these lines, Amy recalled. Rather than coercing people into obedience with a myriad of rules and regulations, with dreadful consequences should one not comply - He taught the Law of Love. It was the only Law which set one free from the tyranny of copious thinking and over-thinking of actions and consequences, binding one in the mind. The Law of Love flows from the heart.

The Law of Love.

The law of love - for one's own sacred Creator divine, oneself and one's neighbour - would liberate and set humanity free. All of creation had in fact been created in love, for love and through love and this was the most important tenet, Amy realised. She felt so much remorse for having held onto the old Law as if her dear life depended upon it. It sadly stifled and undermined the unconditional creative love her sacred Creator is constantly extending to her and to each and every one of us at every moment in time.

Amy now realised that it wasn't through fear that we evolved and united with all that is sacred and divine and with each other as one. But through L-O - V- E. That four lettered word, used and abused over millennia, is what lies within the depths of each and every one of us. It is a love that allows freedom and free will. Love is not fear-based, neither does it seek to control or coerce. Love does not require vengeance not does it seek revenge. Love is generous, love is kind, love is considerate, love is compassionate. It is love which sets one free from the tyranny of regimented rules and unlawful regulations, Amy held and Marie agreed.

She would not ever take any man-made chemicals or medication, but would turn to the most sacred Mother Earth for her medicine. Sacred Mother Earth had a cure for every illness, a medicine for every dis-ease and Amy would turn to her, the next time around, if indeed she had to come back, heaven forbid! But heaven seemed like a very far away fairy-tale place at this minute.

What is this smell? Amy looked around curiously, as a whiff of this something familiar brought her back to reality - or to the here and now - more precisely. She sniffed harder, hoping Marie wouldn't be setting the house on fire. This daughter of hers did keep her on her toes, shall we say. Amy couldn't place the smell, although she had caught a waft of it hundreds of times when still embodied.

Of course, it had slipped Amy's mind that today was the anniversary of her own death. Marie had always performed a ritual either on the day itself or a few days prior, depending on whether schools had broken up for Christmas or not. Marie wasn't keen to perform her annual ritual with the boys in the house. It was a private affair, one which a mother doesn't share, not even with her offspring.

It had been a cold crisp sunny winter's day – the winter solstice – and there were candles burning in every room. Fourteen mystifying years of watching and waiting for Amy, fourteen years of searching, finding and healing for Marie. Both in each other's minds and in each other's hearts. The love which Marie had lavished on Amy, which she thought had been wasted, thrown away in a moment of anger and ingratitude, was there burning bright in both their hearts, in the candlelight. It had not perished, but was kindled like fire with the love Amy now lavished freely on Marie. And which although Marie couldn't see, she could somehow feel.

Chapter 17

The sun reflected a golden reddish glow with a pinkish hue which she remembered marvelling at, when admiring a sunrise or a sunset here on earth. Its bright lustrous light fell on Marie's living room mirror, reflecting an iridescent luminescence everywhere. The candles were burning slowly, their light illuminating the walls, the windows, the doors, the floors and most importantly, Marie whose face shone with an ethereal brightness not of this world.

One could safely say that if in the past Amy saw everything, now she missed nothing!

Marie's whole house bathed in this brilliance - the windows sparkled, the furniture shone -the dishes had been done, the clothes ironed and the carpets hoovered. All in all, it was a picture of domestic bliss. Amy believed Marie was a bit OCD about cleaning, but who was she to point fingers? If this wasn't the pot calling the kettle black, Amy silently smiled to herself, then she didn't know what was. Amy herself had been quite obsessed with having a sparkling clean house at all times whilst on this dense, seemingly solid plane. It were as if the cleanliness of the house reflected the purity of her soul. It was ironic that as much as Marie had rebelled against it, she was now almost a replica of Amy, in this respect. Very ironic, Amy observed extending her spirit to envelope her daughter in her ethereal love. Amy wanted to reassure her daughter that no matter what the house looked like, she, Marie was pure in heart - and very loved, loving and lovable.

Amy wondered what the ritual would be like this year. The ritual always comprised of candles, and these Amy had smelt before she had seen. But were there going to be any surprises this year? Amy wanted to know. Marie was quite an unpredictable one, and always had been. There was always an element of surprise with twists and turns in the plot and when it came to plans with Marie - one learnt to expect the unexpected.

Marie exercised the right which every woman should exercise without being judged - with no valid reason and at very short notice - the right to change her mind. Oh, yes! Amy couldn't keep up with how Marie decided one thing one minute, was hell-bent on it, but changed her mind the next, for no apparent reason. At times such as these, Amy had actually felt sorry for The Man who wouldn't have a clue what to say or do. He found her spontaneity a wee bit confusing, to say the least. He was someone whose outer physical everyday life had to be structured and completely controlled, so he perceived this behaviour as a sign of weakness, rather than a strength - for one had to be confident and courageous to change plans on a whim - being in a constant state of flux, living in a state of perpetual changing and unknowing.

Alas, Marie finally settled down in her eldest son's bedroom. Why in this bedroom in particular, Amy had no idea and, perhaps, neither had Marie. She just watched silently as

Marie perched herself on his freshly laundered bed. Marie communicated with the sacred and divine all the time, in the depths and the silence of her child-like heart.

The Sacred spoke in silence.

She listened.

Marie sat still in union and in communion with her sacred Creator divine - the most sublime prayer of all. She would breathe and be breathed by divine life, love and light reverberating through sacred cosmic sound, realising her oneness with this presence, which was her inherent innate essence.

However, breaking the silence, she sometimes petitioned using words. She would not ask for wealth or riches, nor for flashy cars or big houses, neither for prestige, nor for fame or fortune, but for an inner peace and joy. She petitioned for a unity of heart, mind, body and soul within her own embodiment and a unity of her united embodiment with its Creator, sacred Life, Love, Light divine. She constantly prayed for her two sons so that they would find peace in this turbulent world, be confident and fulfill their life purpose to its fullest. She was happy surrendering her own life into the loving hands of her sacred Father, but when it came to surrendering her own two sons' lives, she silently acknowledged that, she needed more faith than that of a mustard seed.

She always prayed for friends, family and the whole of humanity that peace prevailed in everyone's heart and consequently on earth. If peace reigned in each person's heart, then peace would also reign on the planet. But because people did not strive to have peace in their hearts, then peace did not reign on earth. What people experienced as war, fear, jealousy, anger, hatred was generated by humans whose hearts were unhappy, and did not have peace. When one is at peace and joyous within themselves they are not jealous or envious of others or what others have. They live in harmony with others and with creation, in a state of peace, love and joy, not in a state of fear and war.

She ardently prayed that she would be a living beacon of light shining bright in humanity's dark despair, of which she was deeply aware. She yearned to spread love and light everywhere she went and to touch whom ever she met with peace. The light she would shine, is that which had been placed within her by her sacred Creator divine. She prayed that this divine essence -the Christ-Consciousness - shining within, transmuted fear into love, anger into compassion, despair into hope and death into life for her and for all.

She prayed that her sacred Creator would use her as and when to bring peace, joy and love to the whole of humankind. She prayed that she would continue to be healed from the wounds inflicted upon her and that she would have the courage to take full responsibility for dealing with the pain these wounds procured. She prayed she would be brave to take responsibility for her own well-being and not to be dependent on others for her happiness, healing and wholeness. This is true love of self and others.

She prayed that she would be a good mother, lavishing a pure unconditional love onto her two adorable, beautiful sons whom she loved more than her own life itself. She prayed that whatever had transpired between herself and The Man would not interfere with the plan that life and the Divine had had in store for them, and that they too would know serenity and joy in their hearts. She prayed for The Man that he would begin to see how far apart they had grown and have the audacity to face this truth and do something about it.

Marie felt that he had betrayed her trust for many years, even before they tied the knot, and as much as she had tried to trust him again, she couldn't. Not that she hadn't tried. By Jove, she tried and tried and couldn't have tried any harder. But, as soon as she decided to trust again he'd say or do something to sow seeds of doubt, playing with her mind and messing with her head. So she prayed for clarity. She prayed she would be able to see the truth, know the truth and act from a place of truth which would set her (and him) free. She asked for the courage to bring all of this into being at the right time, for their own highest good and the highest good of all the family.

Finally, she also prayed that she would continue to forgive Amy from a deeper place within her for what she had done that day. Not that she had anything to forgive, she now realised. It was more of a letting go of the effect that Amy's death had had on her, that needed releasing. It felt as if she was almost on the cusp of surrendering something completely and allowing it, together with Amy's corpse, to rest in peace.

She suddenly burst into tears.

This irritated Amy, partly because it scared her to see her daughter in so much pain and not being able to do anything about it and partly because it seemed that Marie cried all the time. This was a habit she needed to kick, Amy remonstrated. It's true that tears released pain and washed away unwanted debris, but Marie's reaction to happiness, to pain, to fear, to ecstasy, to anger, to joy, to love, to gratitude - was to cry. Amy could never tell whether she was crying for joy or for sorrow.

Suddenly something seemed to be happening to Amy.

What is that tugging at her heart or where her heart used to be, pulling at her heartstrings? It was a sweet subtle energy, almost like a breeze, pulling her backwards and pushing her forwards in a soft serene, yet swift swinging movement. Amy had loved the swings when little. She remembered with a fondness taking Marie to the swings on clear-skied starry summer nights. She too would hop onto one, and the two of them would laugh their heads off, swinging with a childlike, joyous abandon. She had always felt free on a swing, especially if there were a gentle breeze which her golden tanned body tickled and teased.

On this side of the veil, Marie sat on the bed rocking to and fro too. Amy heard the gentle sob turn into a cry. She cried louder and louder, praying ardently to be set free. Her heartfelt prayers pierced through the heavens and beyond as her life-long yearning for healing and liberation, for forgiveness (of herself, Amy and all others) were being answered - in one final swift swing - surrendering all that needed to be released.

And just like that, she let go!

She professes not to have seen any flashing lights or to have levitated as some of her friends had boasted they did, but felt a lightness and an uplifting of her spirit. Her soul smiled with ecstasy, whilst she was being set free. As she sat there, Marie felt a presence within her being and with-out. A sweet scent of roses accompanied her every in-breath. The presence seemed to shroud her in its soft and serene embrace, as if she were a newborn baby being lovingly held by the mother who had just delivered her, which wasn't too far from the truth. Suddenly, a rush of dimenthyltryptamine (dmt) flowed right through her, the same as when she had just been born. Her body became one unified sensation, vibrating with a warm cosy feeling like that of when one feels deeply loved or when in love. And she felt completely loved and enveloped in love at that moment in time, as time stood still and all was perfect. She felt her whole being glow with this loving presence, as if it were her very essence. She could hear, as in the gentle whisper of a breeze, the words: 'released… released… released' almost as an affirmation of what had just taken place.

Marie knew beyond a shadow of a doubt that at that moment, on that day, as she sat on that bed, she was liberated. She sat there, motionless. Her heart overflowing with gratitude at her unexpected graceful and seemingly effortless healing of heart, mind, body and soul. She didn't know how many angelic beings or other sacred and divine entities had been in that room that day, but she felt heaven and earth present as she willingly let go of all that no longer served her higher purpose and wasn't for her highest good or for the highest good of anyone.

Oh happy day!

At this point, unbeknownst to Marie, she had set in motion the turning of a key slowly somewhere, somehow also setting Amy free. The gentle swinging movement coupled with what felt like a gentle breeze propelled Amy through an ever-expanding vortex of sound and light. It rang with a symphonic sound of varying pitches, and was swirling with millions of luminous florescent lights made up of various shapes, of minute form. As the form morphed into different shapes, of various sizes and hues, Amy's spirit became the sound, the shape and the form itself. There was a complete union of dance, dancer and the being danced. "When a fruit is ripe, it suddenly and effortlessly falls off the tree. This is how this transition felt for me," Amy described this metamorphosis to her friends when she later transitioned to the next stage.

Amy's whole being was in a complete tizzy as the twirling and swirling made her dizzy. So much had changed, so suddenly. She would have to find her bearings as she wasn't sure she had landed on her feet. She was making a habit of travelling through space head first, it seems! The watching and waiting had come to an abrupt end and like a butterfly, she fluttered her wings, and began to fly high. She felt a surge of gratitude rise within her for this transubstantiation which procured her release from a state of being which had brought her to her knees, on the cusp of despair.

Marie's inner work here and that of Amy there, had brought both of them redemption, at the same time. They were both set free - simultaneously. Amy realised how the effect of one's intentions, thoughts, words and actions, rippled not just within oneself, but in and through the ether affecting everything and everybody else. This was a very profound notion, often overlooked by many, and understood only by a few, Amy reflected.

At the moment, Amy hadn't a clue what would happen next. Would this be the time and space where He would finally come? She would wait for some kind of sign. She had learnt from Marie, the importance of watching for signs and heeding their messages. Would this be the state of being in which she could help Marie, as Marie had helped her just now? She hoped that some time soon she would be able to show her gratitude and reciprocate in some way. She had always promised Marie that she would be a much better mum from the other side and maybe now she would be able to fulfill that promise finally, she hoped optimistically.

So suffice it to say that on that cold sunny winter's day - the winter solstice - the sun shone brightly indeed, in the hearts of these two beautiful women, who had been bound by suffering and pain on parallel planes - one embodied, the other disembodied - waiting to be set free.

And so, their ardent wish had suddenly come to be.

But, where was He? Where was her divine Creator, whom she had waited for a long fourteen years, to come and judge her?

She was adamant that this was the time and the place or space. He had taken His time, but He would come now, she was sure of it. Her guardian angel appeared smiling and serenely welcomed her to the next stage. It greeted her lovingly, yet silently. It warmed Amy with Its loving peace and joy, reassuring her that she was now in the right place. But, it wasn't as yet the right time, to see Him face-to-face – not just yet.

Chapter 18

The yellow and blue book Amy used to read religiously, suddenly sprang to mind. She hadn't been able to remember its name so far, and it was bugging her. She could visualise the cover's colour scheme, as if it were yesterday. What was it called, for crying out loud? The name annoyingly escaped her every time she tried to remember it. Marie had bought it for herself to help with her teaching at the local village catechism centre she attended. Amy had loved it so much that Marie had got her one as a birthday present, Amy recalled joyously going back in time.

Of course, it was the yellow and blue book of *Catechism Stories,* she remembered at long last. Amy used to read it daily on the loo, like many read the newspaper whilst doing their business, first thing in the morning. She remembered a time when she had set herself the task of learning the whole book by heart. How useless it's been so far, Amy reflected regrettably. She had needed to get a life, have some fun, giggles and laughs with some dancing and dining with friends, thrown in for good measure. She wasn't meant to have spent her time indoors solo, learning something which had no practical relevance to her life neither then nor now! It professed to have had the answers to the many of life's most pertinent questions - but in reality, it hadn't a clue. Amy wished she knew then what she knew now.

So far its content had been useless - totally and utterly useless.

"So what happens now?" she asked with a tinge of apprehension in her voice. The question fell on the dark deaf ears of silence. Her guardian angel just smiled silently and lovingly, whilst warmly holding the space. It was still up to her to work it out. Was it possible that the blue and yellow book would give her an inkling of what would or could transpire at this new stage of her extra-terrestrial or other-worldly journey? She doubted it, as it hadn't touched on anything she had been going through on this side so far. It hadn't mentioned the watching and waiting place. It didn't say how you had to watch, when you had to watch, what you had to watch, how to get the most of your watching and more importantly how to get out of the place of watching and waiting. Had this crucial bit of information deliberately been omitted, to keep souls trapped there? Amy wondered. It had asserted, unequivocally, that one would be judged soon after death, so nobody can blame Amy for expecting Him to have come by now.

But He never did!

And now she doubted He ever would.

It had been more years than she cared to remember and still no appearance of the pearly gates of heaven or of her Creator on His golden throne. It's funny how she had seen them in life, but not in death! For in the midst of her hell here on earth, she had seen and tasted heaven oftentimes and felt the Father's loving embrace, and her being filled with grace, many more times than she ever mentioned to Marie or to anybody. And although at times her faith in Him wavered, it hadn't waned, unlike her faith in the catechism stories book and the institution which had it commissioned. Her faith had moved from believing in institutions, tenets, rules, regulations and rituals which were outside of herself - imposed on her, you can safely say, by others, to what she had experienced first-hand, on earth and thereafter.

She had learnt so much in the *thereafter*. For starters, in the watching and waiting place you were completely powerless to procure any influence on anything or anybody in any way. The only influence she had there, was on herself. The only place one can procure change is in their own heart, mind, and soul, very similar to how it is on the earth plane. In fact, this is the whole point of that place and unless these shifts happened within you, you wouldn't be able to move onto where Amy found herself now, Amy realised, quite surprised. It took an openness of heart and mind, a lot of courage, humility and honesty to face oneself in one's totality, allowing shifts to happen. It was akin to moving mountains and maybe these are the mountains He had been referring to when He said that one's faith can move mountains! She did it. She felt and knew that this was the most epic of journeys - back home to Love - to the love within her and to the love which created her.

Smiling at herself and at her guardian angel she acknowledged how far she had come and accepted joyfully her wonderfully renewed spirit. What had taken her lifetimes to achieve and after-lifetimes to procure, she had finally managed to secure - a new liberated state of being, and in a new realm.

This was definitely cause for celebration.

She recognised how, to a certain degree, so much had also depended on Marie. She recalled the frustration of not having been able to influence Marie in any way, as if it were a distant memory, with no bearing on her here and now. Amy had learnt to trust, not through a blind faith, but in having had first-hand personal experience of the alchemy that happened in eternity. If she were to reincarnate, she wondered whether she would bring this inner knowing back with her. She hoped she would, so that none of this wisdom would be lost. But who knows?

Not many possessed the audacity to look within and given a choice they would rather not. In the watching and waiting place Amy had no choice, as she keenly observed what she saw *outside* of her, she watched intently in silence and realised it was a reflection of what was transpiring within her. Only she had the power to procure the changes necessary to making her whole being healed. Only she could get herself ready for when Marie was too. "Here, so much depends on you," Amy said to her guardian angel and it had on earth too, but she hadn't been ready to acknowledge that yet, at the time.

Amy relaxed the intensity of her thinking as her guardian angel held her in Its arms in a warm cosy loving embrace. She melted in Its sweet love. It beheld her, as if she were a newborn babe, whilst she figured out what to do next. She felt as if she were swimming in a sweet, subtle, soothing unconditional sea of love. She felt safe, secure, sustained and at peace as the warm glow emanated in the place where her heart energy vortex was. Her heart had undergone a complete reconstruction and transmuted into a crystalline beacon of sacred life, love and light reverberating within sacred cosmic sound. The bits that had been shattered, lost or misplaced had been put together whilst swirling like a spinning-wheel through the ether from one plane to the next. All was put right. It was the stage of being alright, Amy mused. She had broken free from the dark cocoon, you see. And wings did come fluttering out, as she found herself flying about the ether, through the vortex, to this state - where she starts with a brand new clean slate.

But was this the last stage or were there many others still to go? And more importantly, how will she know? She wished that when she spoke to Marie, Marie could hear her. All she would need to do is ask the question. Marie always had the answer when it came to these things and to many more. Or was she being asked to go within once more? And to look and listen to what resonated within her core?

A thought suddenly flashed through Amy's conscious mind.

She cracked it.

She knew what she was meant to do now and why she had come to this place or rather embrace this state of being. It began to dawn on her what the aim of this more elevated state of being was, although she still had to patiently wait and see, to confirm.

A letter was coming to her... the letter A... it started with an A... A... for... apple, Appleford, Ashford, asbestos, airborne, asshole, aviary, attest, attention... atonement!

Atonement - that was it! She was here to atone for her transgressions not only those she did out of selfishness, self-centredness, self-preservation, fear and a lack of genuine faith, but also for the things she could have done, but hadn't. This state of being begets many questions which she asked herself now. Mainly, what needed to be put right? How would she know? How would she put it right? And how long would it take? How long is a piece of string? is how she answered the last question. She wouldn't have a clue where to start with any of the others.

The only consolation she felt was that at least at this stage she enjoyed an inner peace and her heart overflowed with joy. It was a renewed heart emanating love, knowing it is loved and lovable. Her being twinkled like a star, with a golden glow, filling her whole being and beyond. She couldn't remember when she last felt so content, so fulfilled and so radiant. This was bliss, complete and utter bliss compared to any other memory of the past, whether before or after her suicide. In this state of being she could cope with anything; she could taste the sweetness of heaven and felt it dance in her heart.

To her sheer and utter surprise, she began to recognise some souls that had made it to this place, or state of being too. There were some familiar faces, and although they were quite ethereal rather than made of flesh and blood, they were still recognisable.

The long and short of it was, that here she wasn't on her own any more. She couldn't fathom how she had endured her own company for the last fourteen years or so. And yes, before anybody asked, being alone, she was lonely too! It wasn't like the caption saying, 'On my own, but not lonely!' It had been a very lonely and painful state of being, where she had just been. But, that was all in the past. In the here and now she was the most content she had been since she could remember. It was only now she realised how much she had missed interaction, companionship and possibly friendship .

Here spirits communicated with each other telepathically, with no need for physical bodies, mouths, tongues or lips. They communicated through thought-forms flashing across the ether, as they were made of light. It wasn't like she had to learn a brand new language, as this is our inherent way of communicating, and was before The Split, but she was completely out of practice when it came to interacting with kindred spirits in this way. She had spent the last fourteen years alone in deep thought, processing her most recent past-life. Amy began to feel a hint of excitement, at this brand new stage.

She recognised quite a few people whom she thought would never make it to this place. She had judged them – or misjudged them, rather. Only God knows what resides in the recesses of one's heart, she chided herself and asked her Creator and them in the silence of her soul, for pardon. She was pleased to encounter some other familiar faces and smiled to herself at the prospect that this could be a very happy place.

Alas, now she wouldn't be on her own while making amends for all the damage she had caused, both before and after her untimely death. Here there are others to help her and whom she would help in return. Marie had been very hot on *give and take* and whilst inculcating it into her boys all those years back, some of it had brushed off onto Amy whilst watching and waiting.

"Give and take," Marie would reiterate, explaining to the boys that it was a good skill or attitude, to have in life. She saw it as a way of keeping the life-force flowing freely and quite evenly. It was a good attitude to foster in the after-life too it seemed, as although to Amy's mind it wasn't the ultimate virtue, it was a useful mindset indeed. There was no need for strict solid boundaries and lots of rigorous rules and regulations here, because exchanges were based on the Law of Love.

Here all was enveloped in a sacred life-love-light divine reverberating within eternal sacred cosmic sound. In this state of being, everybody lived in and through this presence, yet experiencing their own unique sacred divine essence.

When enveloped in and coming from a place of sacred light-love-light divine everything flowed in perfect harmony. All that wasn't of sacred life-love-light divine had now been shed and left behind at the watching and waiting place. The memory of her fourteen years of solitary confinement now blended into this bountiful bliss, fading into insignificance. One experienced a unity of their own personal soul - their Christ-consciousness - with the Cosmic -consciousness. Here the micro and the macro united as one, with no division, illusionary or otherwise.

It all seemed so strange that as Marie recognised and acknowledged in her heart of hearts that she had been set free, she sensed her mother had also been. She felt it in her bones, as we say. Marie had come back home to her heart which had ardently been waiting for her return, from her meandering sojourn into the formerly unknown realms of hell. An all-embracing calm, in the stillness, descended upon her. A deep-seated peace, like the one she had known prior to her mum's death, enveloped her whole being in its purity and serenity. She got a taste of the bliss of the heavenly state and it was good, very good. It filled her with hope. With this peace returning to her heart, or her heart returning to this peace she could face anything - even Satan himself, if needs be!

And had Amy got to her promised land where manna fell like snow, where milk and honey flowed as she sat by pastures green, rivers the cleanest and the stillest she had ever seen? Amy was in a good place and this somehow rippled into Marie's state of being. Despite moving up in the world of spirit, Amy was still very close to Marie. In fact, now she was even closer than she had ever been. But, did Marie know? Amy asked, knowing that soon the answer will come. There was no rush to find out. Amy now trusted the process completely and knew that things unfolded as they were meant to unfold, and prayers were answered when the time was right.

Marie felt her mum's presence and knew that that her mum's essence was near. What Marie was unaware of was that Amy was trying to let her know how much she had loved her and how sorry she had been for having hurt her. Amy promised to do her best to make things right.

Little did Marie know that The Man had also been touched by what went on in Mark's bedroom that day. Was it grace, divine timing, serendipity or synchronicity, fate or pure coincidence? Marie didn't have a clue. But she knew that day when he came back home from work, something had shifted - a light illuminated the dark path he traversed - and shone through his eyes. He explained to Marie that he had felt strange sensations during the day. "Strange in what way?" Marie asked. She wanted to know around what time. It had been some time before noon, he said.

Somehow, The Man too had been affected by what had gone on, as difficult as it was to explain. He disclosed how he had felt a sort of a nudge accompanied by a *funny feeling* that seemed to touch that space in his chest - his heart. For the first time in many years, this edifice crumbled and transmuted into love and light. He apologised for the hurt he had caused Marie over the years and asked for her forgiveness.

Marie couldn't believe what she heard that day. These words in way of an apology were like music to her ears. That day a glimpse of hope glimmered in Marie's heart as a shard of remorse shimmered in The Man's. There had been a recognition, an awareness (an acceptance even?) of what he had done - a moment of great grace. Marie had been forgiving.

Yet sadly, the moment dissipated as easily as it had been created and The Man took back the confession and contrition. He continued, a short while after this, as if it had never happened.

Over the years, Marie had tried hard to continue to forgive The Man his transgressions. It had been hard on the best of days, but even harder when she felt he had intentionally deprived her of his attention and affection, which she craved for. He was able to show her respect, and give her attention and appreciation when she threatened some action like leaving or suggesting separation, but would withdraw it as soon as he felt he had reeled her back in. He was very cold and calculating when it came to giving Marie what he knew she needed and craved for. At other times, she wondered whether he had any love to give - perhaps, he was loveless. She tried her best to love him as unconditionally as is humanly possible - but his behaviour was bordering on abuse.

It was abuse.

Marie would have to put an end to this sooner rather than later to safeguard her sanity.

This time it wasn't an unconditional love that was called for. There was accountability and taking responsibility for one's words and actions. Marie had to stand up for herself. She had been used and abused for far too long.

Things had to change. The Man had to change. He had to make amends. Forgiveness didn't mean you didn't try to make things right. In fact, the forgiven in normal circumstances would want to make amends, so sad are they at the prospect of having hurt someone they love. Narcissists didn't. It's not that she had been perfect, far from it, but her intentions were good for as much as she could tell. As much as she aimed at perfection, she had her downfalls too. She had apologised many times over the years for things she had been guilty of and of others she hadn't, just to keep the peace.

They tried to agree on the best way forward, but couldn't see eye-to-eye on how to start rebuilding this dilapidated marriage. He would need to engage in some sort of communication, communion and union coming from a place of love and compassion, not lust and manipulation. She would have to be accepting of his willingness to change and welcome any change no matter how small. And all these conditions had to be happening at the same time. She would have to be patient. But twenty three years of this was taking its toll, and time was running out. Marie was half hopeful they would pull through, and half despairing they wouldn't. It was a shame for as willing to change as his words conveyed, his actions told a different story.

Whilst Marie had been keen to go on a couple's weekend retreat to rediscover the spirituality that had bound them so delicately and sublimely together once-upon -a- time, he was keen on going to counselling. And so to counselling they went.

Amy's guardian angel still hovering about whispered in thought forms that, no matter what, Amy would not be able to influence any decisions Marie made. Neither would she be able to change the course of Marie's destiny but, she would be allowed to protect Marie and her boys in ways she had not been able to before. She would be allowed to be nearby, showering them with love and light and filling Marie with courage and strength. She wouldn't be allowed to stop Marie from making mistakes, but when Marie did, she would help her get back on track in some way or other, helping her get up quicker, heal sooner than she otherwise would have done.

Marie had to learn her lessons in life too, as Amy had done.

But Amy would be there, her rock, constantly by her side. It's a shame Marie would neither be able to see or touch her, but would feel her and in the silence hear her, if she were still for long enough and paid enough attention.

Much more importantly in this state of being nothing that happened on earth would be able to affect Amy's peace, diminish her serenity or jeopardise her bliss. It was not that she cared any less or loved any less. It was that now possessing such inner freedom from expectation, self-centredness, self-absorption and ego-cherishing she could love freely and unconditionally. She would be able to let go of the outcome, not expecting anything in return as she made things right. The only limitation would be, Marie's free will and how open she would be, to be helped. She had to ask for Amy to be able to assist, as Marie's free will was sacrosanct and had to be protected first and foremost at all times.

It would take a while, but Amy was now not in a rush to go anywhere. The warm glow in her heart - LOVE - true love, sustained her and would take her to where she needed to be. She would trust in the power of love with all her heart. In her heart was all the wisdom she would ever need and all the inner-knowing that would see her through this comfortable current state of being.

On the other hand, she also knew that she would see His face one day, but unlike her mother Grandma Jo, who had seen His face and was with Him singing to the children in heaven not long after she died, Amy still had unfinished business to attend to. And she would see this through, for as long as it takes. Sustained by this constant peace and being in this state of unending bliss which nothing and nobody could take away, she would joyfully do her best to restore Marie, as her Marie had restored her on that day.

Chapter 19

Amy accompanied Marie, The Man and the boys on their Sunday outing. It was a clear cold crisp spring afternoon. The Savill Garden was such a stunning place to ramble in, this time of year. Whilst Marie and The Man walked around one of the bigger lakes, the boys scootered in front, behind or alongside the disconnected, discontented couple. They came to the magnificent hundred-foot totem pole which the boys loved. It was a landmark signalling how far they had come, and that there wasn't much left to go.

The Gardens were meticulously planned to accentuate the change of season. Contrasting form and colour danced through the paths orchestrating what seemed like a Garden of Eden or a heaven on earth. Wafting through the pure air was a sweet smelling perfume, enrapturing all the senses with its subtle scent. Mother Earth had come back to life after a long death. Her beauty bedazzled those on this plane and on all others. Both Marie's and Amy's souls sang in ecstasy as they moved through this unsurpassed beauty.

This state of being was like a constant meditative state where Amy was not fast asleep as she had been here on earth, doped up to the hilt. Neither was she as hyper-aware or as ultra-vigilant as she had been during her solitary confinement in the watching and waiting place. Here it was like a constant state of bliss, being in awareness, in the present moment with how things are with nothing to fight or to run away from, embracing all that is, how it is.

She kept herself busy. Sometimes she met others for lunch or to sing and dance. However, more often than not, she gave herself to saving damsels in distress (in whom she could see her former self and Marie), preventing physical accidents, illuminating people in power taken over by greed and a lust for world domination and control, embracing prostitutes in love (knowing that that could've been her), protecting drug addicts (hadn't she been one in her own way? Just because the tranquilisers were legal didn't make them not harmful, Amy realised), shielding women and children from violence, and keeping children safe from any kind of abuse. All this kept her out of mischief and extremely occupied.

Keeping children safe had become a massive issue on earth, as children were being constantly sold as sex slaves all across the globe. Many were being prostituted and raped at very young ages. A few escaped, but most were harmed beyond repair and it seemed that not many people noticed or cared.

But, most of all she would be spending time making it right to Marie – this was her priority. She had always told Marie that she would be a much better mum when *on the other side* and now was her time to prove it, after a long fourteen years of having departed.

Like a mischievous monkey Amy had been wanting to play with Marie, letting her know she was there, interfering in situations where it mattered, poking her nose in where it didn't, minding Marie's business - but she hadn't been allowed to- as yet.

Marie was presently at a crossroads.

Amy felt a great sense of urgency to help her. She had wanted to shout, whisper, whistle or sing the solution in Marie's ear, or do whatever it took to make Marie see she was there with her and for her, wanting to guide her. Amy wished she could share some of the wisdom she had amassed over these years with Marie, but at the moment communication was still difficult as Marie found it very hard to intuit and trust her mother's voice.

Amy wouldn't be able to interfere unless Marie decided, one way or the other, which way to go. Once Marie had made her mind up, Amy would be able to butt in as much as she liked, to help or hinder, depending on who you were in the equation. So in the meantime, Amy had to hold her horses, so that it would be only Marie who would see, decide and act according to what she knew she had to do.

She would only be allowed to reveal herself to Marie once Marie had made the final decision – to be, or not to be in this unhappy, soul-destroying marriage. This is the question which Marie had to find the honest and truthful answer to. It was a decision loaded with a lot of responsibility. Would she be able to act with impunity? Amy asked herself over and over again.

Marie would have to have faith in who she was, and in what she wanted out of life for the rest of her life. She knew that a life of neglect - physically and emotionally, wouldn't do for her in the much longer term -she would end up like her mother, for sure. She had to find a way out and she had to find it quick as time was ticking and the damage escalating.

She was building herself up little by little - making herself stronger in heart, mind, body and soul. It seemed that the wearier the body, the stronger the spirit. Marie had built a strength and developed a patience since youth. Patience is a virtue which takes a lot of patience to cultivate, Amy observed as her daughter trod cautiously and carefully, leaving no stone unturned in procuring the outcome necessary for her survival and, more importantly, that of her two sons.

Marie had to stand firm on her own two feet and face this demon on her own, trusting her inner knowing - intuition or gut feeling - call it what you will. Amy would sometimes choose a song, a number, a word, or a friend who said that which expressed what would be her thoughts exactly! Because she wasn't able to influence Marie's decision directly, she would put subtle hints out there for Marie to pick up. How apt and how close to cheating it all seemed at times, but *all's fair in love and war,* Amy remembered believing back when on earth. She just wanted to reassure Marie that she was not alone.

She would hope that Marie would read into messages left on billboards, notice boards, or number plates, just for her. Would Marie know that the gentle breeze on the day she had been heart-broken would have been Amy blowing a kiss her way? Amy would try stroking Marie's face through the soft hot air brushing against Marie's flushed cheeks, to reassure her of her presence. All dressed in white Amy would appear on the riverbank where Marie walked, making sure Marie knew she was there, where she was, having her back.

Amy could see that Marie had what it takes to extricate herself from this union ravaging her heart, mind, body and soul. But would she ever? She was desperate to find out. She observed how Marie's inner resolve continued to go from strength to strength, the fiercer her inner conflict became. She could feel her faith becoming an inner knowing, not founded on someone else's theories or extrapolations of theories, but embedded in her own personal experience of her own strength and of her Creator's unwavering love which she felt burning within her heart.

She trusted she was divinely protected, because she experienced it, day in, day out, in the little things and in the bigger ones. She trusted in providence not because she had a blind faith in the sacred and divine, but because over the years she saw how she got given what she needed when she needed it, without fail. Her faith was always rewarded in some shape or form. She wouldn't necessarily be given what she wanted, but it would definitely be what she needed. It may not always manifest when she wanted it, but she trusted it would turn up when the time was right.

Some would say she manifested what she dreamt, others that it was coincidence, others that being co-creator with sacred Creator divine she created her own abundant reality in poverty. The fact remained to Marie here on earth and to Amy on the other side, that Marie's faith made things happen and the fact that they happened (not always when Marie wanted them to) turned Marie's faith into an inner knowing by which she planned and lived her life.

Amy saw her own daughter grow in strength and was confident Marie would find, within her, what it takes to follow her inner knowing. She believed that despite the opposition The Man would put up, Marie would pull through. She just needed to take that leap of faith into the unknown, acting on what she knew in her heart of hearts she had to do.

But would she actually find the courage to take that leap of faith necessary to set her free? Would she? Amy, the same as everybody else, wondered. Her guess was as good as anyone´s. She left it at that for now. There was nothing else she could do at this point in time, apart from constantly imbue Marie and the boys with her warm loving embrace.

Why not The Man? To Amy it was heart-breaking that The Man would not allow her energy anywhere near his. Yet, Marie, Mark and David would continue to be strengthened by Amy's loving presence, feeling her essence as if it were in and of them.

As for herself and her own happiness, Amy was overjoyed.

She remembered her Master, Yeshua, The Christ had promised that there were many rooms in His Father's house. It had never been heaven or hell for all eternity as the yellow and blue book professed. That yellow and blue book, left a lot to be desired, Amy thought indignantly. Amy had often wondered about the injustice in punishing a mere mortal to eternal damnation for a transgression which happened in time. Yet, that ungodly institution, the Master's worst enemy - *his church* - had changed His teachings to suit its lust for power and insatiable greed. Selling the idea of an eternal bliss or an infinite damnation, paid. The idea of coercing and controlling through fear remained. Its power had been diminished through the secularisation of Western civilisation, but it still left millions living in fear rather than in the free, liberated state which the Master had envisaged for humanity.

There, in the newfound ethereal community of souls where Amy now found herself, was a certain character whom she had known well on the earth plane. She had been surprised to find him there, almost as if he were waiting for her. Had she had a jaw, it would've dropped as she caught sight of him. She could not believe her eyes, or who she was seeing. He hadn't noticed her at that instant and she thought she would catch him unawares and surprise him - or shock him, a bit later on!

Uncle Don had lived on many years after Amy had gone, but still preceded her to this place. Perhaps, he was fast-tracked? Or hadn't had all the baggage she had brought over with her? As much as him and Amy had shared a strong bond or love shall we say (which neither of them acted upon in the carnal sense), he had been a good husband to Rosie and a great father to Susie and the boys. He had tried his best to live morally and happily.

There were two things which hadn't left Uncle Don after Amy's suicide. The first was a rubber plant which Amy had especially propagated for him from her own one, in the little internal yard she had owned. He had loved that rubber plant and especially after her death, hung on to it for dear life. It were as if through the tree's spirit he could still feel Amy's. His wife had urged him to get rid of it for she knew, like every woman knows, when their husband was in love with someone else. Eventually, he had to relent and Rosie got her way. The tree went and instead, their internal yard hosted a myriad of luscious, colourful plants which satiated the senses, but bore no connection to the deceased Amy.

The second thing he held dear was one which couldn't and wouldn't be taken away by anything or anybody. He had kept it hidden safe in the recesses of his heart, in a space, where nobody was ever allowed to enter. It was an old flame. It still burnt bright. Neither space nor time had withered its light, nor weakened its intensity.

He had thought his heart would break when he heard the news of how she had taken her own life. And the news on that day had spread like wild fire through the four corners of the island, or rather from the island's mouth to its tail, throughout the gills, through to its fins -the island having been shaped like a fish.

To say that he had been shocked is the understatement of the year. He thought that the bond which had existed between them could or would save her. Amy hadn't loved herself the same way him and Marie had, sadly. A bit like Marie, he had hoped his love would be enough, but it hadn't been. He too, had felt betrayed and rejected. And although throughout the years their encounters were less in number, they were by no means any less deep and intensely intellectually stimulating.

It was just that they had been watched like hawks. She, by her husband who although had grown to trust her over the years at times still did turn up at home, unexpectedly, between jobs for a cuppa and a bite. Him, by his extremely suspicious Rosie who had been Amy's best friend once upon a time. It doesn't take a lot of imagination to see why they might not be any more. For many years Rosie had suspected that the two of them had acted on their mutual attraction and didn't realise they never had.

Arguments between him and her ensued. Words were said. Tempers flared. Yet, as they did in those days, they stuck it out, until the end. It was many years after Amy's death – too long to his liking - as he longed to join her wherever she had got to - that they were now in the same realm, at the same time - but not bound by time!

His hadn't been a self-induced passing, it was a cold-blooded murder by a debilitating illness which struck with a vengeance until it eventually got the better of him. Some would argue it was the drugs rather than the illness itself that had finished him off, but the argument was open for discussion then, as much as it is now.

Uncle Don had been a good man in a different way to Mike. Uncle Don, as she preferred to call him (it was his pet name on earth), was the salt of the earth kind of human being. His life had been quite straightforward. He was kind. He was generous. He was spiritual. He was intellectual. The connection they felt was undeniably strong. Since neither of them acted upon it - in itself it wasn't wrong. But the bond was visible and neither could hide, the love and the connection which lay deep inside.

Uncle Don, unlike Amy hadn't hidden it from himself. He acknowledged it. One could go as far as to say, he embraced it. He did not beat himself up about it. What he did do, was try his best not to act upon it. He tried to continue to be loyal and faithful to the wife he had promised years earlier he would be. He was saddened that his heart didn't feel the same way towards her, but there was nothing he could do about it. He now loved her in a different way. He respected her and never stopped being grateful for the three lives she bore them. She too was an innocent bystander, powerless in changing anything or anybody, bar her perception and response (rather than reaction) to circumstances and her outside world.

To be true to his heart, he stopped making love to his wife. His sexual appetite wanted satiating from one source only and if that wasn't forthcoming, then he'd rather die of hunger. He had also stopped sleeping in the same bed as her, blaming it on her copious consumption of alcohol. But was she drinking to drown what her female intuition had picked upon? Or was it the other way around? It was a vicious cycle, one which kept them on a ferris-wheel for a while, both going round in circles, not getting anywhere. His recent decisions stopped the wheel in its tracks. It was the closest he could come to honouring his heart.

Back in the day, it was harder to let your heart have its way. There was not much room for mistakes. Amy had already been bitten by Greg, and had to tread very carefully. It was all well and good edging Marie on to be true to herself but, luckily for Marie she was now living in a different country and in a different era. Amy, on the other hand, had to save face and couldn't afford to fall from grace (as they put it, back in the day), for a second time.

In her and Uncle Don's days, and in the culture they lived in, you didn't really follow the dictates of your heart and if you did you would be deemed improper and ostracised. So you tended to soldier on according to the socially acceptable norms and precepts which would over-ride anything your heart, mind, body and soul wanted or needed. In living life strictly by these rigid rules one would sacrifice the expression of their own unique life-purpose and life-path to suit socially accepted norms and ways of living and being. It was a bit like when one died for the many - the unhappy partner would die to themselves - to preserve the family and the family name. It meant that many people were breathing, but not living - had a heart but were not loving, or being loved. It made one wonder if they had been alive at all, or if they were going through the motions in lifeless, loveless states of being, not knowing whether they were dead or living.

Chapter 20

Like the endless cycles of life and death, without fail, the village festa came round again. This August brought Marie and her now two gorgeous grown sons, almost men, Mark and David back to the island. They not only came for the village festa, but also to catch up with family and friends. They always had the time of their lives in this place - their home from home - and looked forward to their holiday here.

This year uncle Don sat outside his front door from where he could see the statue of Mother Mary being ushered around the village, surrounded by his wife Rosie and some of his children and grandchildren. Unbeknownst to him and to everyone else at the time, this would be his last summer and the last village festa he would be enjoying with his loved ones, on this side of the veil. The following month death would come coldly knocking at his door.

He didn't mind. Instead of trying to fight death, he embraced every single day he was given, strengthened by the fact that he had lived – oh, yes- he had lived. He had travelled. He had loved. He had taken risks, worked hard, read avidly and had some fun along the way, mostly when young. And to one who has lived and has no regrets, death is not as daunting, but just a gentle passing onto the next stage.

He was consoled by the fact that he had always tried to do the right thing, out of a love for others. He was one who always tried to put the shoe on the other foot, making sure nobody suffered unnecessarily or alone. He had always loved his children from the bottom of his heart and would do anything to stop them suffering. He had worked hard all his life so that they all lived happily and comfortably.

His wife had been feisty, loud, loved drinking and dancing, was not very intellectual nor spiritual (like Amy had been), but a salt of the earth woman who loved with all her heart. There were no half measures with her - when she loved, she loved; when she worked, she worked; and when she partied, she partied! She loved life and her family and friends. They were different, very different, but together they had brought up three beautiful children and that was not something to be scorned upon. She had always worked hard to bring bread to the table too. For who she was and what she did, how could he not love and respect her?

Marie, as friendly and as lively as always went up to him for a catch up. She had always been intrigued by this man of few words, who always seemed so calm, serene and peaceful on the outside. She wondered what he was like on the inside. She had always respected him and had silently wished him and her mum were able to make a go of things, as they would have been so compatible, she believed even as a child of ten.

Little did either of them know what lay ahead, as they stood on the street corner to chat. Little did she know that uncle Don would still play a part in her life – well, not directly, but indirectly in some shape or form. Both of them were uplifted by their little friendly hug as they watched the statue moving closer and closer towards them as large as life, as if floating on clouds, as was Marie. For although her outer circumstances left a lot to be desired, her inner world was now vivaciously alive. The deep-seated peace that had inhabited her heart before Amy's suicide had vehemently returned. In and through forgiveness she had come back to her heart's peace, and copious amounts of joy, and for Marie this was the most important thing in life. She didn't need to keep searching, as she had found what she had lost, or it had found her - or a bit of both - who knows!

She knew that outer circumstances constantly changed, and would continue to change, but with her inner light shining bright she could cope with anything. It had seen her through the Amy saga, and she knew it would bring her through any other quandary she might encounter. She had love in her heart - for herself, for her boys and for everyone, really! She hadn't been embittered by life's darker side and had learnt to embrace the shadow as much as the light.

Amy's hazel-green eyed son, bore the statue on his broad tanned shoulder once more, as he had done for many years before. Marie would follow the statue and walk alongside her younger brother in a minute. But, first things first. She had to finish this little conversation with Uncle Don, before they both moved on.

They chatted a little about his illness. He told her that he didn't know how long he would be here for. He explained that he didn't really fear death, although what the next stage beheld, he did not have a clue. The fearlessness of death is the ultimate freedom – they who do not fear death, fear nothing and nobody. This was one of The Master's main messages, but not understood by many. Had that been a wasted life and death here on earth? Marie often wondered over the course of her life.

The Plain Truth magazine which him and Amy had been into for a few years, had had many plain truths in it, but the magazine like Amy's *Catechism Stories* did not give you much to go on, regarding what happens to your spirit when your body died or was killed. It did speak about heaven, but it didn't go into much detail. It just made it seem like this idyllic state where there would be no suffering, pain or death, in which you would be for infinity - your final destination. But it didn't explain all the different states of being in between. It spoke about hell and the gnashing of teeth as the ultimate destination for those who did not comply. And that was all. It was very dogmatic, dualistic and very cut and dry.

Uncle Don wasn't sure, as none of us are, what happens to disembodied spirits after death. He decided to keep an open mind. He trusted that whatever happened he would be supported by the fact that he had tried to live a good life, did as much good as is humanly possible, and avoided doing evil or hurting others with evil intent. He had tried to be as true to his heart as much as it had been socially acceptable at the time – people of his children's generation had so much more freedom to honour their hearts and repair their souls. He took full responsibility for his own well-being and didn't blame his wife for his dissatisfaction with their status quo. Above all, he had always bore in mind that he had his flaws and was no stranger to them.

What he did believe and felt quite sure of, was that he was divine (had a soul) and that the divinity within him would live on and move on to wherever it needed to be, until finally it would reunite with its loving Creator - not that the two were ever separate, as it seems and as we are led to believe -they have always been one. But, having a physical body creates the illusion that the individual soul is separate from the cosmic divine eternal sacred spirit. In death, they would perfectly unite as one and that time would come, one day soon - in fact, it was just round the corner.

The village festa had come to an end, and so had his life a few weeks later. He was calm at his death-bed. He lay blissfully breathing his last, not knowing what to expect, but not scared of it, either. The peaceful angelic look on his face was very uplifting for the people watching him die that day. He had no fear of the unknown, and no attachment to who or what he was leaving behind. He was fearless as to where he was headed and a tranquil aura of peaceful resignation – an acceptance of how things are – surrounded his embodiment as a warm golden glow emanating from his head and hands to his toes.

He hadn't needed to spend nearly as much time as Amy in the watching and waiting place. He had now been in this place or state of being for quite a while. Uncle Don had been very content in this space, moving here, there and everywhere making things right for many near and far. He kept especially close to his daughter, whom he had loved more than his own life itself. She had missed him dearly and spoke of him and to him constantly. There was not one day when Susie didn't address him in some way.

Today, he was in for a surprise. He had been minding his own business as usual and going about helping humanity extricate itself from the depravity it had found itself in, when a kerfuffle caught his eye. There were lots of souls gathered singing their hearts out and clapping profusely. He moved a bit closer to see what the big fuss was about.

He caught a glimpse of a beautiful form up in space making

exquisite shapes, as if dancing - she looked like a sufi dancer with red and gold silk scarfs being waved about gracefully, joining in the mystic dance - and was momentarily mesmerised. Her long black wavy hair bounced up and down as she leapt in space, swirling and turning on what seemed like tiptoes. Spectacles such as this were not a rare occurrence in the circles he frequented, and very warmly welcomed by all and sundry. It must have been the soul who had joined not long ago, whom he had heard about, but had not as yet had the honour to meet and greet, he thought.

He could not believe his eyes. To his sheer and utter surprise it was Amy's spirit leaping, prancing and dancing about exquisitely across the ether, against a starry lit night sky. He couldn't say that his eyes had deceived him, as he strictly speaking had none. It was his perception which recognised his dearly beloved Amy who had made it to this place, or this state of being, at last.

Well not his - she wasn't his then and wouldn't be his now. Here nobody belonged to anybody else. When two united they united in complete and utter freedom. Nobody owned anybody and nobody deemed the other as their own possession. Each person was a pure gift, freely gifted to the other with no expectation or recrimination. All was done in pure love and total freedom. Here each person's unique individual Christ-consciousness, merged with the collective Cosmic-consciousness and all lived in harmony, love, peace and joy, as one. It is the state of being we had enjoyed originally, before The Split. And although this wasn't heaven yet, it was a blissful heavenly state of being.

Not many people believed Amy would make it to this place, as suicide was frowned upon by their institution and deemed as a damnable act of despair – one of the seven deadly sins, which according to the church's teaching could never be forgiven.

No, she should have gone to hell and that's where H*is* church would have put her, if it had its own way - it's what it taught back in the day. How did it not teach that nobody and nothing is beyond our divine Creator's love or beyond His sacred forgiveness? And how much He was into second, third, fourth... perhaps even infinite chances?

Uncle Don got over his surprise-cum-shock quite quickly.

There she was looking at him all coy and shy - smiling from behind her red and gold organza scarf half covering her face. There he was beaming with joy - smiling back. He didn't remember her with long hair, she had always worn it short on the island. She looked so much younger too. He had always thought she looked beautiful, not plain, but beautiful, very beautiful. He couldn't keep his gaze off her, as the glow in his heart began to pulsate not with carnal excitement and passion, but with a sweet and tender love of the heart and soul. He felt alive inside. He felt much more alive than he had done in years. It seemed as if his energy and vibration were suddenly augmented and upgraded just through her being there.

He'd forgotten how beautiful she was. He noticed her red nail varnish and matching red lipstick, which really suited her and realised he didn't know much about her taste in clothes and colours. She seemed taller, slimmer and much more alive than he ever remembered. He couldn't believe that his gaze was resting upon the object of his love, which had been denied him for far too long. He hoped that this wasn't an optical illusion, and that she would disappear in the blink of an eye!

Uncle Don had always been a man of a few considered, well-chosen words and would not say two if one suffices, but on this day there was no shutting him up. Today, it were as if he had wanted to condense a lifetime into one moment and bare his soul to her. Everything that had gone on while she had been away and all the secrets he beheld in the depths of his heart, for decades.

She listened intently especially as he described the time of his death which she had unfortunately missed. It is true that as your life flashes before you as you breathe your last, you carry within your DNA a record of everything you had done in this life-time. What you did, the context in which you did it, the intention with which you did it, all get released in the shape and form of dimethyltryptamine (dmt), which some say is the essence of our soul. Many believe (and some scientific experiments show) that the vast amounts of it present at birth and death indicate that this is true. The euphoria its rush creates as it enters and leaves the body is indescribable and has to be experienced to be believed, Uncle Don explained.

As he spoke she felt her heart vortex sweetly pulsate, the first time in a very, very, very long time. The love denied them by social convention - and judgement and condemnation from various institutions - decided it would not be denied any longer. They both felt love in their hearts. There was no shame or blame, just a gentle resting of the freedom of her soul, in the harmoniousness of his heart.

In this realm everybody was true to their hearts. Here souls realised themselves and were as real and as authentic as was originally intended. They would unite, not through a marriage contract of the physical realm, drawn up by man, but through the Law of Love which needed no written contract nor any external validation or rules or regulations. It all flowed from within one's own soul, and the Law of Love embedded within its DNA. In this unity the many is One, as much as the One is many.

Neither of them knew how many realms there were. Rumour has it, it is seven, and seven to her seemed like a logical number, only because she had thought of the seven years she had spent watching and waiting. No, it was actually seven times two! Then there were all the other sevens she had previously known, which escaped her amidst all the excitement. Amy realised that the realm of watching and waiting, was the second and that now they had ascended to the third realm. Was it possible that there were an infinite number of realms? Nobody knew the full extent of the many mansions, in His Father's house. She'll just had to wait and see. But currently that wasn't scary. She surrendered to the here and now and let it be. In the meantime, she melted ensconced in Uncle Don's long lost tender loving embrace.

Whether they would stay there or not, or how long for, neither of them cared. They were able to be totally present, in the present moment, with no notion of past trauma or future anxiety - together. This was a constant, uninterrupted being in the here and now with a heart full of love, overflowing with a heavenly joy. No matter what happened, this state of being would not be altered. Some would think this boring, but believe you me, if we had a glimpse of this state as we sometimes do, then we would want to be in it forever and ever, as these two.

The first realm which they had both skipped was the *lost souls* realm. The *lost souls* would wander in search of peace in the wrong places, knowing they needed to get to the watching and waiting realm, but not always sure how to get there.

The *lost souls* included those who were completely proud and arrogant, lacking empathy and compassion and those exhibiting narcissistic behaviour. Those who would not take any responsibility for their actions or reactions, but blamed everything on everybody else. Others who were wilfully ignorant of the truth and put many things in place to not see the truth, hear the truth or speak the truth. Others who were naïve and decided to see things as they would like them to be, rather than as they were, also found themselves in the *lost souls'* realm. It wasn't set in stone who ended up where, as many believed. Each case was judged on its own individual merits.

So it wasn't just heaven or hell. As He had said: "In my Father's house there are many mansions," which *His* church (not His at all), could explain, but chooses not to. And although He hadn't made an appearance as yet, Amy knew that she would get there, in her own way when the time was right in the end. But it wasn't the end yet and this wasn't an uncomfortable state to wait in, either - on the contrary, she could taste heaven with every breath as its peace weaved through the whole of her embodiment.

Neither of them knew when they would be made to choose whether to go back to earth or move onto the next realm. This was the stage where that choice would have to be made, sooner or later. Neither of them were partial to the former option, and Amy had vowed to herself, over and over again that if ever faced with that decision, she won't ever come back. But, who knows? You can never say never, right?

Now she would endeavour to give Marie a helping hand with Uncle Don by her side for as long as she could and in every way possible. This was a blessing she hadn't counted upon, one of the after-life's pleasant surprises. Just as she would help him assist Susie, he would help her help Marie and all their other beloved ones still here or there, depending on where you were.

In this realm she would be loved, honoured and respected as she had always longed to be. Her soul's thirst for acceptance, union and communion with a loved one would be satiated, to the brim and overflowing. She could rest by still waters, in the land where abundant milk and sweet honey flowed. And more importantly, not alone.

She was so happy that Marie had journeyed back to herself and found her own inner bliss, traversing the earth with joy in her heart. She was confident that she would find a way forward for she knew her daughter's inner strength, resilience and tenacity, she had helped her build it!

In the meantime, Amy and uncle Don lay naked on the beach, their ethereal light-bodies fully exposed and energised by the warm glow of the mellow sun. The temperature was never too hot, nor too cold. There was no shame, in this state of being very hard to name. They just lay listening to the gentle lapping of the waves singing them sweet lullabies. He would tenderly comb his deft fingers through her dark long hair as his lips brushed against her hot, flushed cheeks, as it were. It was idyllic.

They lay there, not wanting to be anywhere else. They had work to do, but for now they basked in their love's sweet embrace, in this state filled with a heavenly grace. His hands caressed her silky, smooth light body and it felt right.

What was she talking about? Right?

Of course it wasn't right, it was damn'd perfect!

Epilogue

Amy had never thought that she would be the one who would have the fairy-tale ending which read: "... and they lived happily ever after!"

No. She had believed she would remain undeservedly damned forever.

Yet, she had recognised, acknowledged, accepted and taken full responsibility for her attitudes, intentions, words and deeds and held herself accountable for them. She had opened her heart to love and compassion and was well on the way to making things right for her dearly beloved daughter, mostly, and for those others she may also have hurt along the way. Her atonement, when complete, would take her through to the next realm, unless she decided to come back to earth which she could choose to do at that point, as unlikely as it seems.

She would be kept very busy over the next few decades, but there would be no rush as the journey is as valid as the destination, she had always maintained. And this holds true there as much as it does here. Both women had embarked on an epic quest to release themselves from the yoke of slavery dating back generations, breaking cycle after cycle of death, with a rebirth - a resurrection - a new beginning.

Both women may have strayed so much, yet both have loved

so much.

"Liberation is here, not just for me, but for you too, my dearest Marie!" Amy whispered in her daughter's ear, as she smiled and beheld her Marie with as much healing love and compassion as her ethereal being could muster.

Marie felt a sudden shudder run through her spine, uplifting her whole body with a warm deep peace, which permeated her whole being and beyond. "True peace is come to me - it's my destiny," Marie heaved a deep sigh of relief. She felt a lightness of being, and an indescribable joy, up for dancing to any music the next leg of her journey played for her.

About the Author

Born to Maltese immigrants in Australia in the 1960's Mary sailed back to Malta shortly after her fourth birthday with her parents, leaving her grandparents behind. The abundant joy of both families reuniting was a stark contrast to the bad turn that Mary's mother mental health had taken over those years. Mary cared for her ill mother till her bitter end on the 20th December 1993.

It was whilst living in Berkshire that Mary wrote the first Liberation At Long Last by Mary M to commemorate her mother's death by suicide twenty years earlier. Liberation At Last by Mary Mallia is a revised and an updated version. This refreshed version reflects Mary's own journey from a deep grief to a place of wholeness and healing.

Between 2017-2018 Mary started writing poetry. The poetry

written and published so far has stemmed from a lifetime of soul-searching. Mary explores themes like the meaning of life, death, suffering, injustice, abuse, healing, romance, love, human connection, empowerment and enlightenment all thrown into one. She finds inspiration in everything, everywhere.

She now lives in South Oxfordshire where she enjoys walks in the luscious countryside and a living-room with a river view. Writing is her passion and has been since her teens, but she also enjoys dancing, yoga, meditating, cooking and baking. Mary is also a Reiki Master, a British Wheel of Yoga trained Yoga practitioner and teacher and a Holistic healer.

You can connect with me on:

- https://www.facebook.com/mary.mallia.148
- https://www.youtube.com/channel/UC3UBYOcngy87f32iLI
- https://linktr.ee/marymallia
- https://www.instagram.com/marymallia.writer
- https://books2read.com/u/4EJ6QO

Subscribe to my newsletter:

- https://mail.google.com/mail/u/0/#inbox

Also by Mary Mallia

Coming soon….

Lovers and Demons
As Marie and Amy continue to traverse this multiverse, the former on the earth plane and the latter on the other side of the veil, a battle for Marie's soul ensues. Would Amy be able to save her daughter from the furious fangs of the evil forces which assail her, keeping her promise to help and protect her daughter from the other side? Amy's hands are tied, but will she find a way to keep these evil forces at bay? And is this just a war on her Marie, or on the whole of humanity? There might be much more going on than meets the eye.